THE SHADOW GIRL

Also by Jennifer Archer

THROUGH HER EYES

THE
SHADOW
GIRL

JENNIFER ARCHER

HARPER TEEN
An Imprint of HarperCollinsPublishers

HarperTeen is an imprint of HarperCollins Publishers.

The Shadow Girl
Copyright © 2013 by Jennifer Archer
All rights reserved. Printed in the United States of America.
No part of this book may be used or reproduced in any man-
ner whatsoever without written permission except in the case
of brief quotations embodied in critical articles and reviews.
For information address HarperCollins Children's Books, a
division of HarperCollins Publishers, 10 East 53rd Street, New
York, NY 10022.
www.epicreads.com

Library of Congress Cataloging-in-Publication Data

Archer, Jennifer.
   The shadow girl / Jennifer Archer. — 1st ed.
      p. cm.
   Summary: "When Lily Winston's father dies on her seven-
teenth birthday, he leaves behind a mystery about her family's
past—and about the mysterious shadow girl who has followed
Lily and whispered in her ear for her entire life"—Provided by
publisher.
   ISBN 978-0-06-183460-8
   [1. Identity—Fiction. 2. Secrets—Fiction. 3. Love—Fiction.
4. Death—Fiction. 5. Supernatural—Fiction. 6. Family life—
Colorado—Fiction. 7. Colorado—Fiction.]   I. Title.
PZ7.A67462Sh 2013   2012011524
[Fic]—dc23   CIP
                                                              AC

Typography by Torborg Davern
13 14 15 16 17 LP/RRDH 10 9 8 7 6 5 4 3 2 1
❖
First Edition

To Marcy McCay, Linda Castillo,
Anita Howard, and April Redmon.
For all you do, this one's for you.

PROLOGUE

Ty Collier shivered as he paused in front of the Daily Grind coffee shop to wipe his boots on the mat beside the door. Cold weather was nothing new to him; he had grown up freezing his butt off every winter in Baltimore. But this morning something besides the frigid air raised goose bumps on his skin. It was the task ahead of him. And the silence. Noise had always been a constant in his life, so common he didn't notice it until it was gone. City traffic, a raucous family. Ty felt lost without it.

He glanced over his shoulder at the sleepy Colorado town. Even in May, Silver Lake lay tucked under a thin blanket of snow like a dozing cat. But silence has a sound all of its own—something hummed beneath the town's stillness that set his nerves on edge.

Not many cars were out at six thirty a.m. on this Monday morning. Only two were parked in front of the Daily Grind—a black El Camino and a blue delivery van with lettering on the side that read WINSTON CARPENTRY.

Excitement shuddered through Ty. He recognized the van as the one he'd seen in the photograph. The man was definitely here. After a month and a half of searching, he'd finally found him.

Taking a deep breath to steady his nerves, Ty opened the door. A bell jingled to announce his entrance, and warmth rushed forward to welcome him in. "Good morning!" called a woman behind the counter on the far side of the shop.

"Morning," Ty replied, scanning the room. A girl about his age sat on a sofa against the back wall, her feet tucked under her as she typed on a laptop. At a corner table near the front window, three old men chuckled over their coffee. They glanced up when Ty entered, then quickly returned to their conversation.

Ty studied the men discreetly. Two of them had gray beards, but without openly staring he couldn't tell which one was Adam.

As he crossed to the counter, Ty recalled that the lady behind it was named Paula. He'd talked to her over a muffin and hot chocolate yesterday, his first day in town. She'd seemed worried when he told her that he was taking a temporary break from college and was traveling the country, working odd jobs to make money.

"You're too young!" Paula had exclaimed. "What are you? Nineteen?"

"Eighteen," Ty said. He'd waited awhile before asking in an offhand manner if she knew Adam Winston and if she could give him directions to his shop. Ty was afraid to call the number on the website and ask Adam himself. He didn't want to take any risks. Who knew if Gail Withers had set off an alarm? He couldn't be too careful.

Paula told Ty that Adam's shop was behind his house and gave him directions. She also gave him an unexpected bonus, telling him that Adam came into the Daily Grind on Monday mornings to have coffee with his friends. Which was why Ty woke up before the sun this morning and was out the door of his room two hours before he normally stepped foot into the day. He'd rather talk to Adam without his family around.

Ty slid onto a swiveling stool in front of the counter and ordered a coffee.

"You enjoying your stay in Silver Lake so far?" Paula asked as she filled his mug and handed it to him.

"Yeah, it's nice. I went hiking yesterday after I left here."

"Oh yeah? Whereabouts?"

"Some trail at the top of the pass. Still quite a bit of snow up there," Ty said, sipping his coffee. "I'm thinking of climbing the west peak soon. Make it my first fourteener." That part wasn't a lie. Colorado was home to more mountain summits with elevations of at least fourteen thousand feet than any other state, and it was his goal to make it to the top of all of them for his brother, just in case Kyle never got the chance himself. It was something Kyle had always wanted to do.

"Not sure the west peak qualifies as a true fourteener, but it's close," Paula said. "Start early in the morning. The weather's dicey this time of year. We might have snow one day and thunderstorms the next. You don't want to get caught up there when there's lightning."

"I'll remember that. Thanks." Ty propped his elbows on the counter and leaned in closer as Paula filled a jug with tea. When she glanced up, he indicated the three men by the window and asked, "Is one of them Mr. Winston?"

"As a matter of fact, yes. The gentleman with his back to us. He can tell you more about hiking the west peak. Adam lives right at its base." Before Ty could say another word, she called out, "Adam! This young man's looking for you."

The man turned, and Ty's heart skipped across his chest like a pebble skimming a pond. Winston looked exactly like the image in the silver frame on Gail Withers's desk—the photograph she'd tried to hide from him. Curiosity and intelligence blazed in his eyes. Ty had stared at those same dark eyes in half a dozen other photographs of Adam when he was younger; there was no mistaking them.

Taking his coffee with him, Ty started across the room toward the men. "Good morning," he said as he paused beside them. Addressing Adam directly, he asked, "Are you Mr. Winston?"

"That's me." Adam smiled. "Something I can do for you?"

Ty nodded to a table across the room. "Can we talk?"

Adam shrugged. "Sure." He followed Ty to the empty

table and they sat across from each other. Squinting, Adam scrubbed a hand across his beard and asked, "Have we met?"

Ty placed his coffee on the table and took a breath. "No, but you knew my mom a long time ago. My name is Ty Collier. My mother is Jillian Collier. When you knew her, her last name was Steadman."

All the color drained from Adam Winston's face. "What's this about?"

"I need your help with something. I know about your work."

"I'm a carpenter—"

"Your *former* work," Ty interrupted. Winston looked defensive. Nervous. *Afraid.* "My mother always wondered what happened to you. She loved your daughter very much. When I was growing up, Mom talked about her all the time." Smiling, Ty added, "I was always a little jealous."

"Leave my daughter out of this," Adam hissed, pushing away from the table so abruptly the chair legs scraped against the hardwood floor. "Why would Jillian want to find me after all these years?"

Ty hadn't expected such an angry reaction. Determined not to lose Adam now that he'd found him, he said, "My mother doesn't know I've been looking for you. She never talked to me about your work until recently when I read several articles you wrote and mentioned them to her."

"I don't know what you're talking about."

"My brother needs your help. He's only thirteen and—" Ty broke off as a wave of emotion swept over him. After taking a moment to compose himself, he said quietly, "I made a promise to my brother, and you're the only person I know that might be able to help me keep it." Bracing his forearms on the table, he leaned in, adding, "I had to find you, Mr. *Winston*." Adam flinched at the emphasis of his surname, but Ty refused to let him off the hook. "I've read everything about you I could get my hands on, and I know what you're capable of doing."

"You don't know anything," Adam said between clenched teeth.

The man's stubborn refusal to admit the truth stirred anger in Ty. Struggling to maintain a calm tone, he said, "Let me tell you what I know."

"I don't have time for this nonsense," said Adam.

"Hear me out or convince me I'm wrong. I found Ian Beckett and—"

"You've talked to Beckett?" Adam shot up from his chair. Across the room, his friends stopped talking and glanced over. Ty was glad Winston's back was to them so they couldn't see his agitated face.

Hoping to appease the men, Ty smiled at Adam and murmured, "Calm down. Listen, I—"

"You and Beckett stay away from my family," Adam growled, panic simmering in his dark brown eyes. "Do you hear me? Leave us alone." He turned and walked back to his table of friends. The men exchanged a few words that Ty couldn't hear, then Winston left the coffee shop.

"Everything okay?" Paula called out from the counter.

"Yeah," Ty lied. He drained his coffee, then made his way to the door.

"Adam said you're looking for work," one of Winston's friends said as Ty passed their table. "You might try Sal over at the lumberyard north of town."

"Thanks," Ty said, then opening the door, he stepped out again into Silver Lake's startling silence.

1

Lily

I started keeping secrets when I was four years old. Back then, I only had two.

Secret number one was that I sucked my thumb before bedtime while watching the sun melt into the earth outside my window. My parents had warned me that I'd get funny teeth if I didn't stop. They told me in no uncertain terms to keep my fingers out of my mouth.

The girl came while I stood at the window. That's what I called Iris before I knew her name—just *the girl*. She became secret number two. I didn't have to see her to know she was there; I *felt* her.

Sometimes I thought I did see her, though. I'd turn around and we'd be standing toe-to-toe. The girl sucked her thumb like me and mimicked my movements.

Of course, now I know I was only seeing my shadow, not Iris. I can only *sense* Iris. I hear her thoughts in my head. I hear her music, too; the haunting melodies she hums. And I feel her restlessness.

"*Happy birthday, Lily,*" she whispers to me now, her words sweeping through my mind just before my dog Cookie's cold nose nudges my arm. I rub my eyes and pull my iPod earbuds out, silencing Paramore, which was playing on low.

My parents and I live in a cabin my dad built in the Rocky Mountains of southern Colorado. My bedroom is in the upstairs loft. As I roll to face the window beside my bed, the first things I see are the two peaks in the distance, their frosty heads twinkling beneath a hazy wash of moonlight. My parents and I call them the twin peaks, and they're so close together that I used to imagine that they held hands. The west peak changes colors with each season, but the east peak remains black and gray, somber and dark. It's slightly taller than the west peak and stands a step behind, as if to watch over the smaller one. "Good morning," I whisper to them both. And to Iris, whose presence fills me.

At the sound of my voice, Cookie snuggles closer. He turned fourteen a couple of months ago and his joints ache when it's cold outside. He doesn't want me to get up, because that means he'll have to get up, too. The stairs are tricky for him these days, so I don't leave him up here alone.

I hear Mom downstairs in the kitchen making coffee and Dad adding logs to the fire. I'm not ready to go down yet. I'm homeschooled, and I've been getting up before the sun every weekday morning since I was six to do my chores and lessons so I could keep my afternoons free for hiking, or for skating in the winter. But I have today off since it's my seventeenth birthday, and I want to savor the extra time in bed.

I can't be lazy for too long, though. On the day I turned twelve, Dad and I rode four-wheelers up the mountain to watch the sun rise, and we've done it on my birthday every year since. This morning when we're up there, I plan to tell him about my college plans. I'm nervous, but if I can convince him that it's a good idea for me to go to the University of Oklahoma in the fall, maybe he can help me persuade Mom.

I lie very still, listening to the comforting sounds of my parents below, wondering if Iris will go into hiding if I move. That's become her way over the past few years. Dad always jokes that when I became a teenager, I started needing my "space," and I guess Iris does, too. She hovers at the edge of my mind in the quiet hours—early in the morning and before I fall asleep at night. But as my day gets started, Iris dives deeper, goes farther inward. Sometimes I forget that she's with me. Sometimes I convince myself that she's only a dream. Or that I'm crazy. But then for no reason, I become aware of her company again, or I hear her murmuring in my head, and her voice is as real as my mother's or my father's or mine. That's when I remember that she's been there all along, as constant as my heartbeat.

Pulling the quilts snugly around me, I burrow deeper

into the bed. If I have something to say to Iris, all I have to do is think it. She can hear my thoughts, just as I hear hers.

Stay close when we ride up to the lookout, I say to her now. *I'm going to talk to Dad about college and I need your support.*

Her sigh tickles my eardrum as Iris says, *I'm always close. I can't leave you.*

It's the same thing she's said all my life: She can't leave me. She's watching over me, like the east peak watches over the west one. She's waiting for someone, but she doesn't know who. She needs to tell me something, but she doesn't know what.

The way I see it? If anyone's crazy, it's Iris, not me. At least in the last few years she's stopped bringing these things up so much. But sometimes I sense such sorrow in her, like she's lost or lonely, and that makes me sad because I don't know how to help. Like now, for instance, when a shift occurs inside of me, and I feel her retreat to a place I can't reach.

The scent of coffee swirls in to fill the void Iris leaves. I reach for my phone on the nightstand to text my best friend, Wyatt, who lives two miles up the road with his grandmother, Addie. Maybe he'll come with us this morning to give me moral support. This college thing is too important to mess up. If Dad says no, I'm screwed— doomed to spend the next two years at Silver Lake Community College.

I text: *Sunrise @ lookout w/me & Dad. U In? Back b4 u have 2 go 2 school.*

I wait, and a few seconds later my phone vibrates with his response: *thx 4 scaring me shitless @ freakin qtr to dawn.*

I laugh and text: *Lazy ass. Will u go?*

Happy b.day, but no. Must get beauty rest. 50% of big-rig truck wrecks caused by driver sleep deprivation.

I roll my eyes: *Dork. Get up. Going 2 tell dad abt OU. Need backup.*

Another few seconds pass. Another vibration. *Whoa. Wish I cld. Have 2 go in early 4 make-up test.*

I groan. *4 real?*

Yep, Wyatt answers. *Sorry. You'll do fine. B strong.*

I wish I was as confident. *Thx. Go back to sleep.*

Plan to. Sleep-starved teens twice as likely to smoke crack. Bring U cupcake after school. w/sprinkles.

Sighing, I punch in: *Dbl sprinkles.*

So much for moral support. I guess I'm on my own.

Cookie's tail thumps the mattress as I put aside my phone. I laugh. "Thanks, boy. I appreciate the offer. I didn't mean to leave you out. You can ride with Dad, okay?"

Mom's voice drifts from downstairs as I'm getting up. "I dread today, Adam," she says. "I know I shouldn't feel this way, but I can't help it."

"Shhh," Dad says. "Lily will hear you."

"She's asleep. Besides, she listens to music all night."

Cookie pants and stirs. I pat his muzzle to quiet him. Slipping from the bed, I walk to the head of the stairs where I can hear my parents more clearly.

"Don't cry, Myla," Dad says wearily when Mom makes a sobbing sound.

"I'm sorry," she says. "I can't stop remembering."

My muscles tense. Remembering what? Why would my birthday make her cry? Mom is always so emotional. She can obsess over the weirdest things. Once, she burst into tears when I told her I don't like strawberry ice cream—that I'd rather have vanilla. For a long time after that, I wouldn't eat ice cream at all because I didn't want to upset her. Sometimes Mom can be as fragile as glass.

"It's Lily's birthday, honey," Dad says. "Can't you just relax and enjoy it?"

"She's seventeen," says Mom. "How did it happen so fast?"

Dad sighs. "This should be a happy day."

"Happiness doesn't last, you know that." Mom makes a huffing sound. "Everything can change in an instant."

After a long silence, Dad says, "I've been thinking, and I want to tell her."

"No! Adam, you can't."

"Lily is almost an adult," Dad says. "We can't keep her here for the rest of her life. We're in our sixties—"

"That isn't old."

"Maybe not, but we won't be around forever. Besides, she'll want to strike out on her own soon, and I'm starting to think that might not be a bad idea."

"You think she should leave?" Mom asks, radiating

alarm. "But she's so vulnerable."

"The truth will protect Lily more than we can," says Dad. "We have to think of what's best for her."

"We have. Since the day she was born. We gave up *everything*."

Nervous energy bursts inside of me; Iris is suddenly as alert as I am. *What are they talking about?* I ask her. Iris doesn't answer, and her silence causes my skin to prickle. I hold my breath and strain harder to hear over the sudden loud beating of my heart.

"Nothing we gave up was important," Dad says, frustration coloring his tone. "I don't miss any of it."

"So this life we're living is really enough for you?"

"*Lily's* enough," he answers, bringing tears to my eyes.

"Of course she is," Mom says more softly. "I'd leave it all again in a second. You know I would."

Questions collide in my mind. What truth could Dad want to tell me? Why do they think I need protection? What did my parents give up for me?

I start to go down the stairs to ask, but Iris's urgent whisper stops me. *Wait. Listen.* I hold back.

"When do you want to tell her?" Mom asks.

"After we get back from our ride this morning. You and I should do it together."

"Something's happened, hasn't it? You've been tied up in knots ever since you came home from the coffee shop on Monday."

"Nothing's happened. Everything's fine." Despite his assurance, Dad's voice stretches tight. "It's just time. We have a responsibility to prepare Lily. Just in case."

"But what if she hates us?"

"Myla . . . don't you know your own daughter? Lily could never hate us."

Cookie whines, then barks once, short and sharp, calling me back to bed. Mom and Dad must hear him because they stop talking. Dishes start clinking. The television comes on, the volume low. A weatherman predicts more snow later today.

Iris stirs beneath the surface of my skin. *Do you understand any of this?* I ask.

There's something, she says. *Like mist . . . too faint to grasp.*

Confused by her vague comment, I calm Cookie, then head for the bathroom, still trying to sort out my parents' conversation. A few minutes later, I emerge again with my face washed and my hair pulled back into a loose ponytail. Cookie inches to the edge of the mattress as I throw on some jeans, a gray sweatshirt, and a pair of wool socks. I help him hop down onto the rug, and he walks stiffly to the head of the stairs and sits, waiting while I lace my boots. "Come on, boy," I say, and together we take the steps down to the cabin's first floor.

Our living area and kitchen are one big room, connected to my parents' bedroom, the guest room, and the downstairs bath by a short hallway. Dad sits at the kitchen table and he glances up when he hears me, his brown eyes twinkling beneath his bushy gray brows. "Good morning, Doodlebug. Happy birthday."

I smile, but I'm too nervous to hold his gaze. His face shows no sign of the strain I sensed when he and Mom were talking. He's shoving his feet into his boots, yesterday's newspaper folded beside the placemat in front of him.

"Happy birthday, darling," says Mom.

"Thanks." I let Cookie outside, then look across at her. She moves slowly from the table to the sink and back again, her arms crossed tightly. She has on a baggy wool sweater, black sweat pants, and sheepskin slippers. Deep lines I've never really noticed etch the skin around her mouth. Mom looks tired and old this morning.

"Are you feeling okay?" I ask her, wondering if her lupus has flared up again. That led to her rheumatoid arthritis, and now the knuckles on her fingers bulge like knots on a branch. During a flare-up the symptoms are worse.

"I'm fine," she says. "Just a little tired." Her weak smile suddenly widens into a real one. "And excited," she says playfully.

"Excited about what?" I follow her gaze to the floor beneath the coffee table, where I see a box wrapped in white paper and topped with a big yellow bow. "What's that?" I ask, stooping to reach for it.

"Hands off!" says Dad in a teasing tone. "You'll find out later."

Grinning, I stand and walk toward them. I kiss the top of Dad's head, then wrap my arms around Mom. She hugs me a little too tightly as I stare over her shoulder at the framed sketch of a violin that hangs on the wall above the table. Mom did it before her arthritis made sketching and painting too painful. That was her violin in the sketch. She used to play when she was young, but she stopped before I was born to concentrate on her artwork.

"What's for breakfast?" I ask, stepping out of her embrace.

Mom tucks a loose strand of hair behind my ear. "Blueberry muffins. They'll be ready when you and Dad get back from your ride. I'll fry bacon, too, and scramble some eggs." Turning, she straightens the tablecloth, then rearranges the silverware already laid out for three. Without looking at me she adds, "Take it slow, okay? It's dark out there, and the higher roads might still be snow packed."

"I know, Mom. We do this every year, remember?"

The things she said to Dad earlier replay through my mind. What are they going to tell me after we come home that could possibly make me hate them? I want to ask, but something holds me back. Maybe the look of weariness and pain that I saw on Mom's face when I first came down.

Returning to the living room, I let Cookie inside again, then wrap a scarf around my neck, slip into my coat, and pull on my stocking cap and gloves. From the kitchen, Dad calls out, "Are you ready to go?"

"Yes," I say, and silently ask Iris, *What's happening?*

Not sure, she whispers. *Be careful. She's right—everything can change in an instant.*

A chill skitters through me. *What do you mean?*

I listen for an answer, but hear only the steady white noise of her silence.

2

Cookie rides in a crate on the back of Dad's four-wheeler. I follow behind, my headlights illuminating them. Every so often, Cookie turns to glance back at me. His ears flap in the wind, and his teeth are bared like he's grinning.

The lake appears ahead, the water a glossy black ink stain. The sight of it takes me back to the winter I was seven, when I first met Wyatt. His mom had just decided she had better things to do than raise a kid and sent him here from Dallas to live with his grandparents. A couple of days after we met, I taught Wyatt to skate on this lake. He'd never ice-skated before, but when I tried to give him a few tips, he cut me off. He knew what to do, he said. He was a Rollerblader and ice-skating couldn't be much different. He'd show me every trick he knew.

But when Wyatt and I stepped onto the ice, the only trick he did was the splits, and not on purpose. The seat of his pants tore right up the seam, and as he struggled to stand, I caught a glimpse of his Star Wars long underwear. Falling served him right for being such a show-off, so I laughed. But I also offered him a hand. At first he wouldn't take it, but then he laughed, too, and let me help him up. From that day on, Wyatt and I were best friends.

I wish he could've come with us to the lookout point this morning. I'm going to have a lot to tell him when he comes over after school. What's in the box with the big yellow bow, for one thing. Dad's reaction to my college news. And my parents' Big Secret. I shove that last one from my mind, determined to enjoy the ride.

We turn onto the trail that runs along the creek, and aspen trees press in, towering over me, standing guard. I breathe in their spicy scent while listening to the song that Iris hums in my head. It's a favorite of hers, the tempo urgent and powerful.

The trail climbs, becoming narrower and rougher as it winds through the forest. Patches of snow at the side of the road flash by, icy blue in the moonlight. Ragged swatches of purple sky flicker between the branches above. Ahead, the rock dike that snakes through these mountains rises on the left side of the road, while the right side drops into a deep ravine. Soon my headlights expose a place where the edge arcs out to a rocky ledge wide enough to sit on.

Dad slows and pulls in. I follow, easing up on the gas and stopping beside him. We cut our engines, take off our helmets, and hang them on our handlebars.

"Made it just in time, Doodlebug," Dad says, nodding

toward the pink hem of the eastern horizon.

Cookie whines, and I help him out of his crate. "Stay close, boy," I say as we follow Dad to the ledge and sit down to watch the sunrise.

"What's on your mind, Lily?" Dad asks. "You're so quiet I can hear the wheels turning in your head."

Wrapping my arms around my knees, I say, "Remember last August when I talked to you and Mom about going to the University of Oklahoma this fall with Wyatt?"

"Of course I remember," he answers. "I should've been more supportive about that. In fact, I'm starting to think that going away to a four-year school might've been the best option for you." Dad frowns. "But now it's too late, isn't it? I'm sorry."

I shake my head. "It's not too late. That's what I wanted to tell you. I applied anyway. I hoped that if I got accepted, I could persuade you and Mom to let me go."

His brows lift. "And?"

"I got an acceptance letter last month," I say.

"You've been accepted?" He hugs me. "Congratulations, sweetheart!"

"You're not upset?"

"Upset? No. I'll worry about you," says Dad with a chuckle, sitting back. "I'll miss you, too. But it's time for you to go. You should be around people your own age. I know it hasn't been easy for you, living out here so isolated."

Something Mom said to him earlier comes back to me:

21

Is this life we're living really enough for you? Anger rises up in me. Anger at her. Feeling defensive, I say, "I love our cabin. And I love Silver Lake. You know that, Dad. But I feel like I have to go away for a while. I can't explain it."

"You don't have to. You've grown up." Dad loops his arm through mine. "Why OU? I hope you're not just following Wyatt there. You should go to a school that's right for *you*."

"OU *is* right for me," I say. "It's right for both of us. Wyatt and I want to go to another state—just for a change, you know? But it's still close enough that we can drive home if we want to."

"That would be a long drive," he says.

"It's only 491.94 miles. We could make it in eight hours."

"Is that all?" says Dad, sounding amused, his breath a white plume on the cold morning air.

"Not exactly." I grin. "Eight hours and two minutes."

"You really have done your research."

"MapQuest," I say.

"Just so long as Wyatt didn't influence you." He winks.

A laugh bursts out of me. *"Dad.* You know it's not like that with Wyatt and me. We're just friends."

"So you say. But I wonder if Wyatt feels the same."

I bump my shoulder against him. "Wyatt's chasing after a different girl every week. He doesn't think of me like that."

"Okay, okay!" Sighing heavily, he mutters, "Oklahoma. I've never been. It might be a good place for you. . . ." His voice trails, and the humor on his face fades, leaving behind an expression I can't identify.

"Mom won't be as easy to persuade as you were," I say.

"Don't worry about your mother. I'll talk to her."

Gathering my nerve, I stroke Cookie's silky ear and say, "I heard the two of you talking this morning. You said something about the truth protecting me and needing to prepare me for something. What did you mean?"

Dad tenses and inhales sharply. "I'm sorry you heard that, but it's nothing to worry about."

"But Mom said the two of you had to give up everything for me."

"Lily . . ." He hugs me tightly. "Nothing could be more important than you. You can't even imagine what a miracle you are to us. When you were born . . ." Leaning back, he cups my chin in his gloved hand. "You saved us, Lily."

"Dad, you're freaking me out," I say. "What are you planning to tell me when we get home?"

"We'll talk about it later, okay? Everything's fine, and right now, I just want to enjoy the sunrise." He nods toward the sky. "Look."

On the horizon, light erupts, setting the east peak's snowcap on fire. I try to relax as Dad drapes an arm across my shoulder. But for the first time in my life, his nearness isn't enough to make me feel safe.

The trail becomes steeper as I lead the way down the mountain past blue spruce trees, green firs, and towering white aspen, their branches shivering in the wind. Dad follows on his four-wheeler close behind me. The sun is bright enough now that we don't need our headlights.

As I round a curve, a deer darts across the snowy path a few feet ahead. I don't have time to react, but out of nowhere the four-wheeler seizes up, as if someone slammed a foot down hard on the brake. My head whips forward, then back again with the sudden jerk, and the ATV skids sideways, blocking the trail. *Iris*, I think, feeling her terror spike up inside of me. She pressed the brake to keep me from hitting the deer. I'm sure of it, even though she's never done anything like that before.

The roar of Dad's engine drowns out every other noise around me, and a warning catches in my throat as I turn to see him come around the curve. Time slows down. My ears ring and my skin prickles as he yanks his handlebars hard to the right to keep from ramming into me. His four-wheeler tilts onto the two right tires, teeters toward the sharp incline that drops into the ravine at the side of the road, then slams into a boulder. Dad hurtles off the seat toward the trees. Behind him, Cookie flies from the crate and lands in a mound of snow as Dad smashes into an aspen tree at the edge of the slope. The four-wheeler rolls on top of him.

"Dad!" I scream, my boots pounding the ground as I run to him, passing Cookie whose yelps prick me like needle-sharp icicles. I round the overturned four-wheeler and find Dad facedown on the ground, the six-hundred-pound vehicle crushing him. As I drop to my knees beside him, he lifts his head enough for me to see a red gash above his temple where he hit the aspen's trunk. Blood oozes from the wound, soaking a patch of snow beneath his head.

"Lily," he rasps.

"I'm here, Dad."

His face twitches as he lowers his cheek to the cold, hard ground.

"Hold on. I'll get you out," I say, my body shaking.

"No! Don't move anything," he gasps. "My back . . ."

He doesn't have to say more. If I try to move the four-wheeler off him, I could hurt him worse. Panicked, I ask, "What should I do?"

"Get Mom. Call for help."

Cookie's frantic wails shred the last thin thread of my self-control. Sobbing, I say, "I didn't bring my phone."

"My front pocket," Dad says weakly.

I scoot closer and look for a space to slip my hand beneath him. "I'll find it. Don't worry, I—"

"Don't!" Pain and panic flash across his face when I touch him. "It's— Can't reach it," he says, each word a struggle. "Go . . . get Mom."

I swipe at the tears on my face. "I can't leave you and Cookie here."

"Don't cry. Cookie and I—we'll be fine. Please, sweetheart . . . hurry."

Desperate for another way to help him, I squeeze my eyes shut. The scents of the forest fill my senses—moss and pine and rich, damp earth. I hear the tense hiss of Iris's essence. The rattle of tree limbs. Then in the distance, the crunch of snow beneath hooves . . . or boots.

Opening my eyes, I scan the forest in every direction, praying it's a person I hear, not an animal. "Help!" I scream. "Over here! Help us!"

I wait a few seconds for a reply, but know if I stay any longer, I'll risk Dad's life. "I'll be right back. Everything will be okay," I promise him, desperately hoping that's true.

A few feet away, Cookie wails and Dad gasps, "Can you . . . bring him . . . ?"

I run to Cookie and kneel down. He doesn't appear to have any outer wounds, but I have no idea if that's the case internally. I shouldn't move him, but he and Dad need each other, and I can't bring myself to leave him crying in the road. "I'm sorry, boy," I say, lifting him despite his wails. He seems weightless as I carry him to Dad and place him on the ground.

"Lily . . . ," Dad says when I start to turn away. His eyes are closed, the lids quivering like moth wings. "If I don't—"

"No!" I drop to my knees and sweep locks of silver hair off his forehead with trembling fingers. "You'll be okay," I whisper.

"Your mother . . . loves you . . . try to understand. She can't lose you, too."

"She's not going to lose either one of us, Dad. You're going to be okay."

"Trust Mom," he says in a strained whisper. "No one else."

"What?"

"Promise me," he says.

"I promise, but—oh, Dad," I sob, lowering my face close to his.

"We thought we did . . . the right thing." He clutches my wrist. "It was right, wasn't it? You're happy? You're all right?"

Confusion grips me, but before I can answer him or ask any questions, Dad loses consciousness and a voice calls out from the forest on the opposite side of the trail. Turning, I see a hiker emerge from the trees.

Pushing to my feet, I run toward him.

3

"Your mother is finally sleeping," Wyatt's grandmother says as she sits on the edge of the couch beside me. "Won't you let me give you a sedative, too?"

"I want to stay awake until we hear about Cookie." A tear trickles down my cheek. "God, will I ever stop crying?"

Addie's fingers are dry and cool as she wipes the tear away. "It's good to let it all out, sugar."

"Wyatt hasn't called?"

"Not yet," Addie says.

Wyatt volunteered to stay at the animal clinic in Silver Lake and bring Cookie home when the vet says it's okay. Dr. Trujillo called it a miracle that Cookie appears to have survived the wreck with only a few bumps and bruises. But he still wanted to watch him for a while, just in case.

Embers crackle and glow in the hearth across the room. The fire is dying. Addie glances at it, and I know that soon she'll stoke the flames back to life and add another log or two. I hope I'm like her when I'm old. Although she's in her seventies, tiny and thin, with a short cap of snow-white hair, there's nothing frail about Wyatt's grandmother. Her husband had a fatal heart attack in his vegetable garden two years after Wyatt came to live with them, and although a lot of women Addie's age would've moved to town, she didn't budge. She and Wyatt stayed out here alone, practically in the middle of nowhere. I wonder if Mom will stay, too, now that Dad's gone. I can't see it. She isn't that strong.

"You need your rest," Addie insists. "I'll wake you up when Wyatt calls."

"When I close my eyes, I see it happen again," I whisper. I see the deer. My four-wheeler skidding. Dad rounding the corner behind me. He and Cookie sailing through the air in slow motion. I always open my eyes before they land. Then I hear the warning that Iris whispered early this morning: *Be careful. Everything can change in an instant.*

Did she know what was going to happen? She must have. What else could her warning have meant? But then why didn't she tell me?

For the first time in my life, I'm furious with Iris—so angry I want to hurt her. I want her to ache as badly as I do.

Dad died because of you, Iris. Cookie is hurt because of your silence.

I didn't know. . . .

Then why did you tell me to be careful? And what did you mean when you said everything can change?

I remembered something. . . .

What? I demand. I've had enough of her cryptic statements.

A feeling . . . fear. I was happy, says Iris. *And then something terrible happened and I wasn't anymore. . . .*

What are you talking about? Nothing terrible has ever happened to us until today.

She's quiet for a minute, and when she finally speaks, I hear more than her words, I hear her frustration. *Help me remember, Lily. Please . . .*

Before I can press her to explain, the kettle whistles in the kitchen, and Iris startles and curls up inside of me, burying herself deep.

"Will you drink some tea?" Addie asks as she takes the kettle off the stove, silencing its shriek.

"No, but thanks."

"Is there anything else I can get for you?"

"My iPod," I tell her. "It's upstairs on my nightstand."

"I'll bring it down."

As Addie climbs the stairs to the loft, I tug the blanket over my shoulders and shift to stare out the windows overlooking the deck. The dusk sky is a dingy slate gray. Fat flakes drift on the air slowly—almost cautiously—as if out of respect for my grief, they don't want to bother me.

My mind drifts back to this morning. The hiker who came out of the woods and called 911 was a guy not much older than I am. I don't know his name, but even if I never see him again, I'll always remember his kind, dark eyes, and how they kept me from sinking during those long minutes while we waited for the rescue helicopter to arrive. When I was about to hyperventilate, he made me look at him and told me to take deep breaths. He let me clutch his hand while he talked to me in a soothing voice. His strength flowed into me, and I started to believe that he had the power to make everything all right.

After they took Dad to the hospital in Pueblo, the sheriff drove me to meet Mom, Addie, and Wyatt there. I don't know what happened to the hiker.

The stairs creak, and a moment later Addie stands beside me holding my iPod. I take it and thank her, putting the buds in my ears. I find a soft country playlist and push the button to start it, hoping the music will drown my memories of the accident so I can sleep. Soon Iris begins to sing softly along with the song, so I make the music louder. I wish she'd go somewhere far away and stay there. I'm not sure I believe that she didn't know what was going to happen. Her strange excuse about warning me doesn't make sense.

I close my eyes to shut out the world. And close my heart to Iris. But sometime later, as I'm finally nodding off, Dad's voice comes to me, his words woven into the melody that drifts through my ears. *We thought we did the right thing. . . .*

When I awake the next morning on the couch, every muscle in my body is sore, and there's no sign of Addie or Mom. Anxious to check on Cookie, I take a quick shower, then throw on a pair of jeans and an old long-sleeved T-shirt with a pointing finger and the words *You Need a Lobotomy* on it that I stole from Wyatt. Without bothering to dry my hair, I hurry downstairs again and, this time, find Addie sitting at the kitchen table reading the newspaper.

She glances up. "Morning, sugar." Folding the paper, she places it on the table beside her and motions toward the coffeemaker on the kitchen counter. "Coffee's hot. Can I get you some?"

"I'll get it."

"Did you sleep?"

I take a mug from the cabinet. "I didn't wake up once all night." Wondering why I'm still so exhausted, I pour coffee into the mug, then add half-and-half and two packets of sweetener. "Has Dr. Trujillo called?"

"No. Wyatt stopped by a minute ago on his way to school. He said Dr. Trujillo wants you to call the clinic at eight." She glances at her watch. "Just five more minutes."

I sit in the chair next to her. "Where's Mom? She isn't still sleeping, is she?"

"She's outside in your dad's workshop."

"Doing what?"

"I'm not sure. She was up making coffee at five thirty so I got up, too. She took her cup and said she was heading out there. She seemed skittish as a colt, so I didn't question her." Addie shakes her head. "Poor thing."

"I'll check on her after I call the vet," I say. Setting my mug down, I push back from the table and reach for the phone book on the counter behind me.

"Will you eat some breakfast?" Addie asks.

"No, thanks. I'm not hungry."

She catches my attention and holds it as I'm opening the phone book in my lap. "I'm not going to tell you that you'll get over this, because you won't," Addie says softly. "I still miss Dave like crazy, every single day. And even though it's been more than twenty years since my folks passed, I still miss them, too. But with time, the pain will ease up and you'll find yourself remembering the good times with your dad instead of the accident."

I prop an elbow on the table and cover my face. "It shouldn't have happened," I cry. "It didn't have to. I could've stopped it if—"

"Don't, Lily." She squeezes my shoulder. "Blaming yourself won't change a thing. The accident wasn't your fault. You couldn't have known what was going to happen."

She's wrong, but I can't tell her that. If only Iris had given me a clearer idea of the danger ahead before we left, I would've told Dad that I didn't want to go. "Thank you for being here, Addie," I say, wiping tears from my cheeks. "You're the best."

I find Dr. Trujillo's number and call him while Addie busies herself in the kitchen. When I'm off the phone, she asks, "Is everything okay?"

"Cookie was in a lot of pain last night. He's doped up and resting now. Dr. Trujillo wants to keep him another day or two for observation." My voice wavers. "We'll just have to wait and see."

Addie folds a cup towel and lays it on the counter. "I know you're disappointed."

I press my lips together and nod. Putting the phone book away, I cross the room, and take my coat from the rack beside the door.

"Lily." Her solemn voice stops me. "I hate to bring this up, but the funeral home called. You and your mother will need to let them know what to do. If you want to have a service, and—"

"I'll tell her," I whisper.

A cool breeze blows through my damp hair, causing me to shiver as I step outside. The sky is a bright blue. The sun is shining, the thin rays slowly melting the snow away.

I start across the small meadow at the back of the cabin, headed for Dad's shop. It's so strange that nothing looks any different out here. Dad is gone, yet his blue van is still parked at the side of the shop, waiting for him to load it with the cabinets he was supposed to deliver to someone in Pueblo next week.

I pause in front of the building. On the other side of the double garage door that serves as the shop entrance, I hear a scraping noise that makes me think Mom's dragging something heavy across the floor. Wondering what she could possibly be doing, I try to pull the door up, but it's locked. Knocking, I call out, "Mom? Open up."

In a muffled voice, she says, "I need some time alone, okay?"

"What are you doing?"

"Sketching."

I stop tugging on the door handle. Because of her arthritis, Mom hasn't painted or sketched in more than a year. It's a weird day for her to decide she should start again. "Can we talk?" I ask.

"Not now, Lily."

Confused, I walk to the side of the shop. The building only has a couple of small windows up high on each side. Several cinder blocks are stacked against the outside wall. I lift one from the top of the pile and set it on the ground beneath a window, then step onto it and look inside the shop.

Mom's sitting on the floor with her back to me. A long, wide box is open in front of her. The big metal chest Dad used to store his tools. He kept it locked up in the shop's storage closet because he was afraid that someone might break in and steal his tools. I can't imagine why Mom would want to go through it, especially today.

Several items lie scattered on the floor around her. I can't make out what they are, but they don't look like tools. Wondering why she lied to me, I tap on the window, causing Mom to startle and glance over her shoulder. She turns back around and scrambles to gather up the items and return them to the chest.

"Mom!" I call out, my patience dwindling. "Can I just come in for a second? I need to talk to you about something."

"Okay." Pushing to her feet, she closes the lid on the chest, then crosses to the door.

I jump down from the cinder blocks and I'm rounding the corner as Mom comes outside. A breeze blows her silver curls into her face, but she doesn't bother to push them back. "Is something wrong?" she asks, turning to pull the garage door down.

"Yes, something's wrong, Mom. Dad died yesterday. Did you forget?"

Mom flinches. She stares at the door for a moment, still as a statue, and when she finally turns to me, her expression is fixed and unreadable.

"I'm sorry I said that, Mom," I say, my face burning.

She takes my hand and pulls me to her, wrapping her arms around me. "Oh, Lily," she breathes.

Sobs shake my body. "What are we going to do without him?"

"I don't know, darling." She rubs her palms up and down my back. "We're going to miss him, but we'll be okay."

I have a feeling that she's trying to convince herself more than me. "It hurts so much," I whisper.

"I know."

"And Cookie . . . the vet said he can't come home yet. Maybe we can visit him after we go to the funeral home to make arrangements for Dad's—" I can't even say the word. "That's what I want to talk to you about. We need to plan his service. And write his obituary."

Mom goes rigid and pulls away from me. "Your father wanted to be cremated."

Wary of the sudden change in her, I say, "Okay. But the service—"

"There won't be a service. Or an obituary, for that matter." Her voice is flat. "Your father and I have always been private people. He wouldn't want any of that, and neither do I."

"We should do *something*," I say, bewildered by her attitude. "Maybe an informal gathering with his friends, at least. They'll want to say good-bye."

"I mean it, Lily. No ceremony."

"But why?"

"I told you." She rubs her hands up and down her thin arms. "I'm going for a walk, okay?" Turning, she starts off toward the road.

Confusion and anger slam into me so hard I have to pause to catch my breath before yelling, "We can't just do nothing and forget about him! Don't *you* even want to say good-bye to Dad?"

"I already have," she answers without looking back at me, her voice firm and final. But I hear her sobbing.

I turn and start running, my boots pounding the ground as I pass Dad's shop. Stumbling down the hill on the opposite side, I run until my lungs ache and my cheeks sting from the cool air. Until the cabin and Dad's shop disappear behind me. Until I'm surrounded by trees so tall that they block out the white spring sun. When I finally stop, I'm panting. I bend forward at the waist, my hands on my knees.

Iris seeps through my pores and wraps around me, her caress as soft as dandelion fluff. I know she's trying to comfort me, and I wish that I could forgive her, but I can't.

"I'm mad at you," I sob. "You and Mom both. Why is she acting this way?"

You know why, Iris says, her reply a quiet buzz. *She's hiding something.*

4

Maybe Mom's right that Dad wouldn't have wanted a memorial or an obituary, but Addie told me those things are really more for the living, the ones left behind. Some people don't need them to get through grief. Like Mom, apparently. But some people do. Like me.

So on Saturday morning, against Mom's wishes, I have a memorial for Dad at the lake down the road. Wyatt and Addie are with me, of course. And Iris. She hovers just beneath the surface of my senses, dim with sadness, wary of invading my space.

The day is overcast and bleak, cool but not cold. Snow still covers the peaks, but it's all melted down here below. Friends congregate on the lake's rocky shore, as do many of Dad's clients, some I know and some I don't. I spot Sylvie Rodriguez, a girl I worked with at the coffee shop last summer. I haven't seen her more than four or five times since school started last August. Sylvie has cut her black hair to within a half inch of her scalp and added a few red streaks since I last saw her. A blue dragonfly tattoo is visible on the back of her neck. I find myself wondering if it's new, or if it was always there, hidden beneath her hair when it was longer.

Mom didn't come to the service, but that's no surprise. She hasn't spoken to me since she opened the newspaper yesterday and saw the obituary I wrote. I guess she said all she had to say then. Screamed it, really. How I had done the one thing that Dad would've been the most against. How I had invaded his privacy, and hers. I can't remember Mom ever being that upset with me before.

The photograph of Dad and me that I included with the obituary seemed to bother her most of all. In the shot, he and I are standing together next to his van. Behind us, the twin peaks are visible in the distance.

Mom's reaction to the photo keeps nagging me. Yesterday, Iris kept nagging me, too, coaxing me to ask Mom what she's hiding, but I can't bring myself to do it. I can't bring myself to tell her the strange things Dad said before he died, either. Mom's closed-off expression and the fact that she's even more emotional than I am hold me back.

But I can't worry about my mother right now. This morning is for Dad.

Standing at the edge of the lake, I hold the urn containing his ashes close to me and face everyone. When their murmurs fall silent, I pull a slip of paper from my pocket and start to recite a poem by Percy Bysshe Shelley.

After the first line, I'm too choked up to go on. Wyatt appears at my side to save me. Taking the poem from my hand, he reads:

Music, when soft voices die,
Vibrates in the memory;
Odours, when sweet violets sicken,
Live within the sense they quicken.

Rose leaves, when the rose is dead,
Are heap'd for the beloved's bed;
And so thy thoughts, when thou art gone,
Love itself shall slumber on.

As Wyatt's voice fades, I turn to the water and stare at the peaks. Above them, the sky is chalky gray, and the clouds huddle together, as if for support. Around me, the air is so still that when I sling my arm toward the water, the ashes sail out of the urn in a perfect arc. The lake's dark surface ripples when they hit. The reverberation lingers, echoing inside of me.

"Good-bye, Dad," I whisper. "I love you."

In that moment, I feel Iris's warmth and hear her words, hushed and reverent in my head: *I loved him, too.*

Needing her comfort too much to send her away, I mentally fold into her, and when my knees threaten to buckle, it's as if Iris bears my weight and holds me up.

र Ӻ

Sylvie is a high-energy person—a walking nerve ending. She's never struck me as overly sensitive. Sylvie's more of a tough girl. Which is why I know she's sincerely emotional when she walks to the edge of the lake and hugs me as people are starting to leave.

"Sorry, chica," she murmurs.

"Thanks for coming." We step apart.

"I figured you'd need your friends around you," she says in the raspy voice I've always envied. "What happened to your dad just sucks."

I'm grateful for her bluntness and the fact that she's not treating me as if I'm made of glass. "He was the best," I tell her, my entire body throbbing with loss. "I don't know what I'm going to do without him."

We're both quiet for a few moments, uncomfortable with each other all of a sudden. Death does that, I've discovered. Makes it difficult to know what to say, even for no-nonsense people like Sylvie.

Suddenly, she lifts a silver-studded brow, and nudges me with her elbow. "What's *his* story?" she asks in a low voice.

I glance at her. "Who?"

"Mr. Intense."

I follow her gaze past Paula and Sal, and my stomach flips over as I zero in on the hiker who helped me with Dad and Cookie after the accident.

"He's been watching you," Sylvie whispers.

I duck my head, embarrassed. "Everyone's been watching me."

"Not like that. Who is he?"

"He's the hiker who found us on the mountain." I glance at him again. He's talking to Dad's old friend Tony Dimitri, but Sylvie is right; he's looking at me. "I should go say hi," I tell her.

"Sure. Go ahead. I'll call you later." Sylvie waves at Wyatt and calls out, "Hey, Goob!" He glances in our direction and makes a face.

"At least he knows his name," she says smugly. "Guess I'll go see what he's been up to."

As she heads for Wyatt, I start off toward the hiker and Mr. Dimitri, weaving through a scattering of people and acknowledging murmured words of sympathy.

"I missed your name the other day when you were in the coffee shop," Mr. Dimitri is saying to the hiker when I join them.

"I'm Ty Collier." They shake hands. "I'm sorry I didn't introduce myself."

Mr. Dimitri notices me and offers his condolences. I slip my hands into my coat pockets and say, "Don't let me interrupt."

He smiles. "You aren't."

I look at Ty and instantly blush. "Hello," I murmur, mortified by my reaction to him.

"Hi, Lily," he says in that same soothing voice I remember so well. "It's great to see you."

There's something about him that's sweet and gentle, yet also strong. I think again of how much he helped me when Dad was dying, how his calmness kept me afloat when I was about to drown. I was too frantic to notice much about him then, but I take in everything now. Ty isn't tall, but he isn't short, either, and he's thin rather than lanky. Something makes him seem more mature than the guys from town. I try to look at him discreetly as he and Mr. Dimitri resume their conversation. He's a little rumpled, his dark hair longish and shaggy, like he's past due for a cut, and the dark blue shirt beneath his open coat is wrinkled. His eyes are deep set and brown, his mouth wide . . . and disarming. I feel myself starting to blush again and quickly glance up from his lips, noticing the thin scar that slices across his right cheekbone. It looks fairly new.

Mr. Dimitri asks, "Why Silver Lake, Ty?"

"I was just driving through and it caught my attention. I'm a freshman at Columbia but I took this semester off to do some traveling. Silver Lake's a pretty place. I thought I might stay awhile and do a little hiking if I can find work to tide me over."

"Construction?" Mr. Dimitri asks.

"Yeah, that. Or anything, really," says Ty.

Dad's friend pulls a card from his pocket and hands it to him. "Call me later and I'll give you Tommy Carter's number. He's a contractor. He's building a couple of houses right now."

Ty thanks him, then Mr. Dimitri excuses himself and walks away.

"I'm really sorry about your dad," says Ty, his dark gaze roaming my face.

"I never got a chance to thank you for helping me," I tell him. "I don't know how I would've got through it if you hadn't shown up."

"I wish I could've done more." He puts his hands into the pockets of his gray wool peacoat and clears his throat.

The silence between us stretches a few beats too long, making me feel self-conscious and shy. "So you're staying in town?" I ask, just to have something to say.

He nods. "Yeah. I'm renting a place by the community college. Silver Lake Studio Apartments."

"A day or a lifetime?" I say, reciting the corny line from the banner that hangs in front of the building.

He gives a short laugh. "Yeah, it's a real classy place." We both fall silent again, then Ty adds, "If I can do anything for you, let me know. Your mom, too." He glances to where Addie, Sylvie, and Wyatt stand talking to Mr. Dimitri. Actually, Addie is the only one talking. Wyatt is staring at Ty and me and frowning.

"Addie's not my mom," I say, realizing Ty's mistake. "She's a neighbor."

"Oh." He tilts his head. "Hey, how's your dog?"

"Cookie's better. I'm bringing him home from the vet later today."

He grins. "That's great. I've been wondering about him." Thunder rumbles far off in the distance. Ty shakes his head. "You guys have the craziest weather here. It snowed a few days ago, then it was sunny and warmer, and now it's going to rain?"

I shrug. "In the spring it can change from one day to the next."

"That's what I've heard." Ty looks up at an ominous gray cloud. "I guess I better go."

"We probably all should," I say, but I don't want to tell him good-bye.

As if he reads my thoughts, Ty says hesitantly, "Maybe we could meet up sometime while I'm here. Have coffee or something?"

"I'd like that," I tell him, a tiny thrill zinging through me when his face lights up.

"I'd give you my number if I had something to write with," he says.

Sometime during the last thirty seconds, Wyatt wandered up behind Ty. He's pretending to listen to Paula talk to some man I don't recognize, but I know Wyatt. He's eavesdropping on me. Thinking Paula might have a pen in her purse, I call to her and ask, and she pulls one out of the leather bag hanging over her shoulder. I give it to Ty.

He takes a scrap of paper from his pocket and scribbles his number onto it. As he hands it to me, our fingers touch and I almost can't breathe.

"If you can get away, just let me know," Ty says.

I nod, ashamed of what I'm feeling for this guy at my dad's funeral. And then, without warning, I'm crying silently. Tears pour down my face.

Ty backs up a step, but I see understanding in his expression. "'Bye, Lily," he murmurs. "Take care, okay?"

I nod, clutching the paper with his number on it, and watch him walk away.

Not a single drop of rain has fallen yet when Wyatt drives me into town in his rattling truck an hour later to pick up Cookie.

I'm glad to get away, just the two of us. I try to pretend it's just another day, that we're going into town to the hockey rink to shoot pucks on a Saturday morning, and Mom and Dad are at home together, her cooking something deliciously gooey in the kitchen and him out working in his shop.

I can almost believe it. But not quite.

We're both silent as Wyatt turns onto the two-lane highway that runs through town. I lean my head back and stare out the window. Silver Lake sits in the shadow of the mountains. Red-roofed houses lie scattered haphazardly up the sides of the tree-studded slopes. I love the Gothic feel of the town, the familiar dark sweep of scrub oak, faded houses, and old stone buildings.

Soon, Wyatt exits the highway and makes his way along Silver Lake's red-bricked streets. We stop at a light, and Wyatt clears his throat. His knee is bouncing up and down.

"Are you okay?" he asks almost warily.

"Would you please stop that?" I say, tensing up.

Wyatt flinches. "What did I do?"

"Stop being so weird around me."

"I'm sorry. I just—I don't know what to say, I guess. You know. To help you. To make things better."

"You can't make this better, Wyatt!" I say, more sharply than I intend to.

He shifts uncomfortably, an expression of helpless confusion shadowing his face. The light turns green, and he takes off again.

"Nobody can make this better," I tell him, my voice shrill and wobbly. "It's never going to be better."

"I'm sorry. I didn't mean—"

"Quit apologizing! God, Wyatt. I'm the one yelling at you for no good reason. Why do you have to be so nice? Why don't you just punch me or something?"

Wyatt draws back his head and scowls. "Punch you? *Shit*. I don't want to hit you! Why would I punch you?"

"Because . . ." I swallow. "Because if I hurt on the outside, maybe I won't feel this awful pain on the *inside*." Sobbing, I lower my head.

I don't look up again until the truck comes to a stop. We're parked in front of the veterinary clinic, a mud-colored adobe building. I stare at the door.

Seconds tick by, then Wyatt sighs and says, "Jeez, Lil. I'm—"

"Don't say it!" Despite my mood, a smile twitches my lips.

Wyatt grins his sheepish grin. "I was going to say 'I'm happy to oblige, ma'am.' To punch you, I mean." He pulls off the blue stocking cap he always wears and bows in his seat, his sandy hair spiked out all over his head.

And just like that, I feel lighter, a little more like myself. "You're such a dweeb," I say, squeezing the words through my swollen throat. "I don't believe for a second that you were going to say that."

Scowling, he tugs his hat back on. "You wound me. Name one time I've ever misled you."

"This week, or last?" I smirk at him.

Wyatt tilts his head to the side. "So where do you want me to slug you?"

I point at my chin and smile. "Here."

He makes a fist, draws it back, then brings it forward, brushing it against my chin gently. "*Pow,*" he says.

My smile falls away. "I can't believe Dad's dead," I say quietly.

"Me either. It doesn't seem real."

I sigh. "I'm sorry for yelling at you. It's just . . . everything keeps building up inside me. You were just in the way when it exploded."

"Hey, that's what I'm here for."

We climb out of the truck, and I go inside the clinic, while Wyatt spreads his sleeping bag out in the car to make a bed for Cookie. Dr. Trujillo gives me some painkillers, then carries Cookie outside, placing him in the middle of the old bench seat where Wyatt has laid the sleeping bag.

When Wyatt and I take off again, I lean down and look into Cookie's eyes. He licks my cheek, happy to see me. I bury my face in his warm, furry neck and stroke his back while Wyatt drives.

Wyatt is grinning like an idiot when I finally lift my head. "Remember when we dressed Cookie up in a cowboy hat and a bandanna and took him with us to that Halloween carnival when we were kids?" he asks. "He's probably still psychologically warped over it."

As if to prove Wyatt's point, Cookie groans and we both laugh.

Wyatt reaches over and scratches Cookie between the ears. "I wonder if your mom still has those pictures she took of him in his costume."

"I don't know. I'd ask, but she's not speaking to me," I say. "She's the one acting psychologically warped lately."

"Maybe she just couldn't handle the funeral stuff. Too hard."

"Maybe," I say.

He looks back at the road. We ride in silence the rest of the way home.

When we arrive, Wyatt puts Cookie in his pen by the fire while I slip out of my coat and join Addie in the kitchen. She's busy labeling the food people brought while we were gone and putting it in the freezer. Casseroles and soups go hand in hand with grief, I guess.

"Nobody brought desserts," Addie informs me. "I'll make a blackberry cobbler later."

"You don't have to do that," I say.

"Nonsense." Placing another casserole into the freezer,

she adds, "I know there's plenty here for lunch, but I was thinking I'd try to talk your mama into going to town with me for a bite to eat. Give you two a break from each other and get her mind off her troubles for a while."

"Good luck getting Mom out of Dad's shop. Ever since the accident, she's practically living out there. She said she's been doing some sketching and going through Dad's things, deciding what to get rid of."

"Bless her heart. That does it, then; she has to get away. A change of scenery's bound to lift her spirits."

I hand Addie the last labeled bag, and she puts it in the freezer and closes the door. "I know it's hard, Lily, especially since you're also grieving, but try to be patient with your mother right now. I'll head on out to your dad's shop now and talk to her," Addie says. "Wish me luck."

After she leaves, Wyatt and I go to Cookie's pen. Stooping, I murmur, "How're you doing, boy?" Dr. Trujillo warned me that Cookie is still on shaky ground, mostly because he's fourteen, which is something like ninety-eight human years. I reach in and scratch his head. "Nobody understands how tough you are, do they?"

Wyatt crouches beside me, and when Cookie licks my hand, he says, "Rats also show affection by licking."

"*Sick.*" I scowl at him and snort a laugh.

"I'm talking about rats that have been bred to be pets."

"Who'd want a pet rat?"

"Lots of people. Domesticated rats make great companions. They're small, they're smart, they're playful, and they

51

clean themselves like cats." He ticks the points off on his fingers. "I've been thinking about getting one."

I scrunch up my nose. "Well, it's been nice knowing you."

"You'd cash in our friendship over a rat?"

Tilting my head to one side, I squint at him. "Hmmm."

"You have to think about it?" Wyatt clutches at his chest.

"Go ahead. Get a rat. Big Betty will take care of it for me," I say, referring to Addie's cat.

He winces. "I forgot about Big Betty."

Standing, I start for the stairs. Wyatt stopped by his house and changed into jeans and a flannel shirt before we went into town, but I'm still wearing my clothes from the memorial. "Watch Cookie while I change, okay?" I say.

"Sure. I'll put some more wood on the fire, too. It's sort of cold in here."

I head up to my room and exchange my black wool pants and sweater for my oldest, holiest jeans, a Denver Broncos long-sleeved T-shirt, and my knockoff Ugg boots.

Below, the fire crackles as Wyatt stokes it, and I smell the scent of wood smoke. Warm air eddies up to push out the cold. I'm aware of Iris, but we don't talk. It's a careful silence. I guess she's figured out that I'm not going to listen to any more vague warnings that she can't or won't explain.

I forgave her this morning at the lake, and I think she knows that. I still can't imagine why she told me to "be careful" before Dad's accident, but it couldn't have been the deer. Now that I'm thinking straight, I know Iris was telling me the truth when she said she didn't know what was going to happen. If she had, she would've found a way to get through to me. She wouldn't have let Dad get hurt for any reason. I know this because Iris would never hurt *me*, and nothing could be more painful than losing my dad.

Before going downstairs again, I take the slip of paper with Ty's number on it and enter the information into my phone. I don't know if I'm brave enough to make the first move and call him, but I really want to see him again. Ever since he left the lake this morning, I haven't been able to stop thinking about him.

Twisting my hair into a braid, I return to the living room where Wyatt is sitting on the floor next to Cookie's pen. He has the gate open and his hand is resting on Cookie's head. I plop down beside him and cross my legs.

"Who was that guy you were talking to at the lake?" he asks.

"His name is Ty Collier. He's the guy who helped me with Dad."

"Oh, man," says Wyatt. "If I'd known that, I would've thanked him."

"He goes to college at Columbia. Or did. Ty told Mr. Dimitri he took this semester off."

Shifting to look at Cookie, Wyatt says, "So are you going to go out with him?"

"I *thought* you were snooping." I shove him. "He didn't ask me out, he just asked me to meet him for coffee."

"Well, I'd steer clear of him if I were you. I mean, the guy showed up out of nowhere. He could eat babies for breakfast, for all we know."

"Whatever." I roll my eyes.

The door opens and Addie hurries in, followed by a rush of cool air. "I finally wore her down. Your mother's closing up the shop. She asked me to get her purse."

"Doesn't want to see me, huh?" I try to keep my voice light, even though it hurts to think that Mom's avoiding me.

"Give her some time," says Addie, sending me a look of sympathy.

Heading for Mom's bedroom, I find her purse, then bring it to Addie.

She opens the door and steps onto the porch, saying, "Hold down the fort while we're gone."

"We'll do our best," Wyatt says, then in a teasing mock-whisper to me, adds, "Go see if she locked up the liquor cabinet."

Addie shakes her head and mutters something sarcastic about Wyatt leaving for college as she closes the door.

Suddenly serious, Wyatt says hesitantly, "Speaking of college, are we still on for going to OU together in the fall?"

I tell him that I'm not sure I should leave Mom alone so soon after Dad's death, and that maybe I should go to Silver Lake Community College next semester instead. I could transfer to OU in the spring.

He exhales loudly. "Man. It won't be the same without

you. Maybe I should—"

"Don't change your plans because of me, Wyatt," I break in. "Dad said we should do our own thing and not influence the other's decisions." My throat tightens. "We're not little kids anymore. We're not always going to be around for each other."

Wyatt looks like I stabbed him, then he turns and stares into the fire.

"That came out wrong, Wyatt. You know what I meant."

"It just seems weird that you might not always be close by," he mutters.

"I know."

He gives me a sideward glance. "I wasn't seriously considering staying here with you, though. Did you really think I'd give up a semester of beer pong and hot college girls for your sake?"

I smirk at him. "Yeah, I should've known better than that."

Wyatt stands up and stretches. "So what do you want to do this afternoon?"

"Take advantage of Mom being gone." I motion toward the hallway. "Come on."

He frowns. "Where are we going?"

"To look for Dad's spare keys to the workshop. I want to see what Mom finds so interesting out there."

5

After going through all of the dresser and nightstand drawers in my parents' bedroom, I start in on their closet.

Wyatt stands inside the doorway, leaning against the frame. "I don't feel right about this," he mutters.

"You don't have to help," I tell him, shoving hangers across the rod. I understand why he doesn't approve. I feel like a thief as I search inside pockets and shoes. If Mom walked in, she might never speak to me again. I'd be furious if I ever found her nosing through my personal items. How can I expect her to feel any different?

But I can't stop myself, and it doesn't help that Iris is urging me on. She frets through my mind, as anxious as I am to figure out what's up with Mom.

Standing on tiptoe, I snag my finger under the lid of a shoebox on the upper closet shelf and drag it toward me. The movement causes something to slide across the bottom of the box and the rattling sound of metal against metal trips my pulse. I take the box down and pull off the lid. "Here they are!"

Lifting the ring of keys, I turn to find Wyatt watching me with an expression that makes me ashamed of my triumphant feelings.

"Don't look at me like that," I say. "I can't just sit around crying and wondering what Mom's hiding for the rest of my life. That's all I've done for the past few days, and I'm sick of it." I wait for him to speak, and when he doesn't, I say defensively, "Well, what would you do?"

He blinks at me. "The same thing, probably. But maybe you should go to your mom one more time."

"She won't talk to me! She just keeps saying that she's going through Dad's things or that she's sketching when she's out in his shop."

"Maybe she is."

"Then why won't she let me in?"

Wyatt pushes away from the door and sighs. "Let's find out."

Minutes later, memories of Dad wash over me as we enter the shop. "Would you close the door?" I say quickly to Wyatt. "I feel too exposed with it up."

He slides the door down behind us as I wander toward an unfinished cabinet in the center of the room. The scents of pungent wood shavings and Dad's spicy pipe tobacco surround me. Dust motes dance in the blades of light that slice down from the small windows above. Stooping, I run my fingers along the edge of the cabinet. The aspen it's made of is as white and smooth as the petals on the daffodils that have started sprouting in the meadows around our cabin.

For the first time since Dad died, my heart beats at a normal pace. Maybe I've misjudged Mom. Maybe she does spend her days out here just to feel close to him.

No, she's hiding something, Iris insists. *Whatever he was going to tell you.*

Wyatt interrupts my focus on Iris's words. "Maybe we should leave," he says. "It's sort of soon for you to be coming out here."

"No, I'm okay. It feels good to be around Dad's stuff. It's just strange being here without him. This place was always off limits unless he was with me. He said it wasn't safe, and he didn't like anyone messing with his tools." I scan the space around us, the peg board–covered walls with hooks and tools hanging from them, the wood stacked along one of them, Dad's workbench and electric table saw, the paper-thin wood shavings scattered across the floor. Projects he left unfinished. "I feel him here," I whisper.

"Me, too," Wyatt says.

"I think Mom was going through Dad's big toolbox." I walk to the storage closet, the key ring dangling from my fingers. "She must've dragged it back in here." I try each key on the ring until the door unlocks. When I open it, I'm surprised to find *two* metal toolboxes inside—Dad's battered one, and another one just like it that looks almost

58

new. "That's strange," I say, laying my hand on the shiny metal. "I've never seen this one before."

Wyatt helps me tug it out into the room. Dropping to my knees, I insert each key in the latch, and when one of them works, I take a deep breath. "This might sound crazy, but I'm really scared to see what's in here."

"Let me do it," says Wyatt, crouching beside me. The hinges squeak as he opens the lid. "It's just a bunch of clothes."

Iris seems eager but also tense, as I stand and lift out the first piece of clothing and remove the dry-cleaner plastic around it. It's the fanciest dress I've ever seen, except in magazines and on television. The emerald green fabric is covered with tiny green beads.

"Wow." Wyatt blinks at me. "Was that your mom's?"

"I guess."

"I can't imagine her wearing something like that."

I can't see my no-frills mother in the dress, either. She's strictly a jeans-and-sweatshirt sort of person.

I drape the dry cleaner plastic over Dad's table saw and lay the dress on top of it, then lift the next item out of the chest. It's a fitted white blouse. "I guess these clothes could be hers," I say. "But they look like they belonged to someone younger."

"Your mom was our age once," Wyatt reminds me.

I hold the blouse up in front of me. "Yeah, but Mom's sixty years old, and I don't think the styles were like this when she was in high school. I mean, look at the shoulder pads. I'm pretty sure they were popular in the eighties or nineties."

Placing the blouse on top of the dress, I reach into the chest again, take out a plaid wool miniskirt, black leggings, two long baggy pullover sweaters, and a white dress. I add each one to the pile on Dad's table saw. The next item looks larger than the others. A man's red flannel shirt, the fabric soft and faded. On impulse, I slip it on. The shirt feels strangely familiar. Comfortable. Comforting. As I'm rolling up the sleeves, Iris sighs inside my head, as if the flannel against my skin soothes her, too.

"Hey, look at this," Wyatt says, bending over the toolbox. "There's other stuff under the clothes." He sets a small silver jewelry box on the floor between us, then holds up a hairbrush for me to see.

I take the brush from him as he removes a long black case. "What's that?" I ask.

He carries it to Dad's workbench, sets it down, and flips the latches. "Whoa," he says as he lifts the lid. "It's a violin. A Stradivarius. They cost big bucks; pretty much only professional musicians can afford them."

A chill skates across my skin and Iris shivers violently. The hairbrush slips from my fingers and lands on the floor with a *thud*. The violin's amber wood gleams like polished marble, and I have the strangest feeling that I know exactly how it would feel against my skin. Smooth and cool, the neck of the instrument a perfect fit for my hands. Joy surges through me, followed by a feeling of sadness. I don't understand what's happening to me.

"Lil? What's wrong? You're shaking like crazy. Is it your mom's? Didn't you tell me she used to play?"

"Yes, in the school orchestra when she was growing up. But why would she have had such an expensive violin?" Keeping my focus on the instrument, I cross to Wyatt. "This is going to sound weird, but it's like I remember it."

"Just because your mom didn't play it for you doesn't mean you never saw it. She might've shown it to you before she packed it away."

"Yeah, I guess."

A creeping sensation climbs up my spine, and when it reaches the space between my shoulder blades, I feel a firm pressure, as if I'm being nudged to pick up the violin. I jump, unsettled to have felt Iris's touch in such a solid way—if that's what it was. Apprehensive, I reach for the Stradivarius, but quickly draw back my hand after brushing my fingertips across the strings.

But I'm too late.

The brief contact triggers some switch inside of me, and out of nowhere, frantic notes fill my mind, the melody they create too faint to clearly distinguish. I close my eyes and a vision flickers on the backs of my eyelids: *Long fingers quivering across strings . . . feminine fingers tipped by short, glossy nails, holding a bow that simultaneously jerks and glides. And behind the bow, a flash of sparkling green—the dress. The music fades. Applause explodes like thunder.*

Shaken by the memory, I look at Wyatt again. "I think

I did hear Mom play when I was little. I'm pretty sure she was wearing that beaded dress." I gesture toward where it hangs over the table saw. "And she was on a stage, performing for an audience."

His brows lift. "I didn't realize she had *that* kind of talent."

"Neither did I. She only told me she took lessons in school."

"Why wouldn't she have mentioned something like that? And if she was that good, why would she have given it up?"

We gave up everything. Mom's words to Dad that morning of the accident. Was a career as a professional musician part of that "everything"? Why would she have to give it up for me? "She told me she wanted to concentrate on her artwork," I tell Wyatt, trying to tamp down my sense of unease. "But if the memory I just had is real, she was a much better musician than she is an artist."

"Do you think she plays when she comes out here?" he asks, plucking a string gently.

The *ping* of the note vibrates the hushed air around us. I shake my head. "I would've heard her. And anyway, with her hands so crippled, I'm not sure she could."

I step around Dad's old battered toolbox and head for the storage closet. It's dark inside, and the single bulb overhead doesn't offer much light. Finding a flashlight in the corner, I snap it on and sweep the beam across the shelves, scanning rows of jars filled with nails and screws, measuring tapes, extension cords.

Something on the top shelf catches my eye. I stand on tiptoe and reach for it, but the shelf is too high.

"Here," Wyatt says from behind me. "Try this." He drags a stepladder from the corner and positions it near the wall.

I climb up and aim the flashlight above, moving the beam left to right. Four long cardboard tubes are stacked on the shelf. One by one, I hand them to Wyatt, then I step down and we move the tubes into the center of the workshop.

Using my fingernail, I pry the cap off the end of the first one. Inside, paper is curled up like a poster. "This looks like the parchment Mom uses to sketch," I say as I slide it out.

Wyatt reaches for one end. "I'll help you unroll it."

I lay the tube on the floor at our feet alongside the others, then Wyatt takes hold of the edges of the parchment and walks backward. The paper uncurls in my hands. "Be careful not to tear it," I say.

When it's completely open between us, Wyatt says, "Hey, is that you?"

Oh! Iris gasps as I study the girl in the sketch. She's probably twelve or thirteen, and sits in profile, playing a violin. The girl's hair is chin length, just long enough that it falls forward to cover her face so that I only get a hazy impression of her features. Still, our resemblance is unmistakable.

"That must be Mom," I say. "When she was a girl."

"She looks like you."

"Yeah," I say, an odd wariness drifting over me. Returning to the tubes, I open another one.

Wyatt studies the picture and says, "That must be you when you were a baby."

"I guess." In the drawing, my parents and I are standing on a dock that juts out across a lake. Dad is holding my hand.

"Your parents look so young. Where were you?" asks Wyatt.

"I don't know," I say, trying not to cry. I don't understand why the sketches make me feel so emotional.

The next sketch we open is of a colonial-style house on a wide stretch of lawn that's bordered by flower gardens. The last one is a city scene—cobblestone streets and sidewalk cafés in a place unfamiliar to me.

As we're returning the artwork to the tubes, Wyatt says, "At least we know now she wasn't lying. She really has been sketching out here."

"She might've done these a long time ago. They could be old," I point out.

"Yeah, I guess."

We carry the tubes to the storage closet and I put them back on the top shelf. Climbing down from the stepladder, I say, "There's more to all this than I've told you, Wyatt." As I gather up the clothes we found in the toolbox, I explain about the conversation I overheard between my parents on the morning of my birthday.

Wyatt blinks at me, as if trying to make sense of it all.

"That's movie-of-the-week stuff, Lil. What do you think they were talking about?"

"I was hoping you'd have an idea."

"I wish I did."

Realizing how little I know about my parents' pasts, I walk to the worktable and pick up the silver jewelry box. Wyatt comes over and stands beside me as I open the lid. A ballerina pops up and colored jewels wink at me. A ring with a pale green stone lies next to a pair of big silver earrings. I run my fingertips across a turquoise bracelet and a heart locket on a delicate chain. Moving all of the jewelry aside, I find a folded scrap of notebook paper at the very bottom of the box. I set the box down, take the paper out, and unfold it.

"Listen to this," I say to Wyatt, then read aloud the words scribbled in blue ink. "'Good luck, babe. I know you'll do great. Hurry back. I'll miss you like crazy. Love, Jake.'"

Jake. Iris sighs wistfully, then in an urgent whisper adds, *We have to find him.*

Why? I ask. *Do you know who is he?*

No . . . maybe . . . not sure. His name . . . I feel something. She must have known him when we were small. Maybe we did, too. . . .

Understanding that the "she" Iris is referring to is Mom, I try to recall if I've ever heard her or Dad mention someone named Jake. I search my memory for an image of anyone by that name that we knew when I was younger, but don't come up with anything.

65

"So your mom had a boyfriend before your dad," Wyatt says in a matter-of-fact way.

"Not necessarily."

He frowns at the note. "Sounds like a boyfriend to me."

If Jake was Mom's boyfriend before Dad, Iris wouldn't have any memory of him, vague or otherwise. But I refuse to consider that Mom might've been seeing someone after she and Dad married. I don't believe it.

Find him, Iris demands.

I refold the note and tuck it inside the box again. I have no idea how to start to find the guy. I'm not even sure I want to.

I twist the switch inside the jewelry box, and the ballerina twirls. A melody that Iris used to hum begins to play—the lullaby she sang me to sleep with at night when I was younger.

A wave of dizziness rocks me, and a vision appears. *A guy about my age, his face blurred and flickering like an old movie. A flash of teary blue eyes, a shock of black hair falling over his forehead. He reaches out to me, his mouth moving, but I can't hear what he's saying. The guy's face crumples as I lean closer, wanting to comfort him.*

"Lily?" Wyatt breathes.

I blink, and the vision disappears. Wyatt and I are nose to nose, so near to each other that his breath feathers my face.

I stumble backward and glance down at the jewelry box.

The music has stopped. The ballerina no longer twirls. She stares up at me with pinpoint black eyes.

Wyatt stares at me, too, his mouth hanging open.

"Wyatt," I whisper. "What just happened?"

His grin spreads slowly. "That was some kiss. I didn't know you cared."

"Yeah . . . um . . ." I swallow. "Wyatt . . ." Ohmygod. Heat shoots through me as I remember the soft warmth of his lips against mine and how nice it felt. "I'm sorry. I didn't mean—"

"No, it's okay. I liked it." Amusement tinges his voice.

"But I didn't mean for it to happen. It was an accident."

Wyatt laughs. "Yeah, like you fell forward and landed on my lips."

My gaze is drawn to his mouth, and when I realize I'm staring, I look up quickly. What have I done? I'm feeling things for Wyatt that I definitely shouldn't be feeling for my best friend.

He stops laughing. "Hey, not everyone hates the way I kiss," he says, jamming his hands into his pockets, his face beginning to turn red.

"I didn't say that I hated kissing you," I blurt out.

"You didn't have to." He starts for the door.

"Wait, Wyatt." I go after him. "I'm just freaked out. It's just—we're not like that. You know what I mean."

Wyatt stops and looks back at me. "Yeah, I guess I do." He tugs off his hat and drags his fingers through his hair.

"Where did that come from, anyway?"

"Good question," I say with a shaky laugh, my mind searching frantically for an explanation that will make sense to him. "Things have been crazy, and I've been really confused. You've been so great, and I guess—"

"It's okay. You don't have to say anything." Wyatt shrugs a shoulder. "I won't lie, though. I've thought about it before. Haven't you?"

"Maybe." My blush burns hotter. "But we grew up together. I shouldn't have kissed you. We're—"

"Just friends. I know . . ." Wyatt trails off.

Numb with embarrassment, I return the jewelry box to the tool chest. For the first time in my life, I'm self-conscious with Wyatt, and I don't like it. Walking quickly to the violin on the worktable, I close the case and put it in the chest, too, then lock it.

Wyatt watches me closely. "You okay?"

"Yeah." I manage a smile for him. "Let's get out of here before Mom and Addie get back." He crosses to me, and I hand him the key ring. "Would you make me a spare set when you go into town on Monday?"

"Sure."

Determined to act as if nothing happened, Wyatt and I drag the tool chest into the storage closet without uttering a word. He locks the closet, then we go outside, and I secure the door.

I'm glad he can't see my face as he follows me to the cabin because I'm furious. Not at him, at myself. What was

I thinking, kissing *Wyatt* of all people? I *wasn't* thinking. I didn't instigate that kiss any more than I pushed the brake on my four-wheeler to avoid hitting the deer. Iris is guilty on both counts; I'm furious with her, too. Why would she do such a thing?

Suddenly, I'm certain her reason has something to do with the vision I had of the guy with black hair. And sad eyes the color of a bluebird.

6

The outing worked wonders for Mom's attitude. When she and Addie walk through the front door, they're chatting and Mom is smiling. I'm sitting at the kitchen table doing physics homework. Our eyes meet and a silent truce passes between us.

"How's Cookie?" Mom asks, moving toward the open pen by the fireplace where he's resting on his bed.

"I'm sort of worried about him. He's mostly been sleeping since we got home."

"Rest is important for healing," she says, reaching into the pen and petting Cookie.

Addie closes the front door, a sack of groceries propped on her hip. "We had the tastiest chicken salad at that new café on Main." She makes her way into the kitchen and sets the sack and her purse on the counter.

"Don't rub it in—I had a PB and J," I tease.

Addie glances toward the hallway. "Where's Wyatt?"

"He went home so I could finish this assignment. I

don't want to fall behind." I hope she doesn't notice my red face.

"You'll have plenty of time to catch up," Addie says. "No need to hurry just yet if you don't feel up to it."

"I'd still like to graduate next week like I'd planned."

Turning to Mom, I ask, "Do you think that's possible? Me graduating next week, I mean? If not, it's okay. I understand if you don't feel like looking over my assignments for a while."

Mom gives Cookie one last pat on the head, and stands. "You've never made below a B in your life. When your assignments are completed, let me know and I'll give them a look. I have a feeling it won't take long."

"Thanks, Mom," I say.

My parents have been my only teachers since first grade. It's up to them to decide when I'm ready to graduate. Or just Mom now. That's how homeschooling works, at least where I live. The state of Colorado expects me to study four hours a day, and certain courses are required, but that's about it.

"Your father wanted me to make a diploma for you, and he was going to build the frame," says Mom. "I'll still do my part. We can have it framed at Hobby Shop in Silver Lake."

"Okay," I whisper.

Pulling a bag of flour from the grocery sack, Addie clears her throat, then says, "I'm sure you two would like some time alone. After I put this cobbler together, I'll pop it in the refrigerator and you can cook it whenever you're ready. Then I'm going home. I don't want to wear out my welcome."

"That'll never happen," says Mom. "We appreciate all you've done for us, don't we, Lily?"

"You've been great," I say, sending Addie a smile.

Mom tries to help unload the groceries, but Addie shoos her away, so she wanders over to me. "Need any help with your lesson?" she asks hesitantly.

I realize she's trying to smooth out the last wrinkles of tension between us. "No, I'm doing okay," I tell her. "But, thanks."

She glances at the open physics book. "I'm not sure I'd be much help to you with that, anyway."

I know we're both thinking that Dad was the one with a knack for science and math. He taught me those classes. Mom's strengths are history and English and the creative subjects, like writing and art.

And music, I remind myself, thinking of the violin hidden in Dad's workshop.

When the cobbler ingredients are all on the counter, Addie steps out onto the porch to call Wyatt. I try to focus on my classwork, while Mom stares out the windows at the dense blanket of spruce trees beyond the deck. I almost forget she's standing beside my chair until she touches my shoulder.

"Where did you get this?" Her fingers stroke down the sleeve of the red flannel shirt I'm still wearing. How could

I have forgotten to take it off?

"You—um—left Dad's shop unlocked. The wind blew the door open so I went to close it and the shirt was out." Shame rains down on me. I hate lying. Especially to Mom.

She shakes her head. "I remember locking up." After a pause, she asks, "Did you take anything else out of Dad's shop?"

Her sharp tone sparks anger inside of me. "No, Mom! Why do you even care? What's out there that you don't want me to see?"

She pulls her keys from her pocket and heads for the door.

The moment she steps outside, I unbutton the flannel shirt. If it upsets her so much, I'll put it away.

"What's wrong, sugar?" Addie asks as she comes in from outside and sees the look on my face. "Your mother didn't stop to say 'boo' when she passed me on the porch. Is everything okay?"

"She went out to the shop again."

Addie sighs. "I thought an afternoon away from here might put an end to that."

"I know. Me, too."

I'm tugging my arm from a sleeve, when invisible fingers slide down my spine again, caressing the shirt's fabric. Shivering, I pull the sleeve back up my arm.

I know, Iris, I think. *I feel it, too.*

The shirt is like a security blanket, the soft flannel reassuring. It's almost as if it was made for me. Or I was made for it.

Addie leaves early in the evening, and Mom holes up inside the shop until after dusk. I'm not sure what finally makes her decide to return to the cabin, unless it's the sweet scent of Addie's cobbler baking in the oven.

I turn on the television and raise the volume to fill the empty space between us. The silent treatment is our usual M.O. when we're at odds. But tonight it's worse than ever. We can't even look at each other.

On the television, the actors' voices seem too loud and their laughter mocks us. "Lily," Mom says, and I brace myself for the confrontation I've been expecting. But instead, Mom lifts the braid off my shoulder and rubs the spiky ends between her stiff fingers. "You should cut your hair," she says in a distant voice.

I turn to her, anxiety slithering through me. "I don't want to cut it."

"You should." She drops my braid, sits back, and murmurs, "You'd look wonderful."

"I don't think so."

"Your father thought you were adorable with short hair."

"I've never had short hair," I say. "Not since I was a baby."

Mom blinks, and I get the weirdest sense that she just returned from some faraway place. Standing abruptly, she crosses her arms, like she's protecting herself.

"Mom?" I dig my fingertips into the couch cushion.

"The morning of my birthday, before Dad and I drove to the lookout, I heard the two of you talking."

She's quiet for a long time, and then she says, "He was afraid you would."

"What was he going to tell me when we got home?" When she doesn't answer after a few seconds, I try again. "After the accident, before Dad lost consciousness, he said something about the two of you thinking you'd done the right thing, then he asked me if it *was* right and if I've been happy. What did he mean?"

"I don't know. He must've been mixed up." She grabs the television remote from the coffee table and begins flipping through the channels.

"But what were you talking about when you said you gave up everything for me?"

"It doesn't matter now." Mom turns the television off, lays down the remote, and stands, then starts toward the hallway. "Your father is gone and we have to learn to go on without him."

"Is that what you're doing?" I call after her. "Going on with your life by locking yourself in his shop every day?"

The click of her bedroom door is my only answer.

That night, I curl up on the couch close to Cookie's pen, intent on sneaking out to the workshop after I'm sure Mom's asleep.

The log walls creak and groan as the cabin settles in, and quiet yelps slip from Cookie's throat as he dreams by the fireplace. I worry that he might be in pain, but I've already given him his dose of medicine. He's just been so out of it today, so listless.

Iris, though, is anything but lethargic. She's edgy tonight, as restless as the wildlife that creep in the shadows around the cabin after dark. But I'm too tired to try to calm her down. My muscles relax and my eyelids droop.

Just as I'm falling asleep, the fire snaps and flares, and she whispers, *Wake up!*

Startled, I sit upright. *What's wrong, Iris?*

Go. The workshop. Look for answers.

I rub my eyes. *About Jake?*

The secret. He must be part of it.

I stare into the glowing orange embers in the fireplace, feeling reluctant to dig any further. What if Jake wrote that note to my mother? *Babe.* I cringe. If Jake is the young guy I saw in the vision, then they did know each other before Mom married my dad, because he didn't look any older than me. Why did I feel the urge to kiss him? And how is he connected to Iris? None of it makes sense.

Go, Iris breathes.

Slipping from beneath the blanket, I tiptoe into Mom's room. The jeans she wore earlier are draped over a chair in the corner, her ring of keys creating a bulge in one pocket. Holding my breath, I ease across the floor and retrieve the keys without making a sound.

Back in the living room, I take a lantern-style flashlight off the mantel, put my coat on over my pajamas, and stuff my feet into my boots. My breath catches when the hinge squeaks as the front door opens, but Cookie doesn't stir and I don't hear Mom, so I step outside and close the door gently behind me.

Once I'm in the shop, I turn on the flashlight and set it on the floor. I don't want to use the overhead lights and risk Mom looking out and seeing a glow streaming from the windows.

Dragging the toolbox out of the closet, I remove the violin case and the jewelry box and place them on the floor, close to the light. I sit in front of the case, crossing my legs on the dusty plywood planks, and open it. The sight of the instrument's gleaming, honey-colored wood makes my pulse stutter. But as much as I want to, I can't bring myself to touch it again. What if I have another freaky vision of that guy? A part of me is terrified for that to happen. Another part wishes it would so that maybe I can figure out if he's Jake.

Iris flickers inside me like snowy static on a television screen, constant, unbroken. Waiting. I raise the lid on the jewelry box. The ballerina pops up and gives me a blank stare.

"Sorry to bother you," I murmur to the tiny doll. "I'd just like another look at that note, if you don't mind." Retrieving the scrap of paper, I unfold it, place it on my knee. A pencil lies nearby on the floor. Dad was always using them out here; he must've dropped it. I pick it up and trace the name *Jake* on the note, wondering who he might be.

"You know who Jake is, don't you?" I say to the ballerina, staring into her pinpoint eyes. Sighing, I give the peg beside her one twist. She twirls, and music trickles through the quiet workshop like water in a brook.

I flinch at the sound and reach to stop the song, but before I can close the lid, my elbow knocks over the lantern and the bulb flicks off. Darkness swoops over me like the wing of a giant black bird.

The music continues to play, weaving a ribbon of heartache around me so tight that I can't move, drawing me someplace where nothing exists but the melody . . . where nothing else matters.

I'm unsure how much time passes before Iris brings me back. I open my eyes to the darkness again and a sensation that I've traveled to a place I once knew. A place that felt like home.

We have to find Jake, Iris says. *He'll help us.*

I fumble around on the floor until I find the lantern. With one rattle, the bulb engages and faint light quivers. The note from Jake lies atop the violin case. Written in pencil in my own handwriting beneath his name, just above the ragged torn edge of the paper, are the words: *Winterhaven, Massachusetts.*

7

Early the next morning, I wake to pounding above me. My first thought is that Dad is on the roof, nailing down shingles, continuing the project he started before my birthday. But then I remember, and the pain of losing him crashes down around me.

Cookie's whining in his pen. I sit up on the couch. Is he in pain? He slept through the night—maybe he's just desperate to go outside. I reach for my cell phone on the coffee table and check the time. Ten fifteen. I can't believe I slept so late.

As I tuck my phone into the pocket of my baggy pajama pants, the weird things that happened in the workshop last night come back to me. The first time I played the jewelry box, I kissed Wyatt. The second time, I wrote on the note. Does the music throw me into some sort of trance?

Pushing my worries to the back of my mind, I get up and go to the door where I left my boots last night before

I tiptoed to Mom's room to return her keys. As I put them on, the pounding overhead continues.

Entering the pen, I try to coax Cookie out, but he won't budge. He yelps when I lift him to his feet. I stay beside him as he limps into the room, then makes his way onto the porch. When he hesitates at the top of the stairs, I carry him down into the yard and set him in the grass. He does his business, then hobbles over to a patch of shade and plops down with a groan, his head on his paws.

Concerned about him, I say, "What's wrong, boy? Why are you so sad? Does it still hurt that much?" I don't understand. Dr. Trujillo said that Cookie should get a little better every day.

It's warmer than it's been all spring, with only a slight breeze blowing. Wyatt's truck is parked behind Mom's Blazer in the driveway. Knowing Cookie won't go anywhere, I walk to the side of the cabin where I find Mom shielding the sun from her face with one hand as she looks up to where Wyatt is perched on his knees, hammering away at the roof. Wondering if we're back on speaking terms, I try to gauge her frame of mind as I pause beside her.

"Morning," I say.

She glances at me. "Good morning. Did you sleep well?"

"I slept okay." I follow her gaze to the roof. "How'd you manage to bribe Wyatt to do manual labor?"

"He volunteered, free of charge. You're too hard on him. Wyatt's always been a good worker."

"Yeah, but usually for a price. And he takes Sunday being a day of rest to the extreme."

Mom smiles. "Maybe he's maturing."

I snort a laugh, but then I remember the way he looked at me yesterday after that kiss. I didn't recognize *that* Wyatt. Maybe he has changed.

Wyatt's wearing a ball cap with the bill to the back and a short-sleeved T-shirt. The muscles in his arm flex each time he swings the hammer. Crazy questions start knocking around in my mind as I watch him work: What if Wyatt and I hadn't grown up together? What if we were meeting for the very first time?

He lifts his head, catches sight of me, and stops hammering. "Hey." Wyatt sits back on his heels, squinting in the sunlight.

"Hey," I say back.

He flashes a grin, and I cross my arms, embarrassed that my hair is a mess and I'm not wearing a bra. Weird. Wyatt has seen me looking worse than this more times than I can count and I was never self-conscious. Suddenly, I wish that I could remember every detail of our kiss, and that wish startles me so much, I quickly shift my eyes to the ground.

"Come on down whenever you're ready, Wyatt," Mom calls. "I'm sure you have chores to do at home."

"I'll just finish this row," he answers. "If you want me to come back later, I will."

As Wyatt starts hammering again, Mom says to me,

"He's nice to offer, but I can't ask him to finish the roof."
She sighs. "I don't know how we'll afford to hire someone
else to do it, though."

I flash back to Dad's memorial. "I met someone who
might be willing to do it," I say, and tell Mom about Ty
Collier.

She frowns. "I don't know, Lily. I don't like the idea of
hiring a stranger."

"He helped me with Dad and Cookie."

Reluctantly, Mom says, "I'd want to meet him before
I decide. And I'd need references." She hesitates another
moment, then smiles, adding, "I guess you can call him."

I send her a cautious smile back, relieved that she's
more like her old self today. I consider asking about Jake
and Winterhaven, Massachusetts—if she's ever heard of it,
if we've ever been there. But something tells me that Jake
and Winterhaven are connected to the secret Dad wanted
to tell me, and that both might be touchy subjects, like the
red flannel shirt. I don't want to spoil Mom's good mood.

When Wyatt finally comes down from the roof, he carries Cookie into the house for me. Placing him in his pen,
Wyatt asks, "Do you have plans today, Lil?"

"Not really," I say.

"Me, either."

"Could I keep Lily until after lunch, Wyatt?" Mom
asks, sitting on the couch. "We need to call Adam's clients
and look over some paperwork. He had several projects
under way."

"Sure." Wyatt starts toward the door. "I'll call you later, Lil."

"Thanks for your help today, Wyatt," says Mom. "With the roof and with Cookie."

"Anytime." He steps onto the porch and closes the door.

Mom calls me over to the couch, and I'm surprised to see tears in her eyes. "Your father would hate letting down his clients."

"How can I help?" I ask, my eyes filling, too. "What do you want me to do?"

"Nothing right now. I just needed an excuse to steal you away from Wyatt for a while." A tear clings to her lashes, and as she swipes it away, the shadow of a smile curves her lips. "We have some other unfinished business." Reaching beneath the coffee table, she slides out the package with the yellow bow. It's been sitting there on the floor ever since the morning of my birthday, and I completely forgot about it. Holding the gift out to me, she says, "I hope you like it."

I press my lips together and shake my head. "I don't know if I can open it, Mom. Dad should be here with us. Me and my stupid birthday tradition. We should've stayed home that morning."

Mom sets the package on the coffee table. "Come here, Lily." As I settle in next to her, she says, "Your father is still here in so many ways." She gestures around the room, at the view outside the window. "Everywhere I look, I see him. Don't you? He's a part of this cabin and the mountains and meadows he loved so much." She lifts the present from the table. "And he's very much a part of this."

I taste tears on my lips as I unwrap the package. Inside, I find a smaller wrapped box. It's something Dad would do and I'm suddenly laughing as I unwrap it, too. Tingling with excitement, I lift the lid. A ring sits on a black velvet cushion. Symbols are etched into the silver around the band—antelope and stick people, pyramids and spiraling circles. "Oh my gosh! These look like the Indian petroglyphs we saw at Picture Canyon," I exclaim, referring to a day trip we took last year to see the ancient rock art carved into the canyon walls.

"I designed it from the photographs we took." Mom's eyes shine, and I can tell that she's pleased by my reaction. "I know you've never cared much for jewelry, but now that you're older, we thought you might like it. Your father made the band and I did the etching. We took advantage of your afternoon hikes."

I slip the ring onto my right pointer finger. "It's perfect. I'll never take it off." I hug Mom tightly.

"I'm sorry about last night," she murmurs into my hair.

"I'm sorry, too," I say.

"Are you sure you wanna do this?" Wyatt asks when I step onto the porch late in the afternoon, dressed to ride.

"Positive." I take the steps down into the gravel driveway where the four-wheelers sit behind Mom's Blazer. The truth is, I'm *not* sure. Not about riding again so soon. Not about taking the same trail that Dad and I took. Or visiting the scene of the wreck. I'm also not sure that I'm ready to be alone with Wyatt again. But I have to do this. One thing Dad taught me: Postpone facing a fear and it's sure to grow bigger with each passing day.

As I'm climbing onto the seat of my ATV, Wyatt asks, "Did you and your mom get the paperwork done?"

"Not all of it, but we got started." Which is true. We went through everything and made a list of clients to call, invoices we need to pay, and balances due on accounts receivable. In a few hours, I learned more about Dad's business than I've known all my life.

Removing my glove, I hold out my hand to Wyatt so he can see my ring. "Look what Mom gave me for my birthday. She and Dad made it."

Wyatt comes over and slips his hand beneath my fingers for a closer inspection. "It's amazing," he says.

Two days ago, I wouldn't have thought twice about Wyatt holding my hand. But now I'm totally tuned in to how warm his skin is against mine, the rough texture of his callused fingers, how close we're standing. It's unnerving. Confusing. My instincts tell me to break contact and back away *now*, but I can't move. I catch myself wondering what would happen if I leaned in and kissed Wyatt again, but I'm not sure I want our relationship to change. What if it didn't work out and I lost my best friend?

I slip my hand from his, and Wyatt backs up a step as I tug on my glove then twist the key in the ignition. The four-wheeler's engine roars to life.

Seconds later, as we take off, all my apprehensions about riding disappear. One fear down, three to go. Doing something normal feels fantastic. Like so many times in the past, Wyatt follows me down the road, while Iris whistles a tune in my ear.

We move deeper into the forest and the temperature drops at least ten degrees. When the curve in the trail where the accident occurred appears ahead, I slow the vehicle, pull off toward the trees at the trail's edge, and cut the engine. Wyatt stops beside me. We tug off our helmets and hang them on our handlebars.

"This is the place," I murmur.

Wyatt narrows his eyes on mine. "You okay?"

I nod, but every muscle in my body clenches. I take a deep breath and draw in the musk of the forest, remembering it all. *Blink.* I rounded the curve. *Blink.* I saw a deer in the road. *Blink.*

I walk over to the aspen tree Dad hit, sorrow and anger crowding my throat as I run my fingers over a scraped section of bark. It's a small wound compared to what Dad suffered, and that fact makes me want to punch the tree trunk until my knuckles bleed.

I turn and find Wyatt beside me. "It's crazy how one second can change everything," I say, remembering when Mom told Dad that, and later, Iris told me. "It's like my seventeenth birthday triggered something. Like it set some monstrous wheel in motion that I can't stop."

Wyatt's expression spills worry and affection.

"Mom knows I went through that toolbox in Dad's shop," I say, then go on to explain that I forgot to take off the flannel shirt and how strange she acted when she noticed me wearing it.

He frowns. "Why do you think it bothered her?"

I shrug. "I wish I knew."

Wyatt reaches into his jacket pocket, retrieving Dad's workshop keys and an extra set. "Here. I had these spares made for you like you asked."

"Thanks." I put them into my pocket.

"What else did your mom say?"

"She told me I should cut my hair short, that long hair doesn't *suit* me."

"What's that all about?" Wyatt asks.

"Who knows? You should've seen her expression. It was so weird."

Hoping he'll have an open mind, I tell him about my return visit to the workshop last night and what happened. That is, everything other than Iris's insistence that Mom is hiding something. I've never told Wyatt about Iris.

"Winterhaven and Jake must have something to do with what Dad was planning to tell me," I say. "I'm going to ask Mom and see how she reacts. I want to ask her about the violin and other stuff, too. I'm just waiting for the right time. I don't want to freak her out again."

Wyatt blinks and shifts uneasily. Stooping, he scoops a rock off the ground and tosses it down the road.

"What?" I say. "You think Winterhaven's just some random place I scribbled down on paper for no reason? Why wouldn't I remember doing it?"

"I don't know, Lil." He stands. "It is kind of freaky. I mean, you really think something led you to write that down?"

"Do you have a better explanation?"

"Not really. But I'm creeped out by that one, aren't you?"

A burst of cool wind rattles the treetops. Iris's shiver is like a ripple on a lake. Creepy is my normal, I think, wondering what he'd say if I told him about her. "Yes, I'm creeped out," I say instead. "It was completely eerie, but that doesn't mean it didn't happen."

Looking down, he pokes a tree root with the toe of his boot, muttering, "I wish you wouldn't go out there alone."

"I'm not having some kind of wigged-out emotional response to Dad's death," I say softly. "You don't have to worry about me."

"I didn't say I was."

"But you are, and it's okay." I duck my head to capture his attention, and smile. "It's nice that you care. I know this all sounds crazy, but I can show you the note. I've never even heard of Winterhaven, Massachusetts. Why would I just pull it out of thin air? And what about how I reacted to the music box song?"

"I can't explain the music, but maybe you heard your parents talking about Winterhaven sometime in the past. Or you might've heard it mentioned in a movie or something."

"Maybe. But why did I write it down? Don't you think that's sort of random? I'm thinking maybe I've been there before." I cross my arms, my head about to explode from all the questions running through it. "It'll be easy to find out if Winterhaven's a real place, but I don't know how I can prove that it has anything to do with my parents' secret. Or Jake, for that matter. Right now that's just a feeling I have." *Because of Iris*, I think.

"You don't have to prove anything to me," says Wyatt, but he fails to hide his concern.

Humiliated that he thinks I'm losing my grip, I say, "I know you don't believe any of this. But you have to admit that it's a pretty big coincidence that I zoned out twice when the music box played."

"Twice?"

"You were there the first time," I remind him.

He holds my stare. "Wait. When we kissed?"

I've never noticed how green his eyes are. "Yes," I whisper.

"And you think the music had something to do with that?"

"I don't know. Maybe. I mean, you have to admit it was bizarre."

He shrugs.

I don't want to embarrass him, but I will if I tell him it was as if I was kissing the guy with black hair and blue eyes in the vision. "I just don't understand how it happened," I say.

"Maybe we both wanted it to," Wyatt replies, his voice tender and warm.

Suddenly, all of my questions and curiosity, my fears and doubts and affection for him tangle together until I can't sort out one emotion from the other. On impulse, I tilt my face up to his.

Surprise flickers across Wyatt's features. He places a hand on the tree trunk above my head, and I can't move or even breathe as his mouth brushes against mine. I wait for my confusion to clear, to be able to make sense of these new feelings he stirs in me. But if anything, I'm more mixed up than before. "We can't do this," I say. "This is just—it's happening too fast."

Wyatt lowers his arm and steps back, looks away. "Okay," he says quietly. "I get it."

"Don't be mad at me. So much in my life is different now. A part of me is afraid for us to be different, too. One minute I want us to be like we've always been, then the next minute—" I take a breath.

Wyatt's brows tug together, and the tips of his ears turn red. "I didn't start this, Lil. I didn't cause this change between us, *you* did. *You* kissed *me* yesterday."

I can't think of a single word to say as he turns and walks to his ATV. He puts on his helmet, climbs on, and starts the engine. Standing in the middle of the trail, I watch him turn and take off in the direction we came. When he disappears around a curve, I dig my fingers into my palms, trying not to cry.

No more than a minute passes before I notice that the sound of Wyatt's four-wheeler is becoming louder instead of more distant. And then I see him driving toward me again. He pulls to a stop a few feet away from where I stand and takes off his helmet. "Damn it," he says, sounding miserable. "I can't leave you alone. Not here."

Where I last saw Dad alive. I read the words in his eyes, and I love him all the more for his kindness.

I run to Wyatt, throw my arms around his neck, and burst into tears. We hold each other for a long time, but I still sense his confusion, and I'm more afraid than ever of losing the easiness we've always shared.

When I get home, I check my phone to make sure I haven't missed a call from Ty. I called him before Wyatt and I left, but only got his voice mail, so I left a message. I do have a missed call, but it's from Sylvie. She wants to meet in town next week. I make a mental note to call her.

Cookie is awake, but lying listless in his pen. Mom's still napping on the couch. I tiptoe to her closet and place Dad's spare keys to the workshop back inside the shoebox on the upper shelf. Then I throw a load of towels and jeans in the wash, trying to take my mind off the ride with Wyatt.

Iris is impatient, buzzing like a bee beneath my skin. Knowing she won't relax until I research Winterhaven, I go upstairs to my computer. Ever since last night, I've been putting it off because I'm afraid of what I might find— and what my reaction will be. The thought of falling into another strange daze freaks me out.

Sitting cross-legged on the bed, I open my laptop and Google "Winterhaven, Massachusetts." A listing of real estate sites appears, and a link to the town's chamber of commerce. I sit straighter. It's a real place!

Clicking on the chamber of commerce link, I find a photo album with pictures of Winterhaven's main attractions as well as a few places of interest in the surrounding area. It's a storybook town. Colorful shop facades line the main drag, pots of flowers beside every entrance. Homes with huge columns stand watch over cobblestone streets shaded by giant oak trees. A boardwalk curves through a lush green park toward sparkling Winterhaven Lake, a small body of water flanked by tiny pastel cottages.

After browsing through thirty-six unfamiliar images, I click on number thirty-seven and goose bumps erupt on my arms. I stare at the picture of a dock jutting out across an inlet of water on Winterhaven Lake, and a certainty I can't explain washes over me. Somehow, I know that when the water rises after a hard rainfall, a child can sit at the edge of the deck and easily dip her feet in. I know that the lake is freezing cold, even in the summer, and the planks on the deck creak when you walk across them. The wood is weathered, and you have to be careful of splinters if your feet are bare.

I brace my hands on the bed, overwhelmed by sound and sensation: *A gentle lapping of waves against a shoreline of sand and pebbles. The distant putter of a fishing boat motor.*

Masculine laughter. A spray of cold water across my face. Sunshine warm on my back. My toes gritty with sand.

"I *have* been there," I murmur.

Yes, Iris whispers.

In the sketch of myself as a toddler that's hidden in Dad's workshop I'm standing with my parents on a weather-beaten dock. The same dock pictured on the Winterhaven chamber of commerce website.

"Lily? Are you here?" Mom calls from below.

"Upstairs!" I yell, then quickly erase the computer's search history.

Afraid of something I can't name, I swing my feet to the floor and go to her.

8

Yesterday evening, Ty called and said he'd be happy to help with the roof. For the rest of the night, I kept hearing the way his voice sounded when he said my name. And I kept remembering how he looked at me with an intense, single-minded focus when I was standing with Sylvie at the lake. Even now, I get pathetically lightheaded just thinking about it.

This morning when he pulls up in front of our cabin, I go out with Mom to introduce them. It's even warmer today than yesterday. A hummingbird is flitting around the feeder that hangs from the porch eave. Its hyperfast wings are no match for the fluttering in my chest when Ty sees me and his mouth curves into a crooked smile.

I bite my lip and look away for a second to calm down. I don't want to do anything stupid, like trip down the stairs.

In the yard, as Mom talks to Ty, I do my best not to check him out in an obvious way. But it isn't easy. As pitiful as it sounds, I could stare at him all day. His hair is messy, like he forgot to comb it when he got out of bed. All I can say is, tangles look good on him—*really, amazingly good*. He's wearing a white T-shirt, ripped jeans, and black Converse sneakers. His arms are brown and strong—not in a bulky weight-lifter way, just lean, firm muscle. I notice a small tattoo on his right bicep, but can't make out the design without staring.

As I watch him walk around the yard peering up at the roof, it's as if my skin catches fire. There's just something about the way Ty moves, so loose-limbed and sure, that gets to me. He doesn't seem to possess even an ounce of self-consciousness. Then there's his quiet, low voice. And the way his head tilts to one side and his eyes narrow when he talks, like he's daring you to question him. He doesn't come across as unfriendly, just sure of himself.

"I have a couple of other people to interview later today," Mom says to Ty as she leads him back to the front of the house.

She's lying. He's the only person we've talked to about the roofing job. I don't call her on it, though. She's using a cane to help her walk this morning—something I've never seen her do before. I didn't even know she *owned* a cane.

Mom glances at the list of references Ty gave to her when he arrived. "I'll get in touch with a few of these folks this afternoon and let you know tomorrow."

"Cool," he says, and I get the most uncanny sense that although Ty is talking to Mom, he's as tuned in to me as

I am to him. I can almost *feel* his attention being magnetically drawn toward me. "I'd really like to work for you, Mrs. Winston," Ty continues. "I'd do a good job, and I can start right away."

"You're sure you've shingled a roof before?" Mom asks, even though Ty already told her at least twice that he has.

"My parents own rental property," he says. "I started helping my dad with maintenance during high school, and he and I have replaced a few roofs together since then. I also did maintenance part-time on some apartments one of my professors owns." Ty gestures at the page Mom holds. "He's on the list. Dr. Rigsby."

She frowns. "Why aren't you in school anymore?"

"*Mom.*" I glare at her.

Ty isn't fazed. "I'm going back in the fall," he says. "My family's been dealing with some difficulties lately, and I needed to get away."

"You lived with your parents while you were going to college?"

"No, they live with my younger brother in Baltimore. I lived on campus."

"Columbia. Right." Mom analyzes him skeptically. "New York City wasn't far enough away from your family problems?"

"Mom!" I step between them. "I'm sorry, Ty."

"It's okay," he insists, but his jaw clamps tight, drawing my attention to the scar just above it on his cheek.

Mom doesn't apologize for her rudeness. Instead, she sends me a silencing look. "How long do you plan to stay in Silver Lake, Ty?"

"I'm not sure." He glances at me, then back to her. "I can definitely stay another week or so." With a short laugh, he adds. "I wouldn't get far if I left now, anyway. I'm a little short on gas money."

"I can't pay much." Mom quotes a ridiculously low amount.

Ty nods. "I'm fine with that."

"Well, then . . ." She clears her throat. I suspect she was hoping he'd reject her offer. "I'll be in touch," Mom says. Leaning into the cane, she walks toward his car, a not-so-subtle hint that she's ready for him to leave.

Ty and I follow, but I ignore her monotone chatter about Dad's tools and kneepads and nails and her instructions that, if she hires him, she'll expect Ty to clean up and put everything away in the storage shed when he finishes each day.

Clasping my hands behind my back, I risk a sideward glance at Ty and find him watching me, too. We both smile, but I look away first, self-conscious and giddy. I can't recall ever being so aware of another human being in my life.

The three of us pause beside Ty's beat-up old sports car, which is faded turquoise, with double white stripes down the center of the long, narrow hood. It sits so low to the ground that I don't know how he gets around on our rocky dirt roads. It's great, though. It's just like him—cool, but not trying to be.

Mom tells Ty good-bye, then heads for the cabin as he backs out of the gravel drive. Reluctantly, I follow her, pausing when Ty calls, "Hey, Lily!" I look back to find the car stopped and Ty rolling his window down.

I shoot a glance at Mom, but she concentrates on climbing the steps to the porch. "Did you forget something?" I ask Ty.

"No, I wanted to ask about your dog. Cookie, right? I was hoping I'd see him."

"He's inside. He's been so lazy since he came home from the clinic that he hasn't been good for anything," I say jokingly, not wanting to reveal just how worried I really am about Cookie.

"He's better, though, right?" Ty's grimace crinkles the space between his brows in the most appealing way.

I nod. "Yeah. He's getting there," I say, even though I'm not really sure.

"I'm glad." A hint of a smile plays around Ty's lips. He rests his elbow on the opening of the window and drums his fingers on the steering wheel. "Hey, I was thinking . . ." He clears his throat. "Even if your mom decides not to hire me, I hope you'll still call when you're ready to go for coffee."

The fluttering wings in my chest take flight, lifting me off the ground. At least that's how I feel—like I'm floating. "I will," I blurt out, thinking he seems a little nervous. Which is completely surprising and really sweet.

One of Ty's brows lifts as he tilts his head to the side. "Even if your mother doesn't think it's a good idea?"

"She won't care," I assure him, although I know that isn't true.

"After that grilling she just gave me?" He laughs, and I immediately love the sound. It's unrestrained and without an ounce of bitterness.

Wincing, I say, "Sorry about her interrogation."

"I don't blame her. I'm just some strange guy she doesn't know from Ted Bundy; she's smart to be careful."

"Please tell me you aren't *that* strange," I say, teasing. Ty laughs again, and I add, "Mom's just extra cautious lately. Because of what happened. Don't take it personally. I'm sure she doesn't think you're a serial killer."

His face is suddenly serious and filled with compassion. I look down at my boots, struck by emotion again. One thing I've learned about grief—it can catch you off guard and grab you by the throat. "I promise I'll call you," I say, to keep from crying.

"Good," he says. "I'll be waiting to hear from you. 'Bye, Lily."

"'Bye."

He waits three heartbeats before pulling away—I count them. Three wild, pounding heartbeats while we look at each other.

Ten minutes later, I'm in the kitchen washing the break-fast dishes when Mom comes out of her bedroom. My schoolbooks are on the kitchen table. I'm going to try to get back into my routine of working in the mornings for the next few days so that I can finish, turn my lessons over to Mom, and graduate by the end of the week.

She pauses behind me. "I'm still not sure how I feel about hiring Ty."

"Why?" I look over my shoulder at her, my hands submerged in lemon-scented bubbles. "What's wrong with him?"

"Nothing, except that we don't know him. It's only you and me now. We can't let just anyone hang around. Besides, all that talk about his father owning rental property might be pure fabrication and he can't even hammer a nail."

"That's why you check references," I say, with just a hint of sarcasm.

Mom crosses her arms. "I don't know his references, either."

Drying my hands on a dish towel, I face her. "Some of them are professors at Columbia. Jeez, Mom. If you doubt *that*, I'll check the university's website and make sure they're listed. Why are you so nervous and suspicious?"

"Why are *you* so adamant that we hire him? If it's a crush, you're setting yourself up to get hurt. You heard what he said; he's not sticking around. He's going back to New York soon."

Bristling, I toss the dish towel onto the drying rack. "It isn't a crush. And *nobody's* permanent. Dad didn't stick around, either, did he?"

Mom flinches, and I instantly wish that I could snatch the words back. How could I have said something so cruel? Until now, I didn't realize how angry I am at Dad for leaving.

"I'm sorry, Mom. I shouldn't have said that."

Tension stretches between us, wraps around us, tugging tight. The clock ticks steadily. A crow caws outside. Beneath those sounds lies the constant undercurrent of friction that I recognize as Iris. She's nervous about everything, too, lately. Pressuring me to ask Mom about Winterhaven and Jake, to find out what's going on. But I don't think Iris understands Mom's state of mind right now, how easily she might crumble.

A full minute passes before Mom walks to the coffee table and picks up her cell phone. "I'll call his references," she says, avoiding my scrutiny. "If everything checks out, Ty can start work in the morning."

Ty's references had only good things to say about him. Mom said they used words like *diligent, dependable,* and *motivated* to describe him. She's obviously impressed, especially since one of them said that he started college on a full academic scholarship. Mom calls Ty and offers him the job.

On Tuesday he arrives at eight o'clock sharp. I'm already at the table with my work spread out in front of me, and Mom is looking over my assignment. Each time I get up to take a break or tend to Cookie, she watches me as if she thinks Ty's a coyote and I'm a rabbit, and he'll gobble me up.

At least monitoring my every move keeps Mom out of Dad's workshop. She doesn't even escape out there when Ty leaves at three o'clock after clouds move in and it starts to sprinkle.

Disappointed that I didn't get a chance to talk to Ty before he left, I decide to go see Wyatt. I haven't heard from him since our ride up the mountain. I don't want him to think I'm avoiding him.

When I arrive, Wyatt's helping Addie paint the guest room purple. Addie insists the shade is *eggplant* and scoffs each time Wyatt makes a snide remark about the color.

I grab a paintbrush and join them. While we work, Addie chatters on about everything imaginable, but Wyatt barely utters a word, which is unusual for him. I try to draw him into the conversation, without much success. More than once, I catch him watching me, or he catches me watching him, and our gazes lock for a moment before we both look away. Each time it happens, I wonder if his pulse is ticking as fast as mine.

Addie finally runs out of things to talk about and starts singing under her breath, but I'm so caught up in trying to figure out what Wyatt's thinking that I don't pay attention to the song. I also don't notice purple paint dripping from my brush onto the white baseboard until it's too late. I grab an old rag off the floor, and stoop to wipe up the mess when Iris says, *Listen . . .*

I go still and immediately recognize the lullaby Addie

is singing. *It's the song on the music box*, I tell Iris. *You used to hum it to me at bedtime when we were little. It's not so strange that Addie knows it. It's a well-known song.*

Yes, Iris hisses, sounding urgent and confused. *But I remember it on a violin. Did you play it?*

You know I can't play the violin, I silently remind her, baffled by the strange question. *It must've been Mom*, I say.

Then why does the music seem to flow out of me instead of in?

She starts humming along with Addie, and suddenly the tune transforms in my mind. *Notes cry out from vibrating strings and quiver inside of me, the sound as clean and airy as morning light. A hazy image appears. A hand holding the bow as it flies across the strings. Long, feminine fingers so much like mine. Mom's fingers when she was younger, I think, yet it's as if I'm looking down at them like they're my hands, not hers.*

"Oh, Lily! Your jeans!"

Addie's voice breaks my trance. I startle and glance down. I'm still stooping, still clasping the rag in one hand, the paintbrush in the other, but now purple droplets dot one knee of my jeans. "Ohmygosh, I'm sorry! I've made a mess all over your baseboard, too."

Setting the brush in the pan beside me, I rub the rag across the wood, my hand shaking. *Iris, you're freaking me out. What are you trying to tell me?*

I think I'm channeling your memories.

Coldness sinks into my bones. *They aren't mine.*

त ⁊

I'm at the door of the Blazer ready to drive home, when Wyatt steps onto the porch holding a box stamped with Snowflake Bakery's logo.

"I'm almost a week late, but here you go." He comes down the steps and hands it to me. "Happy birthday, Lil."

Inside are a half-dozen red velvet cupcakes—my favorite—the white icing covered with sprinkles. I flash back to my text-message conversation with Wyatt on the morning of my birthday, before my world fell apart. Looking up at him, I blink back tears.

"Double sprinkles," he says quietly. "Just like you ordered."

"You only promised me one." I manage to smile.

"You don't really think I'm going to let you eat cupcakes without me, do you?"

Raindrops suddenly start to fall. We run to the covered porch and sit on the top step beneath the eave, side by side. The rain comes down softly, clearing the air, making everything fresh and new again. "This is a much better gift than the minnow bucket you gave me last year," I say with a laugh, biting into a cupcake.

Wyatt licks icing off his finger and sends me a sideward glance. "You know you loved it."

"Yeah, right. Just what every girl wants."

"You aren't like other girls." His voice drops as he says the words, stroking intimate awareness through me. Holding my gaze, Wyatt lifts the box. "You want another one?"

I laugh at him, my heart pattering like the rain. "You're kidding."

"I never kid about food, Lil, you know that."

Shrugging, I say, "They *are* my birthday present, and I don't want to be rude." I smile and reach into the box.

Just as quickly as it appeared, the awkwardness between us subsides, and as dusk creeps in, Wyatt and I eat another cupcake, knowing that Addie will scold us for ruining our dinner if she catches us. Laughing and whispering like we used to when everything was easy.

I don't tell Wyatt that Ty came to work for us, or that I found Winterhaven, Massachusetts, on the internet. I don't mention the vision that gripped me less than two hours ago while we were painting. I let all of that go. I want to enjoy being just *us*. Right now, that's enough.

Mom has enchiladas in the oven when I arrive home, but I'm not hungry after the cupcakes. She eats only a few bites herself before walking toward the door using her cane, explaining that she's working on a sketch.

"You've been sketching a lot," I say, anxious to stop her, to keep her here. "I'm glad your hands are feeling better. It's been a long time since you've been able to do your artwork. More than a year, right?"

She opens the door and looks back at me, blinking too fast. "Something like that."

"It's weird that the arthritis either bothers your hands

or your hips, but not both at once, isn't it?"

She lifts a shoulder. "There's no rhyme or reason to this damn disease."

Crossing to her quickly, I say, "Can't you sketch in here? You've been spending so much time out there alone. I miss you."

"I don't want to move my things," she says. "I won't be long." Mom gives me a brief hug before stepping out onto the porch and closing the door.

Discouraged, I give Cookie his medicine, then watch television for a while, sitting on the floor and stroking his head. After he goes to sleep, I go up to my room, turn on my laptop, and look at the pictures on the Winterhaven website until I can't hold my eyes open. I fall asleep curled up on my bed, strangely at peace as the images of Winterhaven flicker on the backs of my eyelids like a slideshow.

Sometime after midnight, I awaken to the sensation of Iris shuddering through me, as if she's trying to shake me to consciousness. *Your mother*, she whispers. Something squeaks downstairs—a floorboard or a door—and I realize that I'm hearing Mom creeping into the cabin. *She's back. You can go to the workshop now.*

But the thought of going out there in the dark and possibly falling into another trance disturbs me too much. I'll find a way to sneak out to the workshop again tomorrow. Maybe I can figure out what's going on then.

I try to fall back to sleep, but can't. Instead, I lie awake for a long time, worrying about Mom and pondering the vision I had when I was at Wyatt's today—how it seemed like I was the one playing the violin, not my mother. Of course, that's impossible, in spite of Iris's insistence that she's channeling my memories. I've never played a violin in my life.

9

On Wednesday morning, I try to get Cookie to go outside, but he nips at me. Cookie's never nipped at anyone before, least of all me. I don't think he hurts physically that much anymore; he's been walking easier on his own. It's his state of mind I'm more worried about. It's as if he and Mom are slowly dropping into the same dark pit.

Cookie circles the interior of the pen like he can't find a comfortable spot. I wish I knew how to help him.

Sing him the lullaby, Iris suggests. *It used to calm you when you were out of sorts.*

I begin humming, but the sound of my voice doesn't soothe Cookie.

It's not enough. Something's missing . . . the violin, says Iris.

Her words tap a clogged vein in me, and the music flows free, streaming through me again—the lullaby played on a violin. Soothing. Powerful.

When the sound in my head fades away, I'm left shaken.

With a groan, Cookie finally lies down on the soft pallet in his pen. I pet him for a while, trying to understand what I just heard and what Iris meant. But minutes later, when his breathing steadies, I still don't have any answers.

At a loss, I go into the kitchen and sit down at the table, hoping my studies will take my mind off everything else for a while. As I'm opening my textbook, I hear Ty drive up, and a few minutes later his hammering starts. Mom drags herself out of her room still in her pajamas, looking groggy and pale. She's rubbing the knuckles on her right hand, her fists cradled close to her body.

A heaviness fills my chest. She seems as bad off as Cookie. It's more than her lupus. Dad died exactly a week ago, and I'm having a hard time today, too. I push aside the book on Greek philosophers and the paper Mom assigned before the accident and tell her, "Good morning."

"Morning," she mumbles.

I push my chair back. "Let me get you some coffee, Mom."

"I can get it," she says with a strained smile that doesn't reach her eyes. She pours herself a cup, then turns to me.

I lift my book. "You want to talk to me about this or read over my paper?"

"No, that's okay. When you're through, let me know. That'll be good enough." She shuffles past me to the couch.

I take a breath. "I'm really missing Dad this morning."

"I know, honey. Me, too." Mom sits down, clenching the

mug between her hands, as if its warmth relieves the pain in her fingers.

"I've been thinking about him so much. His life, I mean. There's so much I don't know. Not just about him, but about you, too." Sending her a cautious smile, I continue, "What were the two of you like when you were dating? You've never talked about it."

She lowers the mug to her lap. "I don't know, honey. It was so long ago."

"Did your parents like him?"

"Yes." Her eye twitches.

"Did his parents like you?"

"We got along well enough."

I sigh. "It's so weird. I don't even know what my grandparents looked like. Do you have pictures?"

"We never took many pictures," she says, the words rushing out.

"Surely you have wedding photos. I've never even seen them."

Mom's body tenses, a tiny, almost imperceptible movement, like she's been pinched. She shakes her head, takes a sip, and says, "There aren't any. We eloped."

I know I'm pushing, but I can't stop myself. "You don't even have any from when you were kids? It'd be fun to see what you and Dad looked like back then."

"We never got into photography. I'm sorry." Impatience gives her voice an edge.

I scoot back my chair. "There's not even an old school picture?"

"I'm sure we have a few somewhere, but do we have to look for them right now?" Mom sets the mug down on the coffee table a little too hard. "I'm really not up to it, Lily. Okay?"

It's clear that the subject is closed, as far as she's concerned. Reluctantly, I return to my studies.

Soon the sounds of Ty working lift my mood—and kill my concentration. Each time he walks across the roof, I look up at the ceiling. Whenever he climbs down and passes by a window, I hear the tune he's whistling, then catch myself humming along and tapping my toe to the beat. It's not the noise that distracts me from studying as much as his presence. I can't stop wondering if he's thinking about me, too.

I'd go out and keep him company if I thought Mom wouldn't interfere. I don't want to give her an excuse to fire him, and paying attention to me instead of his work would make it easy for her. Yesterday, she warned me about watching out for "older guys," as if Ty were in his twenties instead of only a year ahead of me. Maybe it's the fact that he's already had a semester of college that bothers her. She's always been overprotective to the extreme. She and Dad both, really.

At noon, Mom and I are making ham sandwiches at the kitchen counter when Ty's hammering stops. A second later, I hear his car door slam. "We should offer Ty a sandwich. He's going to get sick of eating lunch at the Blue Spirit Inn every day," I say, referring to the only restaurant nearby.

"He's just working here for another few days, Lily. I doubt he'll get tired of the Blue Spirit Inn," says Mom wearily. "Besides, he could bring his lunch. Maybe he did."

"I'll go check." Deserting the tomato I was slicing—and Mom's scowl—I hurry toward the door.

Ty is leaning against his car eating a strip of beef jerky. A folded red bandanna is tied around his forehead, to keep his hair out of his eyes while he works. "Hey," I call to him from the porch.

"There you are," he says, a wide smile spreading across his face. "I thought maybe you were allergic to sunshine or something."

"Schoolwork," I say. "Greek philosophy. Plato is kicking my butt."

Ty tilts his head to one side. "'He is unworthy of the name of man who is ignorant of the fact that the diagonal of a square is incommensurable with its side.'"

"Impressive. Maybe I should hire you as a tutor." I'm only half teasing when I add, "What do you charge?"

"I'd do it for free," he says.

I fall into his gaze and wish I could stay there forever, lost in all that soft, dark heat. Blushing, I open the screen door wider and glance down at the strip of beef jerky in his hand. "That's not much of a lunch."

"Don't knock it till you try it. It's not bad, but you might lose a tooth."

Grinning, I ask, "Do you like ham and Swiss? Mom and I are making sandwiches. We can eat on the deck since it's warm out."

Ty pushes away from the car. "Sure."

Five minutes later, I bring a tray filled with sandwiches, potato chips, and soft drinks out to the deck where Mom and Ty are already sitting at the patio table.

Ty stands abruptly to help, his knuckles bumping against mine as he reaches for the tray. We smile at each other as he sits in the chair across the table from Mom and I sit beside her.

"Looks like you're making good progress on the roof, Ty," Mom says.

"I should finish the middle of next week at the latest."

"That long?" She frowns. "Seems like you're moving faster than that."

"He's just one person, Mom," I say in his defense.

"I want to do a good job for you, Mrs. Winston," says Ty, adding, "You're short on a few supplies. If it's okay, I'll quit early this afternoon and go to the hardware store."

Mom takes a soft drink off the tray. "Whatever you need to do. The weather is supposed to stay dry for a while, so I guess there's no real hurry. Adam had an account there. Just have them call if they need an okay."

He nods at Mom, saying, "This looks great," when

I hand him his plate.

Mom opens the potato chip bag and shakes out a few. "I thought we might go into town, too, Lily. I'm in the mood for a movie. We could rent one and watch it tonight."

"Okay." I nibble on a crust of bread, encouraged that she wants to do something besides hide in the workshop or sleep.

She lifts her sandwich, then lays it down again and pushes her plate aside. She's hardly eaten in the past couple of days. "What do you say we rent that romantic comedy you used to love so much? Gosh, I can't remember the title. It was your favorite when you were thirteen or so. You watched it so much I'm surprised you don't have every line memorized."

Drawing a blank, I say, "I guess I've forgotten it."

"Forgotten it?" She sends me a disbelieving frown, and I notice for the first time how bloodshot and puffy her eyes are. "How? You almost wore out the VCR you watched that tape so often."

Tape? VCR? What is she talking about?

Anxious to change the subject, I turn my attention to Ty. "How is it that you can quote Plato? Are you a philosophy major?"

"No, biology."

"Lily was obsessed with that young actor in the movie," Mom says to him, as if she didn't hear us. Her brows shoot up, and she snaps her fingers. "John Cusack. *Say Anything*! That's it. He won an award for his role a few years ago.

Most promising new actor or something like that."

Iris flutters, tremulous and fleeting, as if she senses the tension building.

"Mom, John Cusack isn't young. He's been around forever," I murmur, embarrassed by her insistence that I remember some film that I'm sure I've never seen. "I don't remember that movie at all."

"Good grief, Lily, how can you say—" Mom breaks off, her face going slack, paling. "Never mind. I don't know what I was thinking." Biting into her sandwich, she stares off into the trees beyond the deck.

I can't bring myself to look at Ty. If Mom had to wig out, why couldn't she have waited until he was gone? He starts making small talk about the weather, about how beautiful Colorado is and how much he's enjoying his time here. Filling the silence. Smoothing the ragged edges of strain between Mom and me. Just like Dad used to do.

After a few minutes, Mom pushes away from the table and stands. "Another soft drink?" she asks us.

Ty and I both decline, and she walks around the corner onto the porch. I hear the front door open and slam as she goes inside.

"Make an excuse so you don't have to go to town with her," Ty says, speaking quickly.

"What?" I sit straighter.

"Drive your four-wheeler to the lake. Meet me there."

His sudden invitation zings a thrill straight through me, all the way to my toes. "She'll see your car parked there when she goes to get the movie."

"So she *does* care if you spend time with me." His mouth curves up.

"You've noticed?" I say sarcastically. I start to tell him to meet me at Ponderosa Pond instead of the lake. It's secluded, tucked away in a grove of trees that surround it completely. But it's also been Wyatt's and my secret place ever since we were kids, and I don't feel right about meeting Ty there. What if Wyatt showed up? "Do you know where the springhouse is?" I ask Ty, determined to find the perfect place.

"Yeah, I've seen it off the road by the lake."

"Park behind it," I say, hardly able to believe this is happening. "You'll see a footpath. Follow it past the waterfall. You'll come to a little clearing."

"Okay. I'll wait for you there."

Listening for the sound of the front door opening, I ask, "What time?"

"Two thirty?"

"If I can, I'll be there," I say, knowing I'll find a way to go, no matter what. There's no possibility I'll pass up this chance to be with him.

The front door slams. Ty and I smile at each other, then look away as Mom rounds the corner.

Mom decides not to go into town after all. She says she's tired and just wants to take a nap. I'm worried about her, but not so much that I don't rush out the door the second

I hear her snoring. I push my four-wheeler to the road so I won't wake her when I start it.

For the first time since I was twelve and got into trouble for not wearing a helmet, I forget to put one on. Wind tugs wisps of hair from my ponytail and whips them about my head as I speed along the road. I'm not sure if it's the cool air or the thought of seeing Ty that raises goose bumps on my skin. It's not even two o'clock, and I told him to meet me at two thirty. I think I'll get to the springhouse before him and surprise him, but instead he surprises me. His car is already parked behind it when I arrive. I pull up next to it and cut my engine, then walk the narrow rocky pathway that crosses beneath a small waterfall.

When I reach the clearing, I see Ty throwing rocks across the creek, his back to me. I pause in the shelter of the trees to watch him. It's as if he's trying to torture the opposite bank, pummeling it with stones in rapid succession, bruising the sodden carpet of moss, the fallen leaves.

After a few seconds, he stops chunking rocks and sits down on a boulder at the creek's edge, his forearms crossing his knees. He's not wearing the bandanna now, and as he stares into the trickling water, his hair falls over his forehead, gleaming in the sun. He seems so lost in thought that I almost don't want to disturb him. But the wind does it for me. A gust rushes past me, clattering the tree limbs above.

Ty turns as if startled by the sound, and when he spots me his face lights up and he grins. "Hey!" He pushes to

117

his feet. "You're early."

Starting toward him, I say, "So are you."

He reaches out a hand and helps me across the uneven jumble of rocks in the gulley and over to the edge of the burbling creek. "I was afraid you might not come."

"Mom decided to take a nap instead of going into town so I was able to sneak out." I realize that I'm still gripping his hand, and drop it, although I don't want to. "You have any trouble finding this place?"

"Not at all. It's an amazing spot. Isolated." His eyes meet mine.

"Not always. The bears like it." I point out the green plants flanking both sides of the slender stream and poking up between low-lying, slick gray boulders. "This is a raspberry patch. By mid-August it'll be thick with fruit. More than enough for the bears and us, too."

"I doubt the bears would be happy to share," Ty says with a laugh.

"You just have to hold your ground. Stare them down."

He squints at me, his amused expression doing crazy things to my insides. "You've done that?" he asks, tilting his head to one side.

"Yeah. A black bear came up on me here a couple of years ago. I figured she could run faster over rocks than I could, so I just stayed put and glared at her with my mouth stuffed with raspberries."

"What happened?"

"She eventually took off, and I threw up."

He leans his head back and laughs.

I laugh, too, then go quiet. "I guess you must think it's ridiculous that I have to sneak off to meet up with you."

"Not ridiculous." Ty crouches and dips his hand into the stream, letting the water flow through his fingers. "Maybe a little old-fashioned, but that's cool. It just shows that your mom cares about you."

"I guess. What about your parents? Are they strict?" I cringe inside. Stupid question. He's traveling alone. How strict could they be?

"They probably aren't strict enough," Ty says, as if reading my thoughts. He picks up a stone and tosses it across the stream, lightly this time, but I detect a hint of tension in his shoulders and his words. Sitting down on the boulder, he says, "Come on," then gestures to the space at his side.

Hoping he can't tell how jittery I am, I plop down next to him and grip my knees, fighting the urge to touch his hair and find out if it's as soft as it looks.

Ty begins unlacing his boots.

"What are you doing?" I ask, sending him a suspicious look.

Tugging the boots off, he sets them aside, strips off his socks, and rolls up the legs of his jeans, then lowers his feet into the creek.

"Are you nuts? That water's freezing!" I say.

"It feels good. Come on. You should try it." He grins. "Do something crazy for a change."

"Please. I'm the queen of crazy. Once I dunked my entire

head in the creek in November on a dare."

"Who dared you?"

"Wyatt."

"Ah," he says in a tone that seems to imply he has Wyatt figured out. "The guy who gave me the evil eye the entire time we were talking at your Dad's memorial."

"Wyatt gave you the evil eye?"

"Blond hair? Skinny?"

"That's him. I'm sure he didn't mean anything. He's just protective. We're best friends."

Ty's brows lift. "Best friends, huh?"

"Yeah." Wyatt's expression after we kissed flashes through my mind, and my body tenses with guilt. I have a feeling he'd be hurt if he knew I was flirting with Ty. "Wyatt and I have been best friends since we were this tall," I say, raising my hand four feet off the ground.

Ty shoves his hair back from his eyes, then looks down at his toes in the water. So do I. The sight of his long, bony feet unsettles me in a way that I like.

"So, should I be afraid of him?" he asks, his head still down.

"Who? Wyatt?"

"You said he's protective of you." He slides me a teasing look. "I just thought he might try to protect you from *me*."

I'm not sure I want to be protected from him, but I give Ty a playful shove and say, "I can take care of myself." I duck my head, embarrassed and too aware of him, and when I look up again he's watching me with an amused look that blows every rational thought right out of my mind. "What?" I say, then dip my hand into the water, scoop some up, and splash him with it.

"Hey!" he shouts, laughing and shaking droplets from his hair. "If you're so tough, why are you afraid of putting your feet in a little cold water?"

"I'm not afraid, I'm smart."

He smirks. "I'm not buying it."

Sighing, I remove my boots, peel off my socks, and roll my jeans up my calves, like he did. I lower one foot into the creek beside his and squeal as the shock of cold rushes up my leg. I try to yank my foot out, but Ty gently presses his hand on my knee.

"Count to ten and it won't feel so cold anymore. I promise."

I grit my teeth, stick my other foot in the water, gasp, and start counting.

"Was I right?" he asks when I reach ten and I'm no longer shuddering.

"I have a feeling you always are," I say, heaping on the sarcasm.

"I am." Reaching up, he tugs my ponytail gently and grins. "Don't forget that."

Silence blooms in the space between us, as thick as the spring wildflowers crowding the edge of the creek. I'm amazed that after everything that's happened in my life recently, I can feel this good. My pulse ricochets as I ask him, "Have you always lived in the Northeast?"

"Yep. Eighteen years."

"That explains the accent."

"It's that obvious, huh?" He cocks his head. "You should be used to it. I catch a hint of Yankee in your mom's accent, too."

"That's weird." I slide my toe along the slick, wet surface of a mossy stone. "Mom was born and raised in Colorado. Dad, too."

Ty searches my face, his narrowed eyes touching each feature, forehead to chin. "I guess I imagined it," he says quietly.

Shaken by the intimate way he looked at me, I grasp frantically for something to say to keep the conversation going. I finally settle on school and ask, "What's Columbia like?"

"Fun. Busy. New York has an energy like no place else."

"I'd like to go there sometime. I've never been anywhere, really. Besides Colorado, the only state I remember visiting is New Mexico." My strange snatches of memory surrounding the lake and dock in Winterhaven come to mind, and I add, "And I'm pretty sure my parents and I went to Massachusetts when I was really small. A town called Winterhaven, but I don't remember much about it."

"Winterhaven's near Boston," Ty says. He tosses another pebble into the water, creating ripples around our feet. "Do you have family there?"

"No, my grandparents died before I was born, and Mom

and Dad are both only children. Do you have a big family?"

"Big enough. Four grandparents and a slew of aunts, uncles, and cousins."

"And your parents and a brother, right?"

"Yeah. Kyle." Ty tugs a weed from between the rocks, watching his fingers as he twists the stem into a knot. "Kyle would love it here. He's crazy about mountains. His goal is to climb all the fourteeners in the United States before he's thirty."

"How old is he?"

"Thirteen."

I laugh. "So he has plenty of time."

His fingers still, and it's almost as if he stops breathing. Certain I said something to upset him, I open my mouth to ask what's wrong. But before I can, Ty looks up at me, smiles, and says, "We climbed our first one last year. Mount Muir in the Sierra Nevada Range in California. My parents took us. Kyle kicked my butt. He's a natural."

I notice the tattoo on his arm and realize it's the outline of a mountain range with three spiked pinnacles. The date stenciled beneath it is August of last year. I stroke my fingertips across it, the contact spreading a tingle up my arm. "Is this Mount Muir?"

"Yeah." He gives a short laugh. "I thought about getting a tattoo of each mountain I climb, but I'd be covered from head to toe if Kyle has his way, so maybe I'll just stick to this one."

Relieved that whatever happened to upset him a moment ago has passed, I say, "You should bring your brother here to climb the west peak. It's almost a fourteener."

"I'd like to," says Ty. "Maybe I'll climb it first, though. While I'm here. I've been planning to."

"I can take you up if you want."

"Oh, yeah?"

"I've climbed it at least a dozen times." Reaching for my boots, I say, "You want to go for a walk? I should start home soon, but I could show you around a little first."

"Sure." Ty stands up in the water, but then he grabs my boots from my hand and tosses them back onto the bank. Before I can figure out what he's up to, he takes hold of my arm and pulls me up so that I'm standing in the creek, too close to him. I tilt my head back, look up into his face.

"I owe you something," he says, pointing to his hair, which is still damp from when I splashed him earlier.

I pull back, but he snags my hand. I squint at him. "You wouldn't."

"Wouldn't I?" Ty grins.

"Don't even think about it!" I shout, giggling and trying to squirm free. "You'll be sorry. I mean it!"

"Ooh, I'm afraid!" he says in a shrill, teasing voice, mocking mine. "Make me an offer I can't refuse and maybe I'll reconsider."

"I'll make your lunch again tomorrow," I say, backing away from him. But he holds tight to my hand until our arms are stretched out as far as they'll go between us, and

I can't move another inch.

"My lunch?" He gives an exaggerated frown and slumps his shoulders. "That's not the offer I was hoping for, but your sandwiches aren't bad, so I guess I'll let you off the hook." He drops my hand.

I back toward the bank—one step, then another—keeping him in my sight and grinning so wide my face aches. "I don't trust you."

"Smart girl," he says, advancing toward me slowly. One side of his mouth turns up into a lopsided smile that gives me more of a rush than the cold water trickling over my feet. When I connect with the bank, I crouch and reach back, refusing to take my eyes off him. But instead of grabbing the boots, I quickly swing my arms forward through the creek and send another scoop of water flying up toward Ty's face.

He yells, then lunges.

I fall back onto the bank and he lands beside me. We laugh until my stomach hurts. In the silence that follows, Ty turns toward me, and I feel that same magnetic force drawing us together that I've felt before when I'm with him. When our faces are so close that his breath sweeps my cheek, nerves rush up and I pull back, fumbling on the bank for my boots, choked with embarrassment. What's wrong with me? I wanted to kiss Ty more than anything. Why didn't I?

Minutes later, we're walking down the same path we took to get here. "Thanks for asking me to meet you," I say.

"I thought you could stand to get away for a while." He shrugs. "And I wanted us to have some time together without your mom around." Ty slants me a look, and I try to pretend that it doesn't turn my bones to jelly.

"What?" I ask, my nerve endings humming beneath my skin.

"What, *what*?" he teases. "You keep saying that."

"And you keep looking at me."

He stops walking and covers his eyes with one hand. "I'm sorry. I didn't know looking wasn't allowed."

Pausing on the path, I knock against him with my elbow and giggle, disarmed. "It's not the *fact* that you're looking, it's the *way* you are."

Spreading his fingers, he peeks through them. "Like?"

A wildfire of heat spreads through my body, all the way up to my face. "Like you're thinking something," I say.

"You mean if I want to spend time with you, I not only have to wear blinders, I have to get a lobotomy, too?"

"Shut up." I cross my arms and try not to laugh.

We start walking again, Ty with his hands in his pockets, me with my arms behind my back. "I'm just trying to figure you out," he says after a moment. "I've never known a girl who dunks her head in mountain streams and stares down bears."

I send him a smug look. "That's nothing. Wait until I tell you about the time I wrestled with a mountain lion and won."

He draws his head back. "You're kidding."

I arch a brow.

We reach the place where the waterfall sprays over a jutting cliff above us, just missing the path as it tumbles to a pool twenty feet down the side of the hill. The path follows the cascading water, and it's an easy climb to the bottom. We make our way down.

"Amazing," Ty says when we're standing alongside the pool. "What was it like for you growing up here? I mean, not many people have an entire forest right outside their door."

The air is damp and musky and alive with energy. I breathe it in, feeling revived like I always do when I come to this spot. "I loved growing up here."

"Don't you ever get lonely?"

I think of Iris and how isolated my childhood would have been without her. "Sometimes," I say. "But I've learned to be alone."

I follow Ty across the trail. We climb over a stack of felled limbs that lie crisscrossed like the old pickup sticks Dad and I used to play with. When we reach an aspen tree with letters carved into the bark, Ty pauses to trace them with his finger.

"'L.W. and W.P. were here,'" he reads. "Did you do this?"

"Wyatt and I did when we were eight." I give a short laugh. "Silly, I know."

"Not when you're eight."

"Yeah, you believe nothing will change at that age. That everything will always be good." I hear the sadness in my voice, and shrug.

"Too bad that's a lie, huh?" Ty says.

I nod, wondering what good things Ty has lost.

He sticks his hands into his pockets again and says, "I'll take you up on that offer of climbing the peak together."

"Good. I mean, you shouldn't hike alone. No one should, but especially if you're inexperienced."

"I'm not a *complete* greenhorn," he says with mock offense.

"One fourteener doesn't make you an expert, either." Smirking at him, I add, "Maybe I can show you how it's done this weekend."

As I'm turning toward the waterfall, Ty catches my arm. "Lily." I face him again, my skin tingling where his fingers push against my arm. "I have something to confess," he says. "What I said to your mom about needing to make money for the trip home? That's not really why I'm sticking around Silver Lake longer than I'd planned. I have plenty of money."

"Why are you staying then?" I say in just above a whisper.

He lowers his head and kisses me, his mouth pressing gently against mine. He tastes like chocolate and smells like fresh air and sunshine and shampoo.

Our noses bump when we finally lean apart.

Breathless, I murmur, "You had candy after lunch,"

then think: *Ohmygod, what a stupid thing to say.*

Ty pushes a loose strand of hair off my face and tucks it behind my ear, the corner of his mouth twitching.

We cross the road with our fingers linked, and when we reach the waterfall and the trail beside it that leads to the top, I wish that I didn't have to let go of his hand to make the climb.

10

Mom wanders into the kitchen, leaning on her cane and yawning. I'm sitting on the rug in the living room trying to coax Cookie to play tug-of-war with a toy, but he's not interested.

"Did you have a nice nap?" I ask Mom, hoping she didn't hear me pull up a few minutes ago.

"Yes, just not long enough." She takes a glass from the cabinet over the sink.

I tell myself to stop being so skittish, but I keep imagining that she can read the truth on my face like a flashing neon sign: LILY'S BEEN MAKING OUT WITH TY.

Mom glances over her shoulder as she fills her glass with water from the faucet. "Your hair is damp."

"I washed it." I cringe inside at the lie. But I won't risk saying anything that might ruin my chances of seeing Ty again. I can't remember when I've had as much fun as I did with him today.

Mom shuts the water off and walks to my side. Peering down at Cookie, she asks, "How is he?"

"I think he's depressed. Is that possible?" I scratch the satiny spot between his ears and watch his eyes drift shut.

"He could be," says Mom. "I'm convinced that dogs have feelings just like we do."

"He misses Dad," I say quietly.

"Maybe he does, sweetheart." Mom squeezes my shoulder. "He'll feel better with time." Her slippers make a shuffling sound as she starts off, and the cane taps with a dull inevitability as it hits the floor.

"Where are you going?" I ask.

"Back to bed. I'm not feeling well."

"Do you want me to call your doctor?"

"I don't think it's the lupus," she says. "I might be getting the flu."

I know it's not the flu. Eager to cheer Mom up, I say, "I think I'll go into town and pick up that old movie you were talking about earlier. Would you watch it with me tonight?"

"We'll see how I'm feeling," she says a moment before her bedroom door closes.

Thoughts of this afternoon at the waterfall distract my worries about Mom as I change the bedding in Cookie's pen. I settle him on the soft, clean pallet, replaying in my mind each moment with Ty. I'm so giddy I feel like I could jump out of my skin as I go upstairs to grab my wallet, keys, and phone. Before heading down again, I text Sylvie: *Going*

2 video store. meet me? I hope she can. I want to tell her what happened today.

I'm backing the Blazer out of the driveway when she texts back: *there in 30. merry mushroom after? need pizza fix.*

Braking, I type: *k. see u there.*

Iris is restless during the drive, insisting I'm wasting time. She thinks I should be pumping Mom for more information about the Big Secret, or poking around the workshop some more while she naps. But I can only deal with so much at once, and right now I'm obsessing about Ty. And Wyatt. How I feel tugged toward one, then the other. It's so strange to be thinking about them at the same time. I feel guilty comparing them, but I can't stop.

Soon, I'm pulling into Silver Lake. The only place to rent movies—Play It Again Flicks—is on Main, between Snowflake Bakery and The Pine Shed bar. The Merry Mushroom is across the street. I parallel park at the end of the block behind a mud-splattered truck.

Downtown is usually pretty busy, and this evening is no exception. High school kids and students from the community college shop in the stores and hang out in the cafés, coffee shops, and bars along Main. I walk toward the video store, and through the window, catch sight of Sylvie browsing the aisle in the horror section. She loves low-budget slasher movies, and is especially partial to anything with *dead* in the title. Throw in a zombie or two and she'll even stay home on a Saturday night.

A few minutes later, after the guy behind the counter

132

informs me that they don't have the movie Mom mentioned, Sylvie and I cross the street to the Merry Mushroom.

"I'll split a pizza with you," she says. "I don't eat anything that once had a mother, though, so you'll have to settle for veggie."

"How about sausage on half?" I ask, thinking I'll take some home to Mom.

She wrinkles her nose. "As long as it doesn't touch my half."

We sit in a booth at the front window, and I breathe in the yeast-and-spice-scented air, my mouth watering. Sylvie's black hair is streaked with purple today. She's wearing a leather vest and arm warmers that look like black spiderwebs. Even so, our waitress makes Sylvie look like a Girl Scout. She's emo to the extreme, the makeup around her eyes so dark she looks bruised.

"Keep the sausage far left of center, okay?" Sylvie tells her.

I quietly tap my foot to the beat of the impatient tune Iris hums and stare out the window as Sylvie places our order.

When the waitress leaves, Sylvie's raspy voice cuts into my thoughts. "How are you and your mom doing?"

I turn away from the window to face her. "We miss Dad."

"Yeah," she says, looking sympathetic. "Maybe we could do a movie night? Get your minds on something else? I pop an awesome bag of Orville Redenbacher."

Recalling the blood-splattered scene on her movie's cover, I say, "Thanks, but I'm not sure we're up for it. There's something else that I need your advice about, though."

"Someone wants *my* advice?" Sylvie laughs. "I'll help if I can. Spill."

I glance around the café and lower my voice. "It's guy stuff."

Sylvie's eyes widen. "Okay, who's the asshole?"

"Nobody. It's just . . . I, um, sort of kissed Wyatt."

"You kissed the Goob?" She laughs, then shrugs and says, "Hey, he *is* sort of cute. Totally not *my* type but he's got his own thing going on, you know? Part dork, part jock." She studies me in a way that makes me think she's trying to picture Wyatt and me together, then nods her head slowly. "You and the Goob. I sort of dig it, actually. If you want to hook up with him, I say go for it."

Heat shoots up my neck like a rocket. I nibble my thumbnail.

"Uh-oh." The silver stud in Sylvie's eyebrow catches a beam from the overhead light and winks. "That bad of a kisser, huh?"

"No! I mean it's just . . . Wyatt and I have always been friends. *Just* friends."

Grabbing a glass container next to the napkin holder, Sylvie sprinkles Parmesan cheese onto her palm then licks it off. "If you're confused about it, kiss him again and see how you feel."

"Won't that just make it worse if the person I really want to kiss is someone else?" I draw my lower lip between my teeth.

Sylvie lights up. "Whoa. Who are we talking about?"

"The guy at Dad's memorial," I say.

"*No shit*. Mr. Intense?"

"Ty." Just saying his name makes me feel as if my whole body is smiling. "Ohmygod, Sylvie! Mom hired him to shingle our roof and I can't think straight when he's there. Today I met him at the creek behind the springhouse. We had so much fun and—I don't know. I mean, Wyatt's making me crazy, too. He—"

The emo waitress brings our pizza and saves me from having to say more.

When we're alone again, Sylvie says, "Hello? Are you listening to yourself?" She turns the pizza so that the sausage side is nearest me, then lifts a slice of veggie. "Judging from the way you just gushed all over yourself, I think I know the answer to this, but who are you really jazzed to kiss again, Ty or the Goob? And by jazzed, I mean your toenails catch fire just thinking about it."

The peppery aroma of the pizza suddenly makes me queasy. I lean back, my appetite gone. "I don't *know*. Whenever Wyatt and I are together, I notice things about him I never did before, and I start wondering how it would be if we *were* more than friends." I tell her about the cupcakes. "He's so sweet, and nobody makes me laugh like he does. Plus, we know pretty much everything about each other, so

I don't have to worry what he thinks."

"He's safe, you mean." Sylvie looks disappointed in me. "Safe is a cop-out reason for being with someone."

A little defensively, I say, "But Ty is only going to be here a couple more weeks at most, then I'll probably never see him again."

"So, you're saying you're going to *settle* for Wyatt?"

"No! Is that how it sounded?" I slump back in the booth. "God, I'm so messed up."

"I don't know what to tell ya," Sylvie says around a mouthful of pizza. "But if you ask me, this side trip with Wyatt was inevitable. I've never known a guy who can stay friends-only with a girl forever. They always end up wanting to get their hot little hands in—"

"Hey, Sylvie!" A guy tuning a guitar in the far corner of the café waves her over.

She waves back and says to me, "Speaking of hot hands, I need to make amends with the entertainment. Jonesy called last night and I never called back."

"Sure, go on."

As she leaves the booth, I bite into a pizza slice and stare out the window, disappointed that Sylvie didn't offer any easy solutions to my dilemma about Wyatt and Ty. But it's not her fault. I don't think any exist.

Later, Wyatt calls while I'm driving home. When I tell him I struck out at the video store, he says, "I'll loan you *Superbad*."

I laugh. "That's not exactly the sort of movie I had in mind for Mom."

"What? *You* loved it. You wet your pants you were laughing so hard."

"I did not wet my pants."

"Almost. You knocked over Gram's favorite vase trying to get to the bathroom."

"You are so lame," I say, rolling my eyes.

"It's true! I caught it before it hit the floor. I didn't tell you because I didn't want to embarrass you."

"Yeah, right. Embarrassing me is your favorite pastime."

We laugh, then grow silent. Five seconds pass. Ten. I notice that the late-to-leaf cottonwood trees along the county road are finally budding. Wyatt and I will be graduating soon. Everything's changing.

"You should stop by," Wyatt says.

"I need to work on my paper. And Mom still hasn't called Dad's clients, so I'm going to do it tonight. I don't think she can handle talking to them right now."

"Doesn't sound like a fun job. I'll be thinking about you." Wyatt pauses, then adds in a softer voice, "Of course, I've been thinking about you all day anyway."

"I've been thinking about you, too," I say, wondering if our friendship has been leading us to this new place all along, and our getting closer was meant to be.

"I should go since I'm driving," I tell him.

"Yeah, be safe. I'll talk to you tomorrow."

I put the phone in the cup holder, oddly flattered by the change in Wyatt's voice when he said he'd been thinking about me. But out of nowhere, Ty pops into my thoughts, and I'm confused all over again.

After I get home, I devote a couple hours to my paper, then start calling Dad's clients to tell them that his friend Sal will be in touch about finishing their projects. Sal called Mom yesterday and was nice enough to volunteer to do the work without taking any of the fee. I'm on the phone until close to ten o'clock, and Wyatt was right; it isn't fun. By the time I make the last call, I'm so drained that I can't muster the energy or enthusiasm to go out to the workshop. I know Iris is disappointed, but I can't handle any more stress. I fall asleep curled up on the couch with my clothes still on and Cookie in his pen nearby, whining in his sleep again.

Iris doesn't pester me to go out to the workshop the next morning while I'm working on my paper. I guess she's finally figured out that I won't be able to give my full attention to anything else until I'm finished. I work nonstop until after one o'clock, then slip out of the cabin and take a sandwich to Ty.

When I call out to him from the deck, he starts down from the roof to meet me. I saw him earlier when he arrived and we said hello, but Mom was with me. It's the first time we've been alone since we left the springhouse yesterday,

138

and I feel a rush of anticipation at the thought of seeing him again. I keep remembering Sylvie's question about who I'm more "jazzed" to kiss: Wyatt or Ty? One thing I know—I'd let Ty kiss me right now in a heartbeat if he tried.

Midway down the ladder, he jumps to the deck and turns to me, looking dusty, sweaty, and gorgeous in his torn flannel shirt and holey jeans. His dark hair just misses brushing his shoulders.

"I've been waiting all morning for this," he says.

"I didn't know my sandwiches are *that* good."

"I was talking about seeing you." The smile he flashes is so dazzling it blinds me.

Feeling shy, I give him a sandwich and say, "I'm sorry I've been so busy with schoolwork."

"No problem. I understand. I'm sort of jealous that Plato gets to spend more time with you than I do, but I'll get over it." His eyes sparkle as he takes a bite.

"Plato and I are through." Embarrassed, I quickly change the subject before he can comment. Motioning toward the roof, I say, "How's it going?"

"Okay, but it's warm today." He tugs at his collar. "I was actually roasting up there."

"I'm sure it's warmer if you're working," I say.

"Yeah. It's hard to believe it was snowing just over a week ago." He takes another bite of his sandwich, chews, and swallows. Narrowing his eyes, Ty says, "What did you mean about Plato?"

In a smug voice, I say, "I finished. You are looking at a high school graduate."

His eyes widen. "Just like that? You don't have to take a test or anything?"

"Nope. Just like that." I snap my fingers, feeling different—free.

He beams. "What are you doing this weekend to celebrate?"

"Does taking Cookie to the vet first thing Saturday morning qualify as a celebration?"

"You and your mom don't have plans?" Ty asks, frowning.

"No." I glance away, certain my voice revealed my pathetic disappointment about Mom's apparent indifference.

"Come here." Ty sets his sandwich on the patio table, takes my hand, and draws me nearer to the cabin where Mom can't see us. I back up to the wall, and he kisses me. "I'd like to take you out tomorrow night, graduate," he says, the low vibration of his voice scattering goose bumps up my arms.

"I'd like that." I wipe a smudge of dirt off his cheekbone with my finger and smile. "I hope you'll clean up first, though," I tease.

Ty's lunch break ends too soon. He goes back to work, and I go inside. Late in the afternoon when he leaves, Mom surprises me by heading for the couch instead of the workshop. She curls up under a blanket and stares blankly at the television until it's time for dinner. I offer to bring her a bowl of soup, but she doesn't want anything. She hasn't eaten all day.

Iris comes out of hiding and nudges me. I don't need any persuading, though. If I'm ever going to ask Mom about Winterhaven, it may as well be now. There's not ever going to be a *good* time, and I'm tired of waiting.

"Mom?" Bringing my own bowl of soup into the living room, I set it on the coffee table and sit down on the floor with my legs crossed. "Have we ever been to Winterhaven, Massachusetts?"

She pushes onto her elbow. "Winterhaven? Why do you ask?"

"I found a slip of paper in Dad's workshop with Winterhaven, Massachusetts, written on it." Which isn't entirely a lie. She doesn't need to know that I wrote it.

"What were you doing in the workshop?" she asks, the accusatory tone back.

Scrambling for a reason, I say, "Ty needed a tool."

"I had him take your father's tool chest out of the workshop his first day here. He's supposed to be keeping it in the storage shed."

"He is, but whatever he needed wasn't in there." I can tell by Mom's expression that she doesn't believe me, but I don't care. I won't let her suspicions distract me. "*Have* we been to Winterhaven?" I ask again.

She hesitates, then says, "We flew to Massachusetts once

when you were a baby. To Boston. We were on vacation and rented a car. We might've driven through Winterhaven—we passed through a lot of small towns."

I wonder if the memory I have of the dock and the lake could have taken place on that trip. I start to question her further about it, but I can't do it when I notice that her hands are shaking as she pulls the quilt higher to cover her shoulders. I have a feeling it's fear making them tremble. The same fear I see in her face.

Mom moves from the couch to her bedroom at ten o'clock when the news comes on. I wait until Cookie falls asleep, then go to my sock drawer and take out the spare keys Wyatt made me. Rubbing the metal of one key between my forefinger and thumb, I try to talk myself into going out to the workshop.

Of course, Iris is all for it, encouraging me with tantalizing words: *Everything's tied to the violin. To the music. I feel it.*

The music? I don't understand, I tell her.

But I know by now that Iris doesn't understand, either. Whatever she's channeling, it's only arriving in snatches.

I press the key into my palm. If more clues to the mystery are hidden in the workshop, what will they tell me about my parents? In my mind, I see Mom's gnarled hands trembling as she pulled the blanket higher. That splash of icy blue fear in her eyes. What is she afraid I'll find out? What did Dad want me to know?

Go out to the workshop and see, breathes Iris.

I nibble my lip. *What if the truth is something I'd rather not know?*

Do it for me.

For her? I shove aside the curtain over my window, look out at the moon-bathed peaks, startled and shaken by Iris's plea. I've been assuming she wants to solve this puzzle for me, but she sounds like she has a personal stake in putting it all together. What could she possibly stand to gain from learning about my tie to Winterhaven or who Jake is? Iris isn't even human. She isn't alive. She's . . . I go still.

What are you, Iris?

Shaken, I stare at the shadowy east peak. A silent and brooding presence. Always standing guard. The few times I've asked myself about Iris's existence, I've always dismissed my questions before they could take hold. What am I afraid of? That I'm insane? Or that there might be more to Iris than I ever dreamed?

Something I've never dared to let myself consider pushes to the front of my mind now, refusing to be ignored. "*Who* are you?" I whisper. "Were you ever alive?"

I don't know. Help me remember.

Rain strikes the bedroom window and taps on the roof. A few drops, then dozens, then hundreds. The wind kicks up, and the cabin logs creak, as if complaining. Seems Mom was wrong when she told Ty we'd be having dry weather for the next several days.

I put the keys back in the drawer, anxiety gnawing at

the pit of my stomach. *Maybe it's not the shop we should be searching*, I tell Iris. Returning to the bed, I open my laptop.

For the next hour, I browse the Winterhaven website with thoughts of Ty, of Wyatt and Iris, of my parents and the items in the chest, coiling together like a braid in my mind.

11

Wyatt is busy with school on Friday, so we aren't able to get together. I don't see Ty, either. He calls early in the morning to say that he's not coming to work since it's raining and not supposed to let up all day. He sounds sad and edgy. I ask if he's okay, and he claims he's only tired because he didn't sleep much last night. He asks if we can postpone our date tonight, too, and the moment we hang up, I start imagining all kinds of things. Mainly, that he's decided to leave Silver Lake earlier than he'd planned. I can't believe how much that possibility upsets me.

I spend the day searching the internet for more sites about Winterhaven and doing chores while Mom watches television and Cookie sleeps. Mom hasn't cleaned the cabin since the accident, and it shows. I've been neglecting my chores, too. As I'm working, I have to choke back tears each time I run across something of Dad's—one of his socks I missed the last time I did laundry, clinging to the back of the dryer; his toothbrush and beard trimmer in the down-stairs bathroom; his work boots on his side of their bed.

On Saturday, Mom stays home while I take Cookie to the vet. She's lost interest in everything, even whatever it was she was doing in Dad's shop for so many days and nights.

When I arrive at the veterinary clinic, I'm surprised to see Ty's shabby blue sports car across the street. He's pacing the sidewalk, talking on his phone with his head down, so he doesn't see me. Suddenly, he throws the phone, and when it breaks, he kicks his front tire hard.

I park, climb out of the Blazer, and turn toward the street, calling out to him and waving until I catch his attention. Ty waves back, then bends and grabs his phone off the ground, snapping the pieces back together.

Jogging over, he calls out, "Hey. I remembered you said Cookie had an appointment this morning. I thought you might want some company."

"How did you know my mom didn't come?" I ask, closing the door.

"I didn't." No trace of his anger from a few minutes ago shows on his face as he stops in front of me. "I took a chance. I've missed you."

"You just saw me the day before yesterday."

"For half an hour at lunch. That's not enough." While I'm waiting for my pulse to settle down, he adds, "I'm sorry I had to cancel our plans to go out."

"Is something wrong?" I ask. "I saw you throw your phone."

Humiliation flashes across his features. "I was talking to my dad." He holds out his free hand to show me his cell phone. The back cover is cracked.

"Oh, no . . . does it work?"

Ty pushes a button, then lifts the phone to his ear. "Yeah. That's surprising." He shoves it into his front jeans pocket, out of sight, but doesn't have as much success hiding the distress on his face.

"Is everything okay at home?" I ask.

"As good as can be expected, I guess." His mouth crooks up at the corner and his face brightens. "Anyway, you're here now, so everything's better."

Psyched by his compliment, I open the Blazer's back door and look in at Cookie. "I'm glad you came," I say to Ty. "You can help me get him inside."

Cookie doesn't even complain when Ty lifts him from the seat and carries him into the clinic. The receptionist tells us that Dr. Trujillo had an emergency and he's running a half hour late, so we take Cookie back outside and sit on the lawn beneath a cottonwood tree.

Because it stays warmer in town than on the mountain, the trees bud earlier in the season here. Pale green leaves flicker in the cottonwood tree, and the cool air dances with sunshine. A bluebird sings in the branches, and Iris joins in the song. My fingertips pulse with her trilled melody as I slide them up and down Cookie's spine, and I catch myself wondering if he feels the vibration. If so, he doesn't show it. Cookie doesn't even have the energy to lift his head.

"How's it looking for our hike tomorrow?" Ty asks.

"We're good to go," I say. I slide him a mock-serious look. "I hope you've been working out. I don't want to have to carry you back down the mountain."

Squinting in a way that turns me inside out, Ty leans back on his elbows, his long legs stretched out in front of him. "We'll see who's carrying who. In fact, if you want to race to the top and down, you're on."

"I'll pass." I fake a yawn.

"I think you're afraid," Ty says, looking superior.

"No, I just don't want to embarrass you when I win." He laughs, and after a minute, I ask, "So what's going on at home?"

Sobering, Ty lifts a shoulder. "Mom and Dad are pretty upset with me right now. They don't get what I'm doing here."

"What *are* you doing here?" I ask on impulse. When he doesn't answer right away, I say quickly, "Forget I asked. It's none of my business."

"No, it's okay." He tilts his head back, stares up at the cottonwood's sun-spangled leaves. "My little brother, Kyle, was in a car accident over the Christmas holidays. Kyle wasn't wearing his seat belt. His head hit the windshield, and he's been in a coma ever since."

"Oh my god," I whisper, my fingers curling into Cookie's coat.

Ty exhales loudly. "My parents told me yesterday that

the doctors are saying he won't ever get better. They're talking about turning off the machines he's hooked up to. Mom and Dad want me there to discuss it as a family."

In the silence that follows, sorrow creeps over us, as dense as fog. I take a shuddery breath. "You don't have to talk about this if you don't want to."

"No, it's okay. That's why I took off on this road trip. I couldn't stand seeing my brother like that." He shakes his head. "Pretty weak, huh? But I can't believe they've given up on him so soon. The doctors aren't giving him a chance."

"I'm so sorry," I tell him.

Watching me, he says, "Spending time with you . . . talking. It helps."

"I'm glad. Being with you has helped me, too." My throat closes as I reach for his hand. I want to hug him, but hold myself back. "Please don't get mad at me for saying this, but as much as I don't want you to leave, maybe you *should* be with Kyle right now."

"It wouldn't make any difference. He wouldn't even know I was in the room. I can't help him by being there."

"But maybe it would help *you*. I mean, I wish I'd had more time with my dad. To say good-bye. Even if he might not have been able to hear me."

Ty shakes his head. "I can't do it, Lily. I can't stand seeing my brother lying in that bed. He's only thirteen. He should be playing computer games and hanging out with his friends. I call to check on him every day, but—" Ty drops his chin to his chest. "I'm not running away. It's just—there was only one way I could help him, and now I can't even do that."

"What do you mean?"

"It was just a stupid, desperate idea I had that was a long shot, anyway." He slips his hand from mine, pulls a hank of grass from the ground, and tosses it, watching it scatter. After a minute, he says, "About the hike. I don't want to do anything to get you in trouble with your mom. I shouldn't have asked you to sneak off and meet me the other day, either."

"I'm glad I went," I say.

"Me, too." He looks up and smiles.

Relieved to see the glint return to his eyes, I add, "And don't think you're getting out of the hike. I know you're afraid I'll show you up, but you promised me a race, and I'm not letting you off the hook."

"You want a race? Fine." He reaches up and gently tugs a lock of my hair. "I just hope you know what you're getting yourself into."

"Oooh . . . I'm shaking," I say with a laugh.

Just then, the receptionist pokes her head out of the door of the clinic to call us in. "Ready, Cookie?" I say. But he doesn't budge.

Ty picks Cookie up again and carries him inside.

Early the next morning, I place two lunches and a few snacks in my backpack, make sure Cookie is comfortable, then look in on Mom in her bedroom. "Hey, I'm leaving. Call my cell if you need me."

"I'll be fine. Go have some fun for a change."

I'm completely bewildered. One day she's overly watchful, the next she seems completely disinterested in what I do. I don't know what to expect from her anymore.

"Don't forget to check on Cookie," I say.

The vet confirmed my suspicions—Cookie is physically better and pain-free. So whatever is going on with him now probably *is* depression. Dr. Trujillo said he might be having trouble getting over the trauma of the accident. And he really might be missing Dad, too.

"Don't worry about Cookie," Mom says. "I'll get up in a while and take him outside." I go over and hug her, and as I step away from the bed, she rolls toward the window, her back to me. "You and Wyatt be safe," she murmurs.

It's always colder in the forest, so I tug a gray stocking cap over my hair and head for the door, feeling guilty for lying. But if I tell Mom the truth—that I'm meeting Ty instead of Wyatt—I'm afraid she'll say I can't go. And I know she wouldn't let me hike the peak alone.

A few minutes later at the trailhead, I park next to Ty's car in a small clearing at the side of the road. The driver's door opens and Ty climbs out. Every guilty feeling I had flies from my head as he crosses to me, slinging a backpack over his shoulder. Ty's wearing faded jeans and a blue flannel shirt left unbuttoned over a threadbare white T-shirt that hugs his chest in a way that transforms my legs to string cheese.

I cut the engine and slide off my four-wheeler. "You ready to hit it?" I ask as I lift my pack from the rack behind my seat.

"Lead the way," he says.

"You brought a jacket, right? And rain gear just in case?"

"Yes, Mother. And I put on sunblock." He grins.

I make a face at him, slip the straps of my backpack over my shoulders, and take off at a brisk pace, calling, "Do your best to keep up."

Ty falls quickly into step beside me. "I thought we were racing."

"Let's just say the one who makes it down in one piece without whining wins."

He laughs. "I'll take that deal."

We walk on without speaking for a while. My mind wanders and I relax as we draw deeper into the cool, musky shade of the forest, following the upward incline of the trail. Sunlight blinks through gently swaying tree limbs above. Lacy shadows dance across the ground, dodging our feet. Iris hums a catchy tune, and I realize I'm watching for her silhouette. I'm not three years old anymore; I know it's only my shadow I'm seeing, not her. But sometimes I still gasp whenever I glimpse the dusky stain of my own shape.

Last night, I asked Iris again about her odd snatches of memory and what she had meant about everything being tied to the music. And again, she told me she didn't understand what she was sensing. A tremor started deep in my core, and for the first time, I realized how upset Iris is.

Does she think she's failing me?

"It's so quiet here," Ty says in a low voice, interrupting my thoughts.

"Not really. You're just not paying attention." Stopping midstride, I grasp his arm. "Close your eyes and listen."

I shut my own eyes and zone in on the orchestra tuning up around me. Aspen branches rasping as the breeze rubs them together like a bow against a string. The trill of birdsong. Water tinkling over rock in the nearby stream. The *tap-tap-tap* of a woodpecker.

"Amazing," says Ty, and I open my eyes to find him watching me.

"What?" I ask, afraid to hope that he heard what I did—what I always do when I'm out here.

"I did hear something."

"Really?"

Ty guides my hand to his chest, presses my palm against it. "My heartbeat," he says. "It's all I can ever hear when we're together." He winces. "How cheesy did that sound? Sorry. You make me nervous."

"I make *you* nervous?" I ask, caught up in his stare.

Ty's head lowers and his breath feathers against my mouth before his lips catch mine. I taste his tongue, warm and wet, soft and rough at once. Standing in the middle of the trail, we kiss for a long time, and when we stop, every nerve in my body is electrified.

I keep my hands on his shoulders, and Ty's arms stay around my waist as he looks up into the trees. "The wind in the limbs sounds like cards in the spokes of a bicycle wheel," he says.

"I've never heard that noise."

"You're kidding." He draws back slightly and scowls. "What kid never attached cards to their bicycle wheels?"

"A kid who was fishing and hiking and playing hockey."

"Yeah, right. You play hockey?" He gives me a measuring look of disbelief.

"Ice *and* roller hockey, as a matter of fact," I say proudly. "Why does that surprise you?"

He shrugs. "You don't look like the sort of girl who'd play such a rough sport."

"Meaning, what? That I don't have broad shoulders or tree trunk legs?"

"Well, yeah. Or a mustache." One corner of his mouth quirks up as he pulls the edge of my stocking cap down to the tip of my nose.

I giggle and shove him away, then push my cap up again. We step apart and resume the hike. I spot a familiar wall of granite rising up the mountain side of the trail. Pointing, I tell him, "That's part of one of the dikes that wind through this area. Have you seen them?"

He nods. "They look like the ridged sail on the back of a spinosaurus."

"They do sort of look like that," I say with a laugh. "If you believe in the legend, the wall captured the spirits of the Indians who used to live here, and if you lay your hands on the surface of the rock you can feel their energy inside. The legend also says that if you press your ear against the wall, you can hear the Indians beating drums and chanting."

"My mother believes in all of that metaphysical stuff," Ty says as we stop beside the wall. He places both palms against the rock and goes very still, then suddenly wails and his body starts jerking like he's being electrocuted.

"Very funny," I say, crossing my arms and smirking at him.

He pushes away from the wall, laughing hysterically. "I couldn't help myself. Sorry. I didn't feel anything. It just feels cold." Leaning forward, he presses his ear to the spot above his hands and feigns a serious expression.

"Well?" I ask.

Ty steps back. "I guess my mom's the only one in the family with an ear for music."

"Your mother likes music?"

"It's her life. She's teaches high school orchestra and gives private lessons. She plays all of the stringed instruments. The cello. The violin."

"That's a coincidence." I think of the violin in Dad's workshop. "My mom used to play the violin, too. She doesn't anymore, though. I've never even heard her."

"What about you?" Ty asks with a curious glance and a flicker of something in his voice I can't identify. "Are you a musician, too?"

"No. I asked for piano lessons when I was little, but Mom and Dad said we didn't have room for a piano in the cabin."

We start off again, leaving the rock wall behind. As we climb, the trail becomes steeper and rougher and dotted with patches of lingering snow. We step around large rocks and over the occasional felled tree blocking our path. When we reach an outcropping of rock that offers a view that seems to stretch all the way to the next dimension, we stop to rest. Sitting side by side, we stare out over a sea of evergreen treetops broken only by scraps of pale green meadow.

I take an apple out of my pack and offer it to Ty. He shakes his head, and I'm about to bite into it when I hear a noise on the trail. "Someone's coming," I say, setting the apple aside.

Frowning, he looks in the direction we came. "I don't hear anything."

"No, I'm sure of it." I push to my feet when I see movement in the trees and a patch of blue coming closer. Wyatt appears from around the curve, pausing when he spots us.

"Hey!" I wave and jog to meet him. "What's up?"

"Gran went by your house. Your mom mentioned *our hike*." He glances at Ty and makes a huffing sound. "Gran was worried about you going up the peak alone. So was I. Stupid me, huh?"

"Don't be mad," I say in just above a whisper, hoping Ty won't hear. "Ty wanted to climb the peak, so I offered to take him, that's all. I knew Mom would make a big deal of it, so I didn't tell her." I gesture toward Ty with a tilt of my head. "Come on. Meet him. He's a nice guy."

As if on cue, Ty stands and comes over. "Hey," he says,

offering his hand to Wyatt. "I'm Ty Collier."

The tops of Wyatt's ears turn red as he shakes hands with Ty. Shifting his attention back to me, he says, "Could we talk?"

I look at Ty and wince. "We'll just be a minute, okay?" He nods, and I follow Wyatt to the outcropping of rock where our backpacks lie. "What's going on?"

"Gran's not happy about you lying to your mom. She said for me to find you and if we aren't back in a couple of hours she's going back to your cabin to tell her."

"She'd do that?" I ask hesitantly.

"You know my grandmother. What do *you* think?"

Frustrated, I make my way back over to Ty. "I need to go home."

He frowns. "Everything okay?"

"Yes, but we'll have to save the hike for another day."

Ty pretends not to care, but I can tell he does. I wouldn't blame him if he decided that trying to spend time with me isn't worth the effort.

The return walk down the peak to the trailhead is pure torture, for me at least. Being with Ty and Wyatt at the same time makes me nervous so I start to babble. I tell funny stories about things Wyatt and I did together as kids, but Wyatt remains focused on the path ahead, not amused. He doesn't look up until we reach the trailhead where his four-wheeler is parked next to mine.

Ty draws me aside for a second, saying, "I hope everything's okay at home. I'll call you later, okay?"

I nod. "I'm really sorry about the hike."

"We'll do it another time."

He starts off toward his car, and when he passes Wyatt, they mumble good-bye to each other.

As Ty drives away in his car, Wyatt climbs onto his four-wheeler, stares down at the seat for a minute, then turns to me. "You coming?"

"I'm sorry. I shouldn't have told Mom I was with you and put you in the middle of this. But she has such a weird cautious streak when it comes to Ty."

His brows lift briefly. "Maybe she's smart to, Lil. I mean, what's he doing here?"

"In Silver Lake? Working for Mom, for one thing. Putting a roof on the cabin."

"Yeah, your mom told Gran he's working dirt cheap. She isn't thinking straight or she'd wonder just why he'd do that." He squints at me. "Why do *you* think he's willing to work for next to nothing?"

I shrug. "Because he needs the money?"

"Or wants to be close to you." Wyatt blinks and looks away, his jawline tight.

I cross to him. Take a breath. "We need to talk about things." He turns to me, and his green eyes don't hide anything. I see all of his feelings for me. I'm so afraid of hurting him, but he deserves my honesty. "I'm really confused about us right now," I say. "What happened between you and me—I never expected it, and—"

"What about Collier?" he interrupts, his chin lifting.

I lay my hand on his arm. "I'm confused about him, too. I need some time to think about everything that's happened to me in the past couple of weeks. To figure it all out."

Wyatt pushes a loose strand of hair off my cheek, his fingers lingering beneath my ear. "You don't have to be confused about me, Lil. You *know* me. I'll always be someone you can count on."

He's being so sweet, I want to cry. Lowering my head, I say, "I'm afraid of ruining things—of ruining *us*—the way we've always been."

After what seems like forever, Wyatt bumps me with his elbow, and I look up at him. "I don't like you hanging out with him," he says, "but no matter what, I'm never going to stop tormenting you, if that's what you're afraid of." His cheek twitches.

"Yeah, I live for that," I say with a laugh, pushing the words past the lump in my throat. I nod toward the road. "Let's go home before your grandmother ruins my life."

"Okay."

I climb onto my four-wheeler and start the engine.

Wyatt and I take off, riding side by side, just like we have more than a hundred times before.

12

Mom drives into town for a dentist appointment on Monday morning. Ty calls shortly after she leaves to say he's going to be late coming to work. He has to make another trip to the hardware store.

I curl up on the rug next to Cookie's bed. It hurts to see him so unhappy. He didn't eat his breakfast, and he growled at me when I made him get up and go outside. I know he didn't mean it, but that didn't stop me from crying. Nothing seems right anymore. Cookie isn't himself, and Dad is gone. Mom is like a ghost. I don't trust my emotions when I'm with Wyatt.

Sometime later, I hear a car outside. Hoping it's Ty, I go to the door. Instead, I see Dad's friend Mack Sturdivant climbing out of his white Ford truck.

"Morning, Lily," he calls, slamming the truck door, then moving slowly toward the porch, one hand pressed against the small of his back. He's as stiff, thin, and leathery as the strips of beef jerky Ty eats.

"Hey, Mack," I say, walking down the steps to meet him in the yard.

Wearing a sad expression, he pulls off his cap, and peers at me through his glasses. "Sorry about your daddy. Janie and me were up in Montana visiting the grandkids when Tony called and told us. It just about did me in. Your dad was a good friend." Mack's face reddens and crumples, and all of my emotions from the memorial come flooding back. "You and your mama doing okay, honey?" he asks, pulling a handkerchief from his pocket and blowing his nose.

"We're getting by," I say, choking out the words.

"She here?"

"No, she went into town."

Shielding his eyes from the sun with one hand, Mack looks up at the roof. "Addie's boy finishing that for you?"

"No, sir. Mom hired someone. He's not from around here."

Mack scratches his beard and meets my gaze. "He a kid about your age? Shaggy dark hair?"

"Yes," I say, surprised that he might know Ty.

"I think I met him at the coffee shop last time Tony and I were there with your dad. Apparently, someone had told him Adam might have work. I don't know what was said between the two, but your dad left in a tailspin. I didn't think anything of it until I called him later, and he said the boy threatened him."

I flinch. "What?"

161

"He didn't want to get into details, so I didn't push," Mack says, looking grim. "I just figured the kid might've been a little desperate and lost his cool when Adam didn't hire him."

"Dad didn't mention anything about that," I say, not willing to believe Ty could be the person Mack's talking about. But I'm uneasy all the same. "Are you sure?"

"Yeah, if it's the same kid." His brows tug together. "One thing I do know, from the way your dad talked about him, he wouldn't want that boy out here alone with you and your mother."

"It must've been someone else," I insist. "Ty's really nice. And anyway, you said Tony was with you at the coffee shop, right?" When Mack nods, I continue, "Tony saw Ty at Dad's memorial and left me alone with him. He wouldn't have done that if Ty was the guy who threatened Dad."

Putting his cap on and frowning, Mack says, "Could be that Tony didn't notice your dad's reaction to the kid. Like I said, it didn't register with me until later when we talked on the phone." He pulls a toothpick from his pocket and rolls it between his fingers. "I don't know, honey. You could be right, but I'd feel better if your mom knew about this. Tell her to give me a call, okay?"

"Okay," I say, not sure that I will. I refuse to believe Mack's suspicions. He definitely has Ty confused with someone else, and I don't want him telling Mom any of this. She's already so wary of Ty, if she heard Mack's story she'd fire him on the spot and forbid me to see him without even giving him a chance to defend himself.

After Mack leaves, I use my new keys to get into the workshop. There's an expectant hush in the air that sets my nerves on edge. Leaving the door open, I make my way to the storage closet. I drag the shiny toolbox to the middle of the room, then drop to my knees and open it. I lift out the jewelry box, the hairbrush, and the stacks of clothing.

What am I looking for, Iris? I ask. *If this was Mom's stuff, I don't see how it relates to you or me. Do you see something that looks familiar?*

The violin, she breathes.

I reach for the case at the very bottom of the chest, set it on the floor, then replace everything else and put the chest back where I found it. Certain Mom will be gone for a while, I take the violin back to the cabin.

It's warmer today, so I leave the door ajar. I lay the violin case on the couch, then check on Cookie sleeping steps away on his bed. He moans low in his throat when I touch him. Upset over his sadness, I return to the couch.

When I open the violin case, my breath catches. The instrument is beautiful, with its golden wood and smooth, graceful curves. I remove it from the case, and Iris sighs, *Oh . . .* , as a tingle radiates up my arm.

Shaken by emotions I don't understand, I lift the bow, prop the violin on my shoulder, and settle my chin on the chin rest. I close my eyes and draw a deep breath, then exhale slowly.

Everything except the instrument in my hands

disappears. I no longer smell the scent of this morning's bacon or hear the tick of the wall clock or feel the softness of the couch cushion beneath my thighs. A rush of noise that sounds like applause surrounds me, then slowly fades to an expectant hush as one exquisite note—a quiet plea—stretches into a sweet cry of longing. The music swells until it's all-consuming. White-hot and bright, it fills me up, spills out of my pores, and wraps around me.

The sound of my whispered name brings the world crashing back. I blink. Ty stands inside the doorway, his widened eyes darker than ever against his pale, shocked face. Surprised to see him, I set the violin inside the case and try to stand, but my legs are rubbery, so I slump back onto the couch. "I didn't hear you come in," I say.

He steps toward me. "Why didn't you tell me you can play?"

"What are you talking about? I was messing around."

Ty shakes his head, an amazed expression on his face. "You were incredible. Didn't you hear yourself?"

I heard *something*. Breathtaking music in my imagination. Maybe a buried memory of Mom playing when I was very small, or some random orchestra performance I saw on TV once. "You're teasing me," I say with a laugh. "I must've been terrible."

Sounding awestruck, Ty says, "You're the one teasing. My mom's best students don't compare to you."

"I've never touched a violin until today." I close the case, nervous for some reason. "How could I pick up a violin for the first time and instinctively know how to play? That doesn't make sense."

"I know what I heard." Reaching across my lap, he raises the lid on the case, takes the violin out, and lays it on his knees. "This thing's a piece of art."

I look up at him. "I found it locked in the storage closet in Dad's workshop. It's almost like my parents were trying to hide it from me."

The way Ty is watching me, like he's sort of impressed but also a little freaked out, makes me feel self-conscious. Exposed.

I cross my arms. "Why are you looking at me like that?"

"I'm trying to understand how you can have such an amazing ability and not even know it." He holds the violin out to me. "Once more, okay? Pay attention this time."

My first instinct is to refuse. But then Iris's heat permeates my skin and her breath tickles my eardrum as she whispers, *Please try. I need to feel the music again.*

I look down at the violin and I understand her request. I need to feel the music flow through me, too.

This time, I don't drift away on the notes that bleed from my fingers, I weep along with them. Without even trying, I'm playing the music box song, the lullaby that Iris sang on nights during my childhood when I couldn't sleep.

As the last note drifts into silence, Iris breathes, *I remembered something. Help me . . . what did they do?*

Panic as cold as windblown snow flutters through me. I open my eyes. Who is Iris talking about? What does she mean? She wouldn't have memories separate from mine.

Unless she used to be alive . . .

I avoid Ty's gaze as I stand, return the violin and bow to the case, then run my fingertips across the wood. I have the strongest urge to play it one more time, but I'm afraid to experience those powerful emotions again. I'm afraid of what Iris might be remembering.

I pull my hand back and close the lid, setting the case on the floor beside the couch. "Please take it out of here," I say. "Put it in my dad's workshop."

Ty takes hold of my hand and doesn't let go until I sit down beside him. "You have an amazing gift," he says. "Don't be afraid of it."

"It's not playing that scares me," I say. "It's the fact that I *can*. I must be a freak!"

"No." Ty shakes his head, and his voice is tender as he says, "You're a miracle."

His words take me back to the morning of my birthday. As Dad and I watched the sunrise, he said the same thing: *You can't even imagine what a miracle you are.*

A miracle? More like an aberration. Having Iris in my life isn't normal. *She* isn't normal. Which means I'm not, either, and I just proved it.

Is my musical "gift," as Ty called it, the secret Dad was going to tell me on the morning of my birthday? Did he know about it? Did he know about Iris? Does Mom?

Ty wipes a tear from my cheek with his fingertip, then leans forward and kisses me softly. The next thing I know

I'm kissing him, too, clinging to him, clutching the fabric of his sleeves. But I draw back and shove Ty away when I hear footsteps on the porch. I shift to see the door and find Wyatt standing on the other side of the screen, watching us with a wounded look on his face.

"Wyatt!" I shoot to my feet as Ty scoots to the opposite end of the couch.

Without saying a word, Wyatt turns and starts down the stairs again.

I run to the door. "Come back!" I shout.

But he keeps walking.

Ty sits on the couch, watching me pace as I try to reach Wyatt on his cell.

"Shouldn't he be in school?" Ty asks.

"It's a short week for seniors," I tell him.

"I don't understand why you're so upset that he saw us."

Wyatt isn't answering, so I put my phone in my pocket. "I don't want to hurt him."

Ty cocks his head. "You sure it's not more than that?"

The concern in his voice brings tears to my eyes. I stop pacing and look down at him. "Does it matter? I mean, you're leaving soon. We won't see each other again."

"Says who? We'll stay in touch, Lily. And I might come back."

"I guess, but . . . I'm just confused about everything."

"Are you talking about the way you played? Or are you talking about us?" he asks quietly.

"Both," I say.

I walk to Cookie's pen, and kneel beside it. Reaching in, I ruffle his fur, surprised when he raises his head and his tail starts to wag. I scratch between his ears, and he lowers his head again and heaves a contented sigh. But his tail keeps wagging. *What's got into you, boy?* I wonder, encouraged by the change in him.

Standing, I turn to Ty, knowing that if I keep holding everything in—about my dad's cryptic comments, about Iris, about my mom's weird behavior—I'm going to go crazy. I've always heard that two heads are better than one. Wouldn't three work best of all? Maybe if Ty, Wyatt, and I all put our heads together, we can make some sense of what's happening—that is, if Wyatt ever forgives me.

I motion toward the door. "There's something you should know. Come on. I'll show you."

Cookie needs to go out, so Ty carries him down the steps to the yard. His legs are wobbly when Ty lowers him to the ground, but his tail keeps wagging. A few minutes later he follows us to the workshop, making slow but steady progress.

"He acts like he's feeling a little better," says Ty, as Cookie plops down on the floor.

I lay the violin case next to the chest containing my mother's things. "I know. He had a burst of energy, or something. It's weird."

I turn my attention to the chest and sit down in front of it, next to Ty.

When the music box is out and open between us, with the note from Jake spread across it, I tell Ty about the conversation I overheard between my parents on the morning of my birthday. I tell him about Dad's strange words to me after the accident, too. And I relay Mom's behavior since Dad's death—how she's locked herself in here, and how I watched her from the window going through this chest. I describe the sketches tucked away in tubes on the upper shelf of the storage closet. I decide not to tell him about the strange effect the music box song had on me. I've known Wyatt forever, and he didn't believe me, so why would Ty? I don't want him to think I'm psycho.

He pulls a strand of hair from the brush and wraps it around his finger, looking down at his hands, silent.

"What are you thinking?" I ask.

Ty looks up. "What if they lived there before you were born?"

"In Winterhaven?" I shake my head. "They've always lived in Colorado."

"That could've been the secret they were going to tell you. That they had a different life than they've led you to believe. A life they left."

"I don't know why they'd lie about that."

He lays down the brush, picks up a blue T-shirt, and unfolds it. It's one I haven't seen before. "You said these clothes were your mom's?" He turns the shirt around so that I can see the front. It reads CLASS OF '95. "I'm thinking they could've belonged to someone else," says Ty.

I stare at the shirt, surprised, and my hand trembles as I scratch Cookie's head. "Who?"

"I don't know—a friend or maybe your mom had a younger sister. Or—"

"Mom and Dad would've told me if I had relatives," I interrupt, a note of defense in my voice. "I would've met them. And why would Mom have that person's things? It doesn't make sense."

"Maybe she died."

"*Died?*" I stand abruptly, fighting down a rising sense of unease. "Why would you say that?"

Ty tenses. "Don't get upset." He returns the shirt to the chest. "I'm just tossing out ideas."

"I'm not upset." But I hear the strain in my voice.

He picks up the brush again. "Your mom . . . she looks quite a bit older than my parents."

"She and Dad had me late in life. What are you trying to say?"

"The secret . . ." Ty exhales and gestures toward the chest. "All this. The sketch you found of you and your parents on that dock when you were a baby . . . I'm just trying to come up with an explanation."

"And you think you have?"

"Your dad said something about protecting you. What if your parents did live in Winterhaven and they left because they had to? What if they didn't tell you because it might put you at risk if you knew?"

"What, like they were in the witness-protection program or something?" A sound of disbelief slips past my lips. "That's insane."

"Not really," he says, as if what he's suggesting happens all the time. "It's possible."

I go still as I recall Mack's earlier visit and what he said about Ty. Am I doing the right thing trusting him with this?

Ty must see something in my expression. "Forget what I said. It was just a theory," he says. "You're right—it's crazy. I'm sorry I brought it up."

I stare down at him. What if it isn't a theory? What if Ty knows more than he wants to admit? Dad's voice drifts through my mind, warning, *Don't trust anyone . . .* , and I recall Wyatt asking me to think about why Ty came to Silver Lake, why he's willing to finish roofing our cabin for so little money.

Ty stands and steps toward me, but I back away and cross my arms. "Did you meet Dad once?"

All the blood in my body pools at my feet when he remains silent, his Adam's apple shifting up and down.

"Dad's friend Mack stopped by today before you got here. He said you talked to Dad at the Daily Grind a couple of days before the accident. I told him it must've been someone else."

Ty's chest heaves once. "Lily, I—"

"Did you meet him?"

"I can explain." He reaches for me.

"Don't!" I snap, pulling back. "Why have you been lying to me?"

171

"I didn't lie. I just didn't mention meeting your dad. It didn't seem important."

"I guess the fact that you threatened him wasn't important enough to mention, either?"

"Threatened him? Lily, that's not—" The denial dies on his lips and he blinks rapidly, as if he recalls something he'd rather forget.

"Why did you come to Silver Lake?" I ask, glaring at him. "What did you want from Dad? What do you want from *me*?" I think of the times we've kissed and humiliation threatens to strangle me. Did Ty get close to me for a reason? Does he know something about my parents' past?

"Let me explain," he says again.

"There's no excuse for threatening my dad." I point at the door, wanting him out of my sight. I can't even think straight right now. "Get out."

"Lily—"

"Get out!"

The vein at Ty's temple jumps. Shamefaced, he turns and strides out the door.

Slumping to the floor, I prop my elbows on my knees and bury my face in my hands, too stunned to cry. When the sound of Ty's car engine fades, I force myself to get up and go to the chest, wondering what else I might've missed besides that T-shirt. *Class of '95.*

I take out clothing, piece by piece, studying each item, trying to imagine who it might've belonged to. One name keeps pushing to the forefront of my mind, but I shove it back, afraid to acknowledge it.

I feel the edge of something hard wrapped in a folded sweater and pause to pull the fabric aside. It's a black plastic videocassette. The kind that my parents used to watch in their old VCR when I was younger. Sitting back on my heels, I turn the cassette over in my hands, looking for a label, but I don't find one.

Lying next to the chest, the violin case catches my eye. I feel drawn to open it and take the instrument out, in spite of how much it scares me. Acting on the impulse, I gather my courage, lift the violin from the case, and play again—only a few chords, but they take my breath away.

I'm lowering the bow when something wet sweeps my ankle. Looking over my shoulder, I find Cookie on his feet, licking me, his tail wagging and his eyes shining bright. With a half sob, half laugh, I put the violin away, then turn and wrap my arms around him. "What's happened to you, boy? What's making you so happy all of a sudden?"

The music, Iris says.

I don't have time to watch the video before Mom gets back. She perks up when she notices the change in Cookie.

"I guess the medicine finally kicked in," I tell her, not willing to bring up the violin and other things in the chest just yet, or Iris's claim that the music soothed Cookie and gave his mood a much-needed boost. There's so much I need to understand before I confront her. I want facts that she won't be able to push aside or easily explain away.

If Mom notices that Ty isn't around to do his job, she doesn't mention it. She works on Dad's business files at the kitchen table all afternoon. I realize I'm going to have to wait until tonight when she's asleep to use the VCR.

I try repeatedly to call and text Wyatt but he doesn't answer, so at four o'clock I walk to his house. He isn't there. Addie tells me that he met some friends at the hockey rink.

My stomach flips each time I think of his expression when he caught me making out with Ty. I can only imagine how hurt he must be.

When I ask Iris what she remembered when I played the violin, she says, *I used to play, too. My music meant so much to people. . . .*

I feel a shifting inside me, as if everything I've ever believed about Iris and myself has suddenly changed shape. *You played the violin? You were alive?*

Yes. Her excitement bubbles up like soda water. *But I don't know when, or who I was.*

I can't process anything she says. My mind is stuck on one thought: Iris is a ghost? How is that possible? She seems like a part of me, not something separate—someone who once had a life. *But how do I know how to play, too?* I ask.

Not sure.

My head throbs from all I've learned today. I start up to my bedroom early, hoping Mom will follow my lead so I can sneak downstairs and watch the video. Maybe it will answer some questions. I try to coax Cookie to climb the stairs to the loft with me, but although he seems much more content, he's still exhausted. After taking three steps up, he sits on the stair, unable to go any farther. Hefting him into my arms, I carry him the rest of the way.

Minutes later, after washing my face in the bathroom, I open the door and startle when I see my laptop computer open on my nightstand with the screen aglow.

"Iris?" I whisper.

I didn't open it or turn it on before going into the bathroom, did I? Did she do it through me? Did I forget?

I don't have an answer to that, but I know what she wants. I've been thinking of the same thing ever since Ty left.

Sitting on my bed, I search the internet for "Adam and Myla Winston. Winterhaven, Massachusetts" using several different combinations of their names and the town. I insert the word *carpentry*, thinking that Dad might've worked there, then *artist* after Mom's name. Nothing comes up.

Setting the laptop aside, I lie on my back, pull Cookie into the crook of my arm, and stare at the ceiling. Ty's theories spool through my mind. How can I even consider that anything he says might be true? My parents lived in Winterhaven and ran away to escape some threat? It's a totally far-fetched idea . . . yet it would explain so much.

I think of the T-shirt and who might've worn it. *Class of '95.*

Iris stirs, saying, *It's familiar.*

Her statement lifts my focus to the wall beside the bed where my shadow looms, cast there by the lamplight. The

175

sight of it takes me back to a memory I have from when I was four. Iris and I were playing here in my bedroom when Mom came upstairs.

Smiling, Mom asked, "What's so funny, Lily? I heard you laughing. Who were you talking to? Is Cookie up here?"

"No," I said. "I'm talking to my friend." I pointed at the rug. "That little girl. See?"

"Ah," Mom said. "Your shadow." She winked. "The two of you are like paper dolls, stuck together at the feet. What did you tell the shadow girl that made you giggle?"

"She told *me* something."

"Your shadow isn't a person, Lily," Mom explained. "It's just your silhouette, an outline of you. The little girl is just an imaginary friend."

"No, she's *real*. She told me her name and it's a flower name like mine. It's Iris. Isn't that pretty?"

Energy sputtered in the silence that followed, and I knew it was Iris tickling the hairs at the back of my neck. She was nervous because of the way Mom was staring at us.

"Adam! Would you come up here, please?" Mom called over the deck railing, and I heard something in her voice that made my heart kick my chest. My mother was upset, and I didn't know why. What had I done?

Dad's footsteps were loud on the stairs. "What's going on?" he asked when he reached the landing.

Mom motioned toward me. "Lily's been carrying on a conversation with her shadow," she said in a hushed voice.

"So she has a pretend friend." He shrugged. "She's *four.* It's perfectly healthy."

Mom exhaled a jittery breath. "Tell him what the shadow girl told you, Lily," she said.

"Don't be mad!" I cried. "Iris is nice. She's my *real* friend, not pretend."

"Iris?" Dad's chin jerked up. He shot Mom a look.

She nodded. "According to Lily, the girl said that's her name."

Dad was quiet for a long time. Then he picked me up, hugged me, and carried me to the bed. He told me about shadows. That they're reflections cast by a light. That they can't talk. He was patient and asked me if I understood that the shadow girl wasn't a real person.

Mom watched me closely, her expression scaring me. I could tell that it was important to them both that I believed what Dad had said—that the shadow girl wasn't real. So I answered yes even though that wasn't true.

I knew then that Iris would have to be my secret, but I didn't understand why she made Mom so anxious.

Maybe now I do.

My blood chills as Iris begins to hum, the lullaby faint and wheezy, flickering out and in again like a radio station with poor reception.

Iris, you have to try to remember who you were, I say, desperate for her to disprove my suspicions.

She stops singing, coils tight with frustration. *I can't.*

"*What* are you?" I whisper aloud. *If you were alive, that means you're a ghost. Is that right?*

I'm not sure what I am. We have to find out what they did.

Her words suck the air from my lungs. *Who, Iris? Who are you talking about? Did someone hurt you?*

Something bad happened . . . I can't remember. They made me do something I didn't want to do. . . .

I've never been uneasy with Iris's presence . . . or worried about her. Now I'm both. She asked me to help her, but I don't know how.

Feeling powerless, I sit up and listen for Mom, hoping she's asleep so that I can watch the video. But I hear her stirring below. Popping the iPod earbuds into my ears, I scroll down to a punk rock playlist to drown out my thoughts and make the time pass faster. It doesn't work. Beneath the screech of guitars and pounding of drums, I hear a violin playing the jewelry box song, the same melody that flowed through my fingers today . . . as if by magic.

Something wakes me in the middle of the night. I sit up. The house is quiet.

The earbuds lie on my pillow like a tangled nest. As I slip from the bed, Cookie curls deeper into the blanket. I take the video from my nightstand drawer and go downstairs, careful not to make any noise.

The fire has died, leaving ash in the grate and a smoke-scented chill on the air. Barefoot and shivering, I cross the living room, headed for the television cabinet. Our old

VCR sits on the shelf beneath the television. It's hooked up, although we haven't used it in years. I fumble to turn it on, and a green light spears through the darkness. Shoving the cassette into the machine, I reach for the remote and turn the television on, adjusting the volume to low.

The film is out of focus and blurred, but Mom's voice comes through the speakers.

"I'm so proud of you," she says, sounding distant and scratchy. "I know you're nervous, but I don't have a single doubt that you'll be wonderful."

Iris snaps and sparks like a live wire. My muscles twitch. I hold my breath and look for the button on the remote to adjust the screen's brightness, hoping the image will be easier to see with more background light. But before I can find it, a second voice makes me pause. It's familiar. The voice of a young girl.

"The finale is off," she says. "Would you listen again and tell me what's wrong?"

"Of course," says my mother.

The video flickers, shifts and enhances, as if the person filming did some fine-tuning. Iris shivers as I take in the now-vivid picture, and a thousand needles prick my skin.

It's like I'm seeing myself at the age of thirteen or fourteen years old, but I don't recognize the room in the scene—the dark green velvet sofa, the long flowing draperies behind it, the fancy Chinese rug on the floor. Because *the girl isn't me*. We could be twins, though. Except for her short haircut and her porcelain pale face, we look exactly alike. Her hair is the same dark auburn shade, her eyes the same dark brown. She wears a simple white dress like one I found in the chest in Dad's workshop.

My twin reaches for a violin on a glass coffee table and stands. She looks into the camera and frowns, bites her lower lip as if she's hesitant . . . unsure of herself.

"Take your time," says the cameraman with a tone of encouragement. "There's no need to rush, Doodlebug."

At the sound of Dad's pet name for me, I stop breathing. It's his voice. *He's* filming the scene.

The girl smiles as she looks at my father with loving eyes identical to mine.

Lily, Iris says, her tone capturing my shock as the camera shifts to a woman sitting on the opposite end of the couch. It's my mother when she was much younger. She's radiant, with shiny hair so dark it's almost black and eyes that sparkle with happiness. Scooting to the edge of the couch, she claps her hands together and says, "Aren't you proud of our beautiful daughter, Adam? She's worked so hard."

"Of course I'm proud," Dad answers, aiming the camera again at my twin. "You're going to shine tonight, sweetheart."

Smiling nervously, the girl places the bow against the strings and begins to play the same piece that I played this morning for Ty. The jewelry box song.

I stand frozen in place, listening, stunned, and when she finishes, Mom cheers and Dad exclaims, "Wonderful, Iris!"

A whirlwind spirals up inside of me, and the sound of a gasp spins me around. Mom stands behind me, one hand clutching the handle of her cane, the other pressed to her mouth. Our gazes lock.

"Iris was real," I cry. "You said I imagined her, but you knew I was telling the truth. I had a *sister*! Didn't I have a right to know?"

13

"Lily . . . please don't do this," Mom says, walking past me with her cane.

I whirl around to her, but the television diverts my attention when images of Iris and Mom's smiling face flash on screen. I hear Dad's enthusiastic voice. Their laughter. Sights and sounds of a happy family.

Mom steps in front of the television, blocking my view. "Let this go. No good can come of it." She reaches back to turn off the video.

I rush over to stop her, but I'm too late. "What do you expect me to do? Pretend Iris didn't exist? Well, she did! She still does."

Mom draws back. "What are you saying?"

"The same thing I was trying to tell you when I was four years old." I dig my fingers into my palms as the memory slams into me again. "I told you she talks to me, but you wouldn't listen."

"Do you mean you still think she does?" Mom asks with shock.

"I *know* she does."

The cane thumps the floor as she limps to the couch. "We thought it would stop," she says quietly. "That you'd outgrow it."

My voice rises. "I didn't imagine her, Mom. I'm not crazy. I know her name! Admit it—you and Dad never said it aloud. Not around me, so how else could I have known?" I pause for a breath, and when she doesn't answer, I say, "Why did you keep her a secret?"

She sinks down onto the couch. "You've got to understand—"

"But I *don't* understand! I had a *sister* and you didn't tell me. What were you so afraid of? That you wouldn't be able to move on if you admitted she was here? Because she is." I press my fingers to my temples. "Iris is with me all the time. Inside of me. She's here right now."

Mom goes rigid. "Don't say that! I can't stand it! Iris died. She's gone!"

"*You* can't stand it?" I huff a humorless laugh. "Iris talks to me . . . she whispers and whispers and whispers until sometimes I want to crack my skull open and pull her out, but I can't. I can't get her out, even when I want to be alone and think thoughts she can't hear. That's not possible because she hears *everything*."

"Oh, Lily . . ." Mom sobs, blinking up at me. "We didn't know."

I shake my head. "You and Dad could've helped me, but instead—" The enormity of Dad's betrayal is more painful than hers. I hear him calling Iris Doodlebug. My nickname. *Mine*. "I'm not really surprised that you lied to me, but Dad . . ." My throat closes.

"Please don't blame him," Mom says in a quivering voice. "Your father wanted to tell you, but I wouldn't let him. This is my fault. All of it. From the very beginning."

"Why did you and Dad hide your past from me? Why can't Iris move on? Why can't *you*?" When she turns away, I start for the stairs to the loft, pausing at the landing to glance back at her. "How did my sister die?" I ask.

"She had leukemia."

"When did she die?"

"May nineteenth. The year before you were born. She turned seventeen on May sixth."

"May sixth is *my* birthday," I say.

"The two of you were born on the same day," Mom explains, sounding wrung out and ancient. "Eighteen years apart."

My mind stumbles over that freaky twist of fate. "What did Dad mean when he asked me to reassure him that the two of you had 'done the right thing'?" I ask.

In a harsh whisper, she says, "I don't know." But I don't believe her.

"He was going to tell me about Iris when we got home, wasn't he? How can knowing about her protect me? That's

184

what Dad said to you that morning—that the truth is my only protection."

No answer.

Trembling with anger, I say, "Did the two of you run away to Silver Lake?"

Her head jerks toward me. "Run away? I don't know what you're talking about."

"Stop lying! Did you even know how to play the violin or is that a lie, too?"

"I played," Mom says. "When I was a girl. But not like Iris. Nobody could play like her."

"I can," I say. "I played today." But I'm not sure she hears me.

Covering her face with her hands, Mom starts weeping again. "Iris helped me, but I couldn't help her. So I did what I had to. I don't regret it. You don't know how it is to lose a child. I couldn't just let her go. I couldn't."

Confused by what she's saying, I cross to the couch and sit beside her. I push her hair back, still upset, but hurting for her, too.

"Your father and I—we loved her so much." Mom lowers her hands, and her eyes meet mine. "We love you, too, Lily. *I* love you. But it's been so difficult." She cups my cheek. "How can I move on when I see her every time I look at you?"

Her comment stings like a slap, but she's my mother, and I can't stand to see her in so much pain. Taking her hands, I say, "You said you don't regret what you did to help Iris. What do you mean?"

I can tell my words don't reach her. She squeezes her eyes shut, caught in a landslide of mindless grief.

"I'm so sorry," Mom whispers, gripping my fingers. "We never imagined that Iris would haunt you. In a way, she's haunted all of us."

I lie in bed next to Cookie for an hour listening to my iPod with the volume turned up so I won't hear Mom's crying or Iris's frenzied pacing around in my mind. When the playlist ends, I pull the earbuds out. The house is quiet. Iris is, too.

I go downstairs again and find Mom asleep on the couch, tossing restlessly. On the coffee table beside her, her vial of sedatives sits next to a stack of books.

I pick up the VCR remote and turn on the television, muting the volume. After hitting rewind, I retreat to a corner chair. The tape makes a whirring noise as it scrolls back to the very start of the cassette, and when it finishes, I click play.

Over the next several minutes, my sister's life unfolds before me, beginning just after her birth. I'm completely aware of Iris watching along with me, mesmerized by each image on the screen, as numb with shock as I am.

In the video, our parents are so young that I almost don't recognize them. They're all smiles and wonder as they wiggle Iris's fingers and toes, their joy so overwhelming I can almost feel the warmth of it flowing from the television set.

On the couch, Mom murmurs disjointed sentences in her sleep as I watch Iris grow into a toddler, surrounded by my parents and other adoring people I don't know. A young woman with frizzy brown bangs and squinty eyes behind funky glasses who resembles Dad. A tall, skinny man with big ears and a grin that covers half of his face. An older couple about the age my parents are now. I wonder if they might be my grandparents.

Yes, Iris says. *I'm not sure about the other two. So much is still hazy.*

Envy spears me. Iris knew our grandparents. Why haven't *I* ever met them? Or these other people who were once important in my parents' lives? Why weren't they ever even mentioned?

What else do you remember? I ask.

We were happy. Then something bad happened. I was so scared.

You got sick.

Something else. Something they made me do.

Dreading her answer, I ask, *Who? Mom and Dad?*

Not sure. I don't think so. Maybe . . .

Iris's anxiety becomes my own as, on the screen, I see her splashing in a lake, and I realize that she's the girl in all of Mom's artwork. Shaking, I fast-forward through her childhood until she's almost the age I am now. She's standing on a stage, wearing the green beaded dress, the violin and bow in her hands. Behind her, a black man dressed in

187

a tuxedo sits at a glossy piano. I use the remote to ease the volume up slightly as they begin to play.

The music drifts over me like a warm breeze, and despite everything that's happened tonight, I gradually feel uplifted. At peace. I think of the change in Cookie after he heard me play this afternoon—the bolstering effect the music had on his mood.

"Oh, darling. I'm sorry," Mom murmurs, and I drag my gaze from the television to look at her. She's sitting up, a dark silhouette in the shadowed room, her voice distraught. My spirit tumbles again. Pushing from the chair, I go to her.

There are so many things I want to ask her. Why did she and Dad leave their old life behind? Why did they have me after Iris died? Was I just her substitute? A baby conceived to fill the void Iris's death had left in their lives? If so, I failed. Mom said she loves me, but does she love me as much as she loved my sister?

Sitting beside Mom on the couch, I watch Iris on the screen and jealousy stabs me again and twists the knife. I take in her chic haircut, her poised posture, her grace and confidence. No wonder I don't measure up to Iris in my mother's eyes. I look exactly like my sister, but she was everything I'm not. When Mom looks at me, she must only notice what's missing.

"Forgive me," Mom whispers.

"Please don't cry anymore," I say. "I'm not mad at you or Dad. I just need to understand what's happening."

The light on the television screen flickers, illuminating

her face, and I realize Mom's watching Iris. She's asking for my *sister's* forgiveness, not mine.

Resentment fills my chest and hardens like concrete. But it just as quickly crumbles when I notice the deep creases of worry on Mom's face and the sharp glitter of anxiety in her eyes. Encouraging her to lie down, I say, "You don't have to worry anymore, Mom. Iris is happy."

She clutches my arm, blinks up at me. "Is she, Lily?"

I focus in on the essence of my sister, aware of Iris's distress. "Yes," I tell Mom. It isn't a complete lie. I know Iris has moments of happiness.

"How do you know?" Mom asks.

Measuring my words, I say, "I sense her feelings and hear what she's thinking in my head. You said that she haunts me, but it isn't like that. It's—" I glance at the girl playing her soul out on the screen. "It's like Iris is more than a ghost—like she's a part of me."

"But you said she's in your head. That she won't stop whispering. She must be so tormented." Mom cups my cheek with her cold, trembling hand. "You both must be."

"No, Mom. I was upset when I said that. Sometimes I do wish she'd let me have a minute to myself, but I would never want her to go away forever."

The music ends. Applause erupts. On the television screen, Iris bows.

"She's always been my friend," I whisper. "I love her."

In the video, my sister lifts her head and peers out at the audience. The applause intensifies. Iris looks directly into

189

my eyes and smiles as a soft voice inside my mind says, *I love you, too.*

I sit on the porch, wrapped in a blanket, waiting for the sunrise. Iris hovers at the edge of my mind.

So many lost memories . . . , she says sadly. *Why can't I remember more than glimpses . . . the music . . . Jake?*

Maybe it's just going to take time for the rest. I sigh. *The things in the tool chest are yours, aren't they? Jake wrote the note to you.*

Yes.

You loved each other.

Like crazy, Iris says.

I want to ask more, but she curls into that dark, silent place where I can't reach her, as if she wants to be alone with her memories of Jake.

I pick apart all I know, piece by piece. For some reason, I keep returning to the odd coincidence that Iris and I share the same birthday. I once wrote an English report about a science fiction and fantasy writer named Emma Bull. She said that "coincidence is the word we use when we can't see the levers and pulleys." Could there be a reason our birthdays are the same? Does that commonality have anything to do with why we've connected so strongly?

Tangled up inside, I call Addie as the first rays of light peek over the eastern horizon. She's always up before dawn, and answers on the first ring.

"Something happened last night," I tell her. "I really

need to talk to somebody. Can you come over?" I burst into tears.

Addie says she'll leave right away.

While I wait, I go check on Mom. She's still sleeping so I put Cookie in his crate and go upstairs to change into jeans and a long-sleeved shirt. Twenty minutes later, I hear a car outside.

Rushing downstairs, I pull open the door. Wyatt is climbing the steps behind his grandmother. I'm so glad to see him that I run past Addie and throw my arms around him. "Thank you for coming."

As we step apart, he lowers his eyes. "I can only stay a little while before I have to leave for school."

Addie reaches for the door, saying, "Where's your mother?"

"Sleeping on the couch. I'm worried about her. She's totally out of it." My voice cracks as I add, "Before she fell asleep, she couldn't stop crying."

Inside, the three of us pause, our eyes on Mom. Then Addie shrugs out of her coat, whispering, "Help me get her to bed, Lily."

Wyatt goes out to the porch as Addie and I rouse Mom and take her to her room. She curls up on her bed without a word.

I follow Addie back to the living room, and call Wyatt inside. "What happened?" Addie asks, leading me to the couch and drawing me close to her.

There's no way to prepare them for the truth, so I just come out with it. "Last night I found out I had a sister. She died of leukemia before I was born. I guess talking about it was too much for Mom. She just—she fell apart."

Addie doesn't attempt to hide her shock. "They never told you before?" she gasps.

Pressing my lips together, I shake my head.

"Why not?" Wyatt asks.

"I don't know." I twist my fingers in my lap. "I kept asking but she got really upset and said a lot of things that don't make sense."

Addie hugs me. "When everything settles down and your mother's emotions aren't so raw, maybe she'll be ready to talk about it. She's suffered a lot of loss." She sits back. "What can I do for you, sugar?"

"Nothing. I guess I just needed to tell someone. I feel so alone. I'm sorry I made you come over here."

"No, I'm glad you called. You've been through a lot, too. More than your share."

"Would you mind staying with Mom while I take a walk? I need to get out of here, and I don't want her to wake up to an empty house."

"Sure," Addie says. "Take your time."

Turning to Wyatt, I ask, "Will you come?" I bite my lip.

"If we hurry," he says, still looking injured.

I grab my jacket off the hook by the door and slip it on, then Wyatt follows me outside. The dawn is milky gray, the sky streaked with tenuous light. We take the steps down into the yard and walk in the same direction without even discussing where to go. I know we'll end up at Ponderosa Pond, our spot, the place where we learned to swim and skip stones across the water, where we shared secrets about broken rules, first beers, and first crushes—Wyatt's on Kelsey Redgrave in fourth grade, mine on Zac Efron, who I'd crushed on after seeing him in *High School Musical*. I've never told Wyatt my *biggest* secret, though. Today I'm finally going to.

Wyatt and I reach the pond in ten minutes. I stare across the murky green water, smelling a faint scent of fish in the air. My eyes are so tired, my lids scrape like sandpaper each time I blink. "I can't believe how stupid I've been," I say. "I should've listened to you. Ty doesn't really care about me. He was only using me."

Wyatt startles, alarmed. "What are you talking about? Are you okay?" His eyes narrow. "If he hurt you—"

"He didn't. I'm fine." I tell him about Mack's visit. "When I asked Ty about threatening Dad, he didn't deny it; he just looked guilty and wanted to explain."

Wyatt utters a sound of disgust. "What did he say?"

"I didn't give him the chance—I told him to leave. I didn't want to listen to his excuses. But now I wish I had. I want to know what he and Dad argued about and why he came here."

"No, you did the right thing. He probably would've lied, anyway. He already proved he can't be trusted."

I watch Wyatt closely. "So, you're not mad at me?"

He squints and scratches his chin. "Hmm. I need some time to think about that."

"Don't tease," I say, crossing my arms. "Not now. I really need to talk to you about my sister."

Sobering, Wyatt says, "You must be freaking out."

"It seems impossible. Why would they hide her from me?"

Wyatt shakes his head. "Those things we found in your Dad's workshop. The clothes . . . the violin . . . I guess they belonged to her instead of your mom?"

"I guess. She was wearing two of the dresses in the video. And the violin—she played it, and ohmygosh, Wyatt! She's incredible. But there's more about her I haven't told you." Fighting a flutter of nerves, I take a breath, then say, "I've known Iris most of my life. I was four the first time I remember talking to her."

"What? But you said she died."

"She did."

Wyatt's look of bafflement turns to disbelief. "Come on, Lil. Are you saying she's a ghost?"

"I don't know what she is, exactly. But we communicate. It's like she's inside me."

He blinks, silent, waiting for the punch line.

Desperate for him to believe me, I say, "I'm serious. I knew Iris's name when I was little, even though nobody ever said it to me." I tell him about the warnings she sent me before Dad's accident and that she pressed on my brake to keep me from hitting the deer. "And she made me write *Winterhaven* on that note," I finish.

Wyatt shifts his attention to the water.

"You don't believe me."

Rubbing a hand across his face, he says, "Listen to yourself, Lil. Maybe . . ." He exhales.

"Go ahead and say what you're thinking."

"Don't get mad," he says slowly, "but maybe the next time your mom goes to the doctor, you should see him, too. You've had some hard stuff to deal with lately. First your dad, then Cookie, and now this."

Heat crawls up my neck. "I don't need a straitjacket. I'm not imagining things. I can understand your doubts, but I thought you'd at least try to have an open mind. Didn't you tell me once that something like forty percent of city police departments use psychics to help solve crimes?"

"More like thirty-five."

"I remember you talking about a case you read where a woman led the cops to a lake where a victim was buried."

Wyatt shrugs. "They get lucky sometimes." He gestures toward the road. "Let's go talk to Gran about this, okay? I'm a little freaked out."

My blush burns hotter. "Explain how I knew my sister's name before anyone ever told me about her. When I was a kid, I even mentioned Iris to my parents and they got all weird about it."

"You must've heard them say her name sometime and

you just don't remember."

"No." I shake my head. "What about everything else that's been happening?"

"Like what?"

"For one thing, the visions."

"Visions? What do you mean?"

I rub my palms up and down my arms, chilled by the cool morning air, in spite of my jacket. "I told you about them. In the workshop. Writing on that note . . . ?"

Wyatt clears his throat. "I guess I didn't realize you *saw* something when that happened."

Eager to make him understand, I say, "It's sort of like I have memories, but now I think they're actually *Iris's* memories. I think she transfers them to me somehow. You were with me the first time. Remember how I zoned out that morning when we played the jewelry box? When the music started, I saw a guy's face and that's when I kissed you. But it was like I was kissing someone else, not you. I think it was the guy who wrote the note to Iris. Her boyfriend, Jake."

Wyatt's eyes are narrowed, his jaw clamped tight. "So your ghost sister *made* you kiss me?" he says. He turns his head, as if he's too humiliated to face me.

Wincing, I say, "I'm sorry, Wyatt. I'm just telling you the truth."

"I get it." His voice is pinched. "You wish you'd never kissed me and don't want a repeat. Well, there won't be one, so you can relax."

I touch his shoulder. "I didn't say that. I just—it was only at first that I felt like I was kissing Jake. Then it was you. And I wouldn't mind if it happened again, but I can't think about that right now." I sigh. "Please don't be upset."

A scowl darkens his face. "I'm trying to understand, but you're not making it easy. You say you wouldn't mind if it happened again, but I saw you making out with Ty, and now you tell me that when we kissed the first time you felt like you were kissing some other guy. What am I supposed to think?"

Knowing I don't deserve Wyatt's understanding, I say, "I know this is messed up. *I'm* messed up."

He looks down at his boots.

Birds chirp high in the branches overhead. On the opposite side of the pond, two deer pass between the trees. I hear a splash as a fish jumps in the water near the shore where we stand, rippling a perfect circle on the surface of the pond.

"I'll go with you to talk to your mom if you want," Wyatt mutters after a minute. "We'll figure this out."

Relieved that he's not going to walk away, I say, "Thanks, Wyatt. You're awesome to offer, but right now I just need you to talk to *me*. About Iris. All of it." Ducking my head, I catch his gaze.

"Sure." He kicks a rock. "So . . . uh . . . has she made anything else happen since she hit the brake on the four-wheeler? Besides forcing you to kiss me, I mean?" His mouth slants into a smirk.

"I can play the violin," I say, choosing to ignore his sarcasm. "I'm not sure if Iris is playing it through me or what, but I'm almost as good as she was. Possibly *just* as good. The first time I picked up her violin I knew exactly what to do. I didn't even have to think about it."

He frowns and gnaws his lower lip.

"What?" I say.

"I don't know. This is all pretty weird. Maybe I should see that video."

"You should." I want to tell him that the music was like a balm to Cookie's spirit, and how hearing Iris play it on the video had a powerful effect on me, too, but I don't. He already thinks I've lost it. I don't want to convince him he's right. "Come over after school and I'll play the violin for you," I say.

"I'll try." I get the impression that he isn't sure if he should be worried about me or laugh in my face.

"I *can* play," I say, feeling defensive. "Ask Ty. He was there. He heard me. He said I was wonderful."

"Yeah, I saw how wonderful he thinks you are." Wyatt jams his hands into his pockets. "Sorry. That just slipped out."

"No, I'm the one who's sorry."

"I said it first."

With a flustered laugh, I say, "That depends on when you started counting." We stare at each other. The air is so thick with tension, I can barely breathe. "Promise you won't tell your grandmother about any of this, okay? I'm not ready to talk about it with anyone except you."

"Sure. Okay. I won't say anything."

We start walking at the same time, careful not to look at each other. Hating the awkwardness between us, I reach over and grab the tie dangling down from Wyatt's stocking cap and give it a tug.

He slides me a crooked smile.

I smile back. *Progress.*

14

When we get home, Mom's up and sitting at the kitchen table in front of a plate of bacon and eggs that haven't been touched. Addie stands at the sink washing dishes and chattering like a magpie. Mom responds to her questions with brief, quiet answers and downcast eyes.

I go upstairs and bring Cookie down. He's not as spunky as he was yesterday, but at least his tail thumps the mattress when he sees me, and that gives me hope that he's going to be okay.

After Addie and Wyatt leave, I go straight to the shower, and as the hot water sluices down my body, I cry until I'm numb. Wyatt didn't believe me. Ty and my parents betrayed my trust.

Why didn't you move on after you died? I ask Iris. *What kept you here?*

Jake, she says. *And something unfinished. I have to watch over you.*

When I ask, she's unable to say what needs finishing, or why she feels I'm in need of her vigilant eye. She only knows that she has to see Jake.

I'll try my best to find him. Maybe he can answer our questions, I say.

Her excitement soars through me like a shooting star, and I'm suddenly afraid of getting her hopes up. Iris hasn't remembered Jake's last name. I have no clue how to begin looking for him.

I step from the shower and wrap up in a towel. Downstairs, Cookie barks once, as if calling out a greeting, and I hear a car engine outside. Doubting Mom will answer the door, I dress quickly. But the doorbell never rings.

I'm heading for the stairs when Iris whispers, *The window.*

The urgency in her tone sends me hurrying to the window at the far side of my bed. I peer out at the meadow across the road where Mom and Ty stand facing each other in the pale spring grass. Mom leans on her cane, her posture rigid. She jabs a hand toward Ty and says something. He jams the hammer he's holding into his tool belt and says something back.

Mom lifts her cane, takes a step toward Ty, and says something else that sends him walking past her, headed for the cabin. Mom stays in the meadow, watching him.

I exhale the breath I've been holding. *Iris, what's happening?*

I don't know.

Dad's toolbox sits on the ground beneath my window. Ty reaches it, puts the tool belt inside, closes the box, and picks it up. Taking long strides, he starts around to the front of the house.

I run downstairs and throw open the door as he's rounding the corner. "What's going on?"

He glances down at the toolbox and mumbles, "I need to put this away."

I wait in the yard, but when he returns from the storage shed, Ty passes by, heading for his car without uttering a word or even casting a look my way.

Starting after him, I say, "Why were you and Mom arguing? Where are you going?"

He opens the car door and moves to climb behind the wheel, then pauses. "Your mom asked me to leave."

"She—why?" Anger flares in me. "Did you threaten her, too?"

He looks so sad that I almost regret my harsh question. "I shouldn't have come back. I don't want to upset you anymore," Ty says.

I'm torn between wanting to hurt him, and wanting to throw my arms around him and tell him I'm sorry. "What's going on, Ty?" I ask, unable to disguise my frustration. "I didn't let you explain before. Now's your chance."

"I'd only make things worse between you and your mom," he says, sounding miserable. "I hate to leave town like this, but maybe it's best."

"Leave Silver Lake? Right now?" He nods, and

something hot and sharp explodes in my chest. "I won't see you again?" I'm surprised that possibility upsets me so much after what he did.

"I should be with my family," Ty says quietly. "I'm heading back tomorrow."

"But you can't! I mean, we haven't—" My voice breaks. "I don't even know why you came here."

"It doesn't matter anymore."

"You were right about the clothes in the chest," I say quickly. "It turns out I had a sister who died before I was born. The violin was hers. Tell me the truth. Did you know about her?"

The sound of gravel crunching on the road draws our attention, and we both shift to see Mom making her way toward us. "Come inside, Lily," she says.

I return my focus to Ty, lowering my voice so Mom won't hear. "At least tell me if you got what you came for—whatever it was you wanted from us."

He shakes his head. "No, but I found something else important. Something I'd never put at risk." Getting into the car, Ty starts the engine, then lowers the window. In a thick voice he says, "'Bye, Lily."

I watch his car disappear down the road, trying not to cry and wondering what he meant. Was he talking about me? How could his being here put me at risk? I turn to my mother, and my tears slip free. "What were you two fighting about?"

"Forget him, Lily. It's for the best."

"For you, maybe, but not me! Dad knew Ty, didn't he? Did the two of you live in Massachusetts before I was born? Did you come to Silver Lake after Iris died?"

"Lily . . . stop." Her face crumbles. "I'm not going to discuss this. You're upsetting me."

"*You!* What about *me*? Do you think all your secrets and lies aren't upsetting? It's not fair! I have a right to know. Why did Ty come here? To find Dad? Does it have something to do with Iris?" I give her a minute to answer my rapidly fired questions, and when she doesn't, I say, "What really happened to her, Mom? Was her boyfriend involved in it? Do you know Jake?"

Mom recoils at the mention of his name. I think she's surprised at how much I've learned.

I wait another few seconds for her to answer, then stomp past her. "I hate you right now. I really do. I'll just find out on my own."

"You'll only get hurt if you listen to what he says. You trust people too easily."

"You're right. I trusted *you*," I shout, running up the cabin steps and onto the porch.

"Stay away from Ty," she calls after me. "He used you. He used both of us."

Pausing at the door, I look back at her. "How, Mom? *What is going on?*"

She opens her mouth and takes a step toward me. But just when I think she's finally going to talk to me and give me some answers, she draws back. "I'm your mother," she says. "You have to do what I say. I don't want you talking to Ty Collier anymore, do you understand? Your father would agree with me about this."

"No, I don't understand. I don't understand anything." I walk into the cabin and slam the door.

Ty doesn't answer any of my calls. I'm so upset that while Mom is napping, I take one of her sedatives from the medicine vial and gulp it down with a glass of water. Thirty minutes later, I understand why she loves them so much.

The fog is quiet. It absorbs all sensations. Weightless and numb, I curl into the vaporous mist and sleep for hours or maybe only minutes, until the haze parts and a guy's face appears, hovering above me . . . a vision . . . a revelation . . . the answer to a thousand prayers. I've been waiting for him all of my life. Searching for his blue eyes in every person I've met since I was little, longing to touch his black hair and feel it brush my cheek.

Jake, I whisper to the wavering apparition. *Jake Milano, I love you. Don't let me go.*

I wake up with a jerk, and sit straight up in bed, wide-awake now, stunned. The slant of sunbeams through my bedroom window tells me I haven't slept long. "Milano," I whisper, and Iris spins like a cyclone inside of me. "That's Jake's last name, isn't it?"

Yes! she breathes. *We thought we had forever . . .*

Not only do I know Jake's last name, I remember him. I *know* him. The sound of his laughter. The scratch of the rough calluses on his palms, the soft touch of his fingers. I know the press of his mouth and the warmth of his body. He loves to drive too fast and sing too loudly and push himself to the point of puking as he runs around a track. He's afraid of failing, of not meeting his parents' expectations. And he's afraid of losing the girl he loves.

But he knows he's going to.

"Oh my god," I whisper. The memories seem to be as much mine as Iris's. But how can that be? How can I know these things if Jake is from my sister's past, not mine?

We have to find out what happened to you, Iris. It's weird, but I feel like I'm a part of it somehow. What should we do?

Jake can help us, she says with certainty. *Somehow, I know it.*

"Someone else can help us, too," I say aloud.

I can't let Ty leave Silver Lake. Not until he tells me what he knows about my parents.

I call Silver Lake Studio Apartments' office and ask the desk clerk if Ty checked out. When she says he hasn't, I start making plans to slip away to see him. Mom doesn't make it easy for me. She stays close all day, keeping an eye on me. In the evening, I lie and tell her I'm driving into town to meet Sylvie, and she insists on going along. I tell her no, and we have another argument that sizzles like the lightning splitting the sky outside.

When she forbids me to leave, I get so angry that I bolt

upstairs to my bedroom, determined to grab my keys and go anyway. But the sight of my open laptop in the middle of the bed stops me short. The Winterhaven Chamber of Commerce site is up on the screen. Not again. Did I pull up the site earlier today? Did Iris do it?

Don't leave. Look for Jake first, she pleads.

A crash of thunder rattles the windows and rain taps the roof as I settle in front of the computer. A search for "Jake Milano, Winterhaven, Massachusetts" produces a link to a store called Milano Lawn & Garden Center. The contact information doesn't include any names, only a phone number and an email address.

The rain falls harder, transforming the windowpanes into wavering dark pools. I place my fingers on the keyboard, ready to send an email, but I don't know what to say. So instead, I type *Iris Winston* into the search box, realizing that if my sister was a child prodigy violinist, articles might've been written about her. Nothing relevant appears, so I type: *child prodigy violinists in the 1990s*. Links fill the screen about child prodigies in general, about savants and extreme precocity in children, but nothing specific to Iris. I skim past a Wikipedia entry about a little boy in France, and another about an American girl I once saw featured on the news. I'm about to give up when, at the very bottom of the screen, the name *Iris* jumps out at me in a link to a YouTube video.

EXTRAORDINARY 6-YEAR-OLD VIOLINIST IRIS MARSHALL.

Marshall, not Winston. Disappointment swells in my chest, but curiosity makes me move the mouse over the link and click.

A still image of Iris—my Iris—standing on a stage backed by a blue velvet curtain appears. Her violin is poised beneath her chin, the bow touching the strings, her face the definition of concentration. My pulse rushes to catch up with my stampeding thoughts as I start the video and Iris begins to play. And when the performance ends, I can hardly sit still.

Iris is bursting with excitement, too. *That was me,* she says.

I stare at the screen. *But our last name isn't Marshall, it's Winston.*

It wasn't then.

The sound of water running in the bathroom downstairs drifts up to me. I could feel Mom's fear when she insisted I stay away from Ty. What does he know about her past that she doesn't want me to find out?

Determined to get some answers, I type "Adam Marshall" into the computer. The links containing that name fill two screens. The mouse shakes as I position it over the first link and click. A photograph of a sprawling campus of one-story buildings in a landscaped setting appears. The sign at the entrance reads CELL RESEARCH TECHNOLOGY. A scan of the text beneath the picture explains that the place is some sort of lab in Boston—a bio-tech firm. Adam Marshall is listed as a lead research scientist, on staff from 1986 until 1994.

Iris shudders. *There were animals in cages, and a man. The animals didn't like him.*

An uneasy feeling drifts over me, light as a cobweb, tangling me in its delicate snare. *What man, Iris?*

I can't remember his name. . . . He scared me.

Sitting straighter, I look for photographs of the scientists and staff, hoping Iris will be able to identify the man she mentioned, but there aren't any pictures. Closing out the site, I open the next link to an article in a scientific journal written in 1987 by Adam Marshall, Ph.D. When I catch sight of a small picture of the author to the right of the text, a cold fist squeezes my throat. Thick, dark hair without a speck of gray. Pale skin, unlined. No beard. Only the dark brown eyes are the same. They're the gentle, curious eyes that belonged to the father I loved and trusted.

I shift to the text:

> *Studies involving specialized DNA technology . . . in my attempts to produce multiple exact genetic duplicates of endangered species . . . the benefits of taking the next step would need to be weighed against possible moral and ethical consequences. . . .*

I start again at the beginning, trying to comprehend the meaning of what I'm reading. It seems impossible that Dad headed up a team of scientists at that Boston lab before I was born. That he oversaw a project to try to save animals from extinction by reproducing them genetically. But as I study the picture again, I know without a doubt it's Dad. The same man who couldn't stand to pull a thorn out of Cookie's paw because he was afraid of hurting him.

Exiting the website and closing my laptop, I scoot off the bed and look for my bag but can't find it. Deciding I must've left it by the front door, I go downstairs and see it tucked into the corner of the couch. I grab it and quickly peek in on Mom. She's completely knocked out.

I take my raincoat from the closet by the door, put it on, and slip outside, pulling the hood over my head. The storm has eased, but raindrops still plop onto the slick fabric of my coat, and cool night air chills my cheeks as I let myself into Mom's Blazer. The door clicks shut.

Without turning on the overhead light, I dig inside my bag for my keys, dumping the contents onto the seat, riffling through gum wrappers, receipts, pens, a pad of paper, my wallet. The keys aren't there. And Dad's van keys are on the same ring.

I bang my palms against the steering wheel. Mom must have them. She knew I wouldn't stay away from Ty.

I go back inside and look through her purse, but don't find my set or hers, either. In spite of the fact that she's sleeping only inches away, I check her jacket pockets and peek inside her nightstand drawers. Finally, I search the kitchen. But the keys are nowhere to be found.

I'm so mad at Mom, it's hard not to slam the door as I

leave the cabin and take off on foot down the road toward Wyatt and Addie's. With any luck, Addie will be asleep; she's an early-to-bed, early-to-rise sort of person.

The fresh scents of damp earth and rinsed air swirl up as I walk. Silky meadow grass swishes as the breeze combs through it, and my boots make a soft, measured thump as I make my way up the road. I'd normally be comforted by the familiar smells and noises, but not tonight. I half expect an invisible hand to lunge out of the shadows and grab me, yanking me down to some cold, dark place. *Iris, I'm afraid. Why do you think Dad and Mom changed their last name?*

The same reason they ran away and came here.

Yes, I say. *And I'm starting to think that had something to do with you. But what?*

I sense her mulling over the question as I round the bend, breathing a sigh of relief when Wyatt's house appears ahead. All of the windows are dark except the one in his bedroom. Trotting the rest of the way, I jump up to tap the pane, hearing the chatter of a voice on his television inside. "Wyatt, it's me." I wait, and a few seconds later, the blinds raise and his face appears. "Come outside."

He lowers the blinds, and I walk around to the front of the house. As I'm climbing the stairs, Wyatt steps onto the porch, propping the screen door open with his shoulder. Addie's orange cat, Big Betty, meows as she creeps out between his bare feet. She comes toward me, weaves around my ankles, her coat as soft as fog.

"You cut your hair," I say.

211

Lamplight from the living room casts a glow around Wyatt's bare shoulders. He looks different somehow. Older. Maybe because he isn't wearing his hat. Or maybe it's his expression—the way he's looking at me. Wyatt can grow sideburns. I never noticed before. My pulse kicks up and my focus lowers as if drawn by gravity. I've seen Wyatt's skinny white chest too many times to count. We spent almost every day of last summer and the summers before that swimming in the pond or splashing around in the creek. But tonight his chest doesn't seem skinny as the shadows flicker across his skin. I'm suddenly feeling insanely awkward yet drawn to Wyatt at the same time, with him standing half-naked only a couple of feet away. But now's not the time to be thinking such thoughts.

He pushes the screen door wider. "You want to come in?"

I shake my head. "I can't."

"What's up?"

"Where do you want me to start?" I pause, struggling to find the right words. "I wish everything could be like it was before Dad died. I don't even know who I am anymore."

Wyatt steps closer, easing the screen door shut behind him. "What's wrong, Lil?"

"I need to go to Silver Lake, but Mom hid all the keys. Will you take me?"

"Why'd she hide the keys?"

"She doesn't want me to see Ty."

Wyatt scowls, and after a drawn-out silence, he asks, "Is that why you want to go to town? To see *him*?"

"Yes, but not for the reason you think. He knows about Mom and Dad's past and what really happened to Iris. I'm sure of it."

"I thought your sister died of leukemia."

"That's what Mom said."

"And you don't believe her?"

"I don't know what to believe."

Wyatt exhales loudly. "I'm sorry, Lil, but I'm on your mom's side. Why would you trust what Collier says over her? I mean, the guy threatened your dad. He's up to something."

"Mom's lying, and I think he knows why. I've tried calling and texting him, but he won't answer."

"Why can't it wait until tomorrow?"

"He's leaving in the morning." I step closer. "Please, Wyatt? I've got to talk to him before he goes, or I may never figure this out."

Scrubbing his hand through his hair, he says, "Come on, Lil. Don't do this to me. Let me take you home. I'll get my keys."

As he's turning toward the door, I place my hand on his arm to stop him. "If you think I want to see Ty for any other reason, you're totally wrong."

I wait for him to give in and say he'll take me, but Wyatt doesn't budge.

"Never mind. I shouldn't have asked you. I'm sorry, Wyatt." I turn and take the steps down into the yard.

"Wait up," Wyatt calls after me. "I said I'd drive you home."

"That's okay," I say in a matter-of-fact tone. "I'm not going home."

"You're *walking* into town? In the dark? That's crazy! It'll take over two hours."

"I'll be fine," I say, then take off at a jog.

I slow my pace the second I'm out of sight of Wyatt's house. An owl hoots from a nearby tree. A coyote howls in the distance and a second one answers the call. Frogs croak in the murky rain water in a gulley at the side of the road.

I press on for at least ten minutes before deciding Wyatt was right about walking to Silver Lake being insane.

Stopping in the middle of the road, I lean my head back and scream as loud as I can, hoping it'll make me feel better. It doesn't.

I spin on my heel and start toward home, crunching gravel beneath my boots. But, I've only taken a few steps when I hear the rumble of a motor moving closer, then the faint sound of music. Headlights glimmer in the trees beyond the bend, and then I recognize the old Kings of Leon song that's playing. They used to be Wyatt's favorite band before they "sold out and went commercial," as he always says.

I move to the side of the road and wait. When Wyatt reaches me, he pulls to a stop and lowers the volume. "Okay, you win," he calls out the window. "I'll take you to town."

Jogging around to the passenger door, I get in. Wyatt's wearing his usual hat now, yet in so many ways he still doesn't seem like the same guy I knew a month ago. Or even last week.

"Why do you have to make everything so difficult?" he says, clearly put out with me.

"I know. I'm sorry." I cross my arms and settle in.

"Coyotes prowl after dark; you know that. There've been, like, thirty incidents of people getting attacked."

"Thirty people have been attacked this year?" I say, sending him a startled glance.

Watching the road, he says through gritted teeth, "No, not this year. Period."

"In the entire history of the world?" I smother a laugh. "Gee, that's enough to scare the crap out of me."

"That's only *reported* attacks," he says, sounding defensive.

I hide my smile. The cab of the truck smells like corn chips and dirty gym socks. Crushed fast-food wrappers litter the space on the floorboard around my feet. I'm not sure what it says about me that I'm happy to be sitting in the familiar mess alongside Wyatt, but I am.

"This better be *really* important," he mutters.

"It is. Thanks for caring whether or not I'm eaten by a coyote." On impulse, I reach across the seat for his hand.

Wyatt tenses and I pull my hand back, realizing my mistake. He's still not over catching me with Ty. Eager to fill the silence, I tell him about everything I've learned since the last time we talked.

His eyes widen. "And you think Collier knows something about all this?"

"He must. I mean, there's the confrontation he had with Dad, and then his argument with Mom today. Not to mention how desperate she seems to keep us apart. And the theories about Mom and Dad's past he came up with when we were looking at the stuff in the chest . . . it almost seemed like he was trying to lead me toward something he already knew."

Wyatt squints at the dark road with his lips pursed. It's so quiet that I can almost imagine we're hurtling through space, the last two people in the universe. The lights of Silver Lake appear ahead of us, twinkling like multicolored stars against the black canvas of night. "Where's Collier staying?" he asks.

"In those pay-by-the-week apartments near the campus. I think they're on Pine Street."

"I know the place."

I barely hear him over the pounding of my heartbeat.

15

Ty opens the door, sees me standing on the stoop, and takes a quick step back. "Lily . . ." His voice trails as Wyatt moves out of the shadows behind me.

Motioning us in, Ty closes the door and stares at it, his back to us. In that moment, I forget that Wyatt is with me. I have the strongest urge to reach for Ty, to make him look at me. It's impossible to believe that he was only pretending he cared about me because he wanted something.

"You know about my dad's past, don't you," I say. He turns around, and I tell him what I found online. "What were you and Mom arguing about in the meadow?"

Dark circles rim Ty's eyes. Exhaling, he says, "I told her if she won't tell you the truth, I will."

"I knew it," I say with a sinking feeling.

"Lily, I—" Something behind me diverts his attention. "Hey!" Ty yells, bolting past me. "Get your hands off my stuff!"

I swing around. I didn't even realize Wyatt had left my side, but he's standing at the kitchen table holding a newspaper clipping. More clippings and a scrapbook are scattered across the table beside him.

Ty tries to grab the clipping from Wyatt's hand, but Wyatt holds tight to the scrap and backs up to the wall. "It's your dad's obituary," Wyatt calls to me. "Look at that stuff on the table. He's been collecting all kinds of information about your family."

I cross to the table and look down, my gaze skipping over loose photocopied articles containing image after image of Dad when he was young. I've suspected that Ty's reason for coming here has something to do with my father's past, but that doesn't ease the gut punch of seeing the proof.

"Lily, wait," Ty says as I open the scrapbook.

A reflection of my own younger face jumps out at me. I know instantly that it's Iris, not me. My sister sits in a chair next to a piano, a violin lying across her lap. A smiling young woman stands next to her.

I feel unsteady as I turn the page to a magazine photo of Iris, posing again with her violin. She was probably eight years old at the time. An article fills the facing page, but I don't pause to read it before moving farther into the book where I find a newspaper story containing a picture of Iris performing onstage when she was a teenager.

As I flip through page after page, more images of my sister flash before me: Iris standing between Mom and Dad on a groomed lawn in front of a two-story house that seems so familiar I can hear the squeak of the screen door when it opens; Iris with a group of other young musicians, all of them holding instruments, all of them dressed in black and white; Iris and a young man with wavy black hair and startling blue eyes smiling out at me from a homemade Christmas card addressed, "To Jillian," and signed, "Love, Iris and Jake."

Jake. Iris's whisper of his name skims a tingling sensation along the surface of my skin. As if she's speaking directly to him, she says, *A part of me couldn't forget. . . . I've been waiting. . . .*

I brush my fingers across Jake's image, so stunned I'm dizzy. Ty and Wyatt are talking to me, but their words don't register. Slowly, I flip to the back of the book, and when I reach the final page a ringing noise fills my ears. Iris's obituary is one column wide and three paragraphs long, with her picture at the top. My vision narrows until "Iris Marshall" is all I can read.

When Ty touches my arm, I turn and look up at him. "You knew about her, too," I say, as the ringing in my head subsides.

He nods. "I've known about her all of my life. Before I was born, my mother was your sister's music teacher." He takes the scrapbook from my hands, closes it, and puts it on the table. Lowering his head, he exhales a quick rush of air. "I can explain all of this."

Wyatt is by my side in the time it takes to blink. "You can come up with more lies, you mean. Just like you lied to Lily about meeting her dad and the reason you came to Silver Lake. I bet you never even went to Columbia. I bet those references you gave Lily's mom weren't professors at all; they're probably in on this. And the poor little brother in a coma's probably made up, too."

Ty recoils, and I snap, "*Wyatt!*" But what if he's right? The truth is, the thought crossed my mind, too.

"No." Desperation strains Ty's voice. "I didn't lie about Kyle or anything other than why I came here. I just—I didn't tell you everything because I hoped your mom would. You should hear the truth from her, not me."

"What truth, Ty?" I gesture toward the table. "Why are you collecting information on Dad and Iris?"

Wyatt slams Dad's obituary down on the table. "No lies this time."

Ty nods once and draws a breath. "Before my parents married, my mother lived in Boston and worked as a music teacher. Twice a week, your mom brought Iris in from Winterhaven for private lessons. She was only five when they started working together, and by the time she was seven, Mom knew that Iris had outgrown her; she needed a teacher with more skills and experience who could develop her gift in a way my mother couldn't. So Mom sent her to the New England Conservatory in Boston."

He pauses, and I say, "I get why your mother followed Iris's progress, but why did she keep all those articles about Dad?"

"Those are mine."

"You're obsessed." Wyatt almost spits the words as he walks to the ratty-looking sofa and plops down. Glaring at Ty, he adds, "You were stalking Lily's dad, weren't you."

Keeping his gaze on me, Ty says, "I did come here to find your dad, Lily, but it's not how it seems."

I want so much to believe him, but every new thing I learn just makes Ty look more guilty. "On the morning of the accident . . . were you following us?" I ask.

"No." He shakes his head. "I was hiking, that's all. I had no idea you'd be up there. I know this looks bad, but I can clear everything up."

"Then do it," I say, joining Wyatt on the couch.

Pulling a chair over, Ty turns it to face us and sits down. "It's a long story."

"We're not going anywhere," Wyatt snaps.

Ty looks from me to Wyatt, then back again. "I grew up hearing stories about Iris. Mom had recordings of her music that she played a lot. I wasn't all that interested until Kyle got hurt and Mom started playing the CDs in his hospital room. I doubt he hears them, but Mom thinks he does. She believes that your sister's music has some sort of positive effect on him. She said it impacted a lot of people who heard it."

I sit straighter, thinking of Cookie's progress after I played, and the peace I felt when I heard Iris playing in the video. "What kind of positive effect?"

"She says his vital signs improve for a little while, like he's calmer or something."

Ty's face flushes and he has to look away to compose

himself. Despite everything, my heart goes out to him. I don't know Kyle, but the thought of him lying in a bed, completely at the mercy of a bunch of machines to keep him alive, makes me want to cry, too.

Wyatt scrubs a hand over his face. "I don't get what all this has to do with you coming to Silver Lake."

Glancing at him, Ty says, "I'm getting to that." He shifts his focus back to me. "Iris's music—the more I heard it, the more it blew me away. Mom started talking about Iris all the time again. I think it helped take her mind off Kyle. This time I listened, and I started thinking about how Iris and Kyle both had terrible things happen to them when they were so young, and how, in a way, that connected them." Blinking, he continues, "I couldn't stand seeing my parents' grief. I wondered how your mom and dad had managed to go on after Iris died. Mom had told me how close she used to be to your parents, and I thought maybe it would help if they talked."

"So that's why you tracked Dad down and came here?" I say quietly, aching for him. "To ask my parents to talk to your folks?"

"That's part of it."

Wyatt huffs his disbelief. "You came all this way for that? The Winstons have a phone."

Casting a look in Wyatt's direction, Ty says, "I would've called, but when I mentioned the idea of talking to the Marshalls, Mom said that she didn't know where they were. That nobody did. They vanished off the face of the earth a few months after Iris died and nobody's heard a word from them since. So I started searching for information. Partly because I really did want them to talk to my parents, and partly because it was a way for me to escape what was happening to my family."

Digging my fingers into the couch cushion, I ask, "Why would they have disappeared?"

"Mom thinks it might've had something to do with your mother having a miscarriage about three months after Iris died. She thinks they might've wanted to start their lives over some place where they wouldn't have any reminders of your sister."

I shake my head. "Mom didn't miscarry. I was born less than a year after Iris died."

"Yeah, I know," says Ty. "I think they lied about the miscarriage."

"Why would they do that?" asks Wyatt, scowling. "And why would they change their last name?"

"I'm not sure yet."

"But you have an idea, right?" Wyatt says with a hint of sarcasm.

"I'm not sure," Ty says more firmly. He seems to brace himself for my reaction when he adds, "Your mother changed her first name, too. She used to go by Melanie, not Myla. Melanie Marshall. She taught art at the high school in Winterhaven."

I'm hit by a shock wave of disbelief. After seeing the video, after all the information I found online, I don't have any reason not to believe him, but it's so hard to accept what he's telling me. "How could they pretend that they're someone they aren't? My whole life—my identity—it's all a lie." I stand and turn away.

Wyatt pushes to his feet and wraps an arm around my shoulders. "There's got to be a good reason. This might sound stupid, but maybe they entered the witness-protection program or something. Maybe they did it to protect themselves."

I was joking when I said the same thing to Ty yesterday. But now I grab on to that possibility because it's the only one I can process. "That has to be it," I say, looking up at him.

The wooden chair Ty's sitting in creaks, drawing my attention to him. He shifts uncomfortably. "That's not it, Lily. I'm betting they were trying to protect someone by running away, but not necessarily themselves."

"Then, who? Me? What would they be protecting me from?" But the instant the question leaves my mouth, I recall Dad's comment to Mom about the truth being my only protection.

Ty breaks my gaze and looks down at the floor. I can tell he's still holding out. But why?

"What's with all the riddles, Collier?" Wyatt says. "If you know something, why don't you just spit it out?"

"Dad told his friend Mack that you threatened him at the coffee shop," I say.

"I think maybe your dad just *felt* threatened," Ty

explains. "Maybe he was afraid I'd expose his identity, or that I'd go back home and tell people where he was. I never said that, though."

"But if your mom and my parents were such good friends, wouldn't Dad believe he could depend on you?" I ask. "Why would he get so upset?"

Ty's jaw tightens, but he doesn't answer.

Wyatt utters a sound of disgust. "So much for telling Lily the truth. There's more to all of this, and I think you know what it is."

"Is he right, Ty?" I ask.

"I've told you all I know for certain," he says. "Your mom is the only one who can fill in the rest of the blanks."

I lift my hands, drop them. "But she's not talking! I've given up on getting any answers from her."

"Let's get out of here, Lil," says Wyatt. "I'm pretty sure you're not going to get more answers out of him, either."

Ty doesn't dispute Wyatt's comment, so I follow Wyatt to the door.

"There is one more thing, Lily," Ty says, following us. "You have an aunt in Winterhaven. Your dad's sister."

"Dad didn't have a sister," I say, confusion tearing me apart.

"I've met her," he says. "Her name is Gail Withers."

The name strikes inside me like a match. A memory flares, illuminating a freckled face, a riot of brown hair. The flame snuffs out, and the vision dies with it. Iris strokes an icy finger down my spine, freezing each vertebrae from my neck to my tailbone. *Aunt Gail,* she whispers. *I remember her. She's in the video . . . when I was a baby.*

At the door, I catch my breath and pause. "I want the articles," I say to Ty, motioning at the table.

He goes to gather the loose ones, slips them into a folder, then brings it to me. He gives me a pointed stare, quickly shifts his gaze to Wyatt, then back to me again. I finally get it—Ty has more to tell me, but he's holding back because Wyatt's here. Whatever he knows about Dad, he thinks I might not want Wyatt to hear it, which gives me a sick feeling that it must be something really bad.

Wyatt opens the door and we step across the threshold. He pauses and looks back at Ty. "I'm sorry about your brother," he says. "But Lily and her mom can't help you. It's time for you to go back to New York or Baltimore or wherever you came from."

Halfway home, Wyatt glances at me across the cab of the truck and asks, "What are you thinking, Lil?"

Neither of us has spoken a word since we left Ty's apartment, and I'm so caught up in my thoughts that I jump at the sound of his voice. I press my palms against the folder in my lap. "Everything he said . . . it's too much to take in. I don't even know where to start."

"I know your parents. If they uprooted their lives and lied to you, there's a good reason for it. I still think the most logical one is the witness-protection program. We should just ask your mom flat out."

"I guess, but the way she's been acting, I doubt she'd answer us." I nibble my lip. "What if I do have an aunt in Massachusetts? And maybe an uncle and grandparents and cousins?" My laugh sounds cold and sharp. "Wouldn't it be crazy if I've been alone my whole life when I have this huge family I could've been a part of?"

"You haven't been alone," says Wyatt softly. "I'm your family and you're mine."

"I know that," I say, my throat so tight with emotion I have to squeeze out the words.

I turn my attention to the windshield and the dusty ribbon of road unfurling ahead of us. As much as I want to believe that Wyatt is right about the witness-protection program, it doesn't make sense. Why would Mom be so terrified for me to find that out? And why would she feel a need to protect me from Ty?

The motor hums as we rumble along the bumpy road. "My parents lived a very different life before I was born," I say. "What Ty said about Mom teaching art in Winterhaven . . . it makes sense. She's been an artist my whole life. And those sketches we found in the workshop. All of the things Ty said fit, Wyatt. I'm really scared." I blink at him. "What does it all mean?"

"We'll get to the bottom of it." He turns off the county road and onto our lane. Glancing across at me he adds, "You and me together, okay?"

Minutes later, Wyatt swings his truck into our gravel driveway, turns off the headlights, and kills the engine.

"I'll go in with you, and we can look through those articles," he says.

"We don't have to tonight. It's really late and you have graduation practice tomorrow."

"You sure? I don't mind."

"I'm sure," I say, knowing that I'll do it on my own after he leaves. "Wyatt, thank you."

"Don't thank me. I'll always be here if you need me. That'll never change."

Shadows carve dark hollows beneath his cheekbones. In his expression, I see all the things that I've always loved about him, and more. I'm not sure I'm being fair to Wyatt since I still have feelings for Ty, but I don't back away as he leans closer and cups my face. He traces my lower lip with the pad of his thumb, and I stop breathing.

"I'm not good at this, Lily," he murmurs.

"You're wrong about that," I say in just above a whisper, smiling.

Wyatt slides his hand to the back of my head and brings our faces so close that our noses touch. "I'd never lie to you. I'd never try to hurt or confuse you."

But he *is* confusing me. As our mouths meet, and I taste his lips and our breaths mingle, I can't understand what's happening to me. How can this be Wyatt who is turning my body to liquid heat? How can I be kissing him back as if I'm starving for him? How can I feel what I'm feeling for

228

Wyatt when Ty still owns a giant piece of my heart?

Shaken, I pull away, my heart in my throat.

"Wow." Wyatt exhales. "Was that Iris or you?"

"Me." I feel myself blush.

"And you were kissing . . . ?"

"You."

He grins. "I hoped you'd say that." Reaching back, he opens his door.

Wyatt is out of the truck, around to my side, and opening the door before I can move. He takes my hand to help me climb down, and we walk into the cabin together.

I lay the folder on the coffee table, then peek into Mom's bedroom. She's still asleep, snoring softly. Closing her door, I return to the living room and whisper to Wyatt that everything is okay.

"I'll come by after practice tomorrow," he says. "We'll figure all of this out, Lil. I'll even try to talk to your mom, if you want."

Still dazed by our kiss, I nod, unable to speak.

"Well, see you later." His gaze roams my face. "Don't forget my graduation ceremony tomorrow night."

I stand at the front window and watch him drive away, stunned by what happened between us in the truck . . . and how he made me feel.

I don't go to bed after Wyatt leaves. Propped up against a pile of pillows on my bed with Cookie stretched out at my side, I stare down at the folder of articles Ty gave me, afraid to open it. My parents have betrayed my trust in so many ways. I'm not sure how many more of their lies I can handle.

Cookie sighs so deeply he moans. "I know what you mean," I murmur, stroking the velvet oval of his ear. My lips still tingle from Wyatt's kiss. I want to regret what happened, but I don't. Still, I'm torn. Shouldn't my new feelings for Wyatt erase all my feelings for Ty? Even though I kissed Wyatt and liked it, it's Ty I want to talk to now. Ty's voice I want in my ear, his dark eyes I want to look into. The same dark eyes that calmed me that morning on the peak when Dad was dying and I was out of my mind.

I want so much to believe that his feelings for me really kept him from leaving Silver Lake. I can't stand thinking that he had an ulterior motive for getting close to me. Could it be true that he only came here to persuade Mom and Dad to talk to his parents?

"Iris," I whisper aloud, and hold my breath.

She's here, of course. The white noise that I've become accustomed to, the constant snowy static in the background of my mind that's easy to ignore because it's always there. "Is this how you felt about Jake?" I ask.

There's a break in the hiss, a hiccup so brief that I might've missed it if I hadn't been desperate to hear. And in that tiny space of time, the sighed words: *Find him.*

I'll try. Hoping for a miracle, I ask, *Did Ty's story bring back any memories? Other than our aunt, I mean?*

A reporter . . . he said my music had an incredible soothing effect. I played for patients in hospitals . . . nursing homes.

Mom said you helped her, I say.

Her lupus. The music made her forget the pain for a while.

Encouraged by how much is coming back to her, I ask, *What else, Iris? Who is the man who scared you? What did he make you do?*

Can't remember. Jake will know. . . .

Dread presses down on me as I open the folder in my lap. At the top of the pile of clippings I find an article from a 1993 newspaper about an investigation of Dad's research. I stare at it for a full minute, hesitant to read what's there. Finally, I take a breath and start at the top.

Words swim before me . . . *independent stem cell studies . . . raised ethical questions . . . gene manipulation on a human subject . . . led to child's early death . . . cleared of misconduct . . .*

I sit back against the headboard, sick inside. I don't completely understand what I read, and I'm not sure that I want to. What kind of man *was* Dad back then?

Iris's answer brings relief, if not understanding: *The same man you knew.*

Desperate to believe her, I skim the article again, then with an unsteady hand, grab my phone off the nightstand and punch in Ty's number. He answers after the first ring. "I was just about to call you," he says.

"Don't leave in the morning. I read the first article. It was about one of Dad's projects." My voice falters as I add, "A little boy died, Ty."

He hesitates, then says, "We need to talk. I'll come out there. I didn't want to tell you about it in front of Wyatt."

"It's bad, isn't it."

"Don't worry." He exhales. "It wasn't your dad's fault. I'll tell you what happened."

"Okay, but I don't want to risk Mom hearing us. Meet me at the Daily Grind at six thirty. I want to leave the house before she wakes up. If I can't get away for some reason, I'll call you."

"I'll be there," Ty says.

We hang up. I need to find those keys.

16

I leave Mom a note saying that Paula called from the Daily Grind and asked me to fill in for a sick employee. It's something I do sometimes, since I worked there last summer, so I think she'll buy it. I spent all night looking for the keys, but didn't find them, so I walked to the main road and caught a ride on the six o'clock bus that shuttles county workers into town each day.

I arrive at the coffee shop before Ty and choose the table farthest from the counter. Other than Paula and her employee Rhonda, who are busy preparing for the morning rush, I'm the only person in the coffee shop. I order two hot chocolates and wait.

Minutes later, Ty arrives. I melt like the marshmallows in my mug when he steps inside the door and sees me and his mouth tilts up into a lopsided smile. There's a part of me that can't help being drawn to him, no matter what he has or hasn't done.

He hurries over to the table and sits across from me. "Hey."

"Hey." Motioning toward the mug in front of him, I say, "I took a chance and ordered you a hot chocolate."

"Thanks." He lowers his head to blow into his mug.

Now that we're alone, I'm self-conscious and off balance. I can't stand to think of him leaving today. Watching him, I say, "So . . . tell me about my dad."

Ty looks up. "Your dad was a genius," he says without hesitation. "He was also ethical, but he'd bend the rules if it was the only way to help someone. Some people might have a problem with that, but not me. That's why I was researching his work, and why I had to find him—for Kyle's sake."

"So you did have another reason for coming here."

He nods. "The stem cell research he was doing in the early nineties? What he did for that boy? It had to do with healing brain injuries like Kyle's."

I take a moment to let that sink in. "Surely that sort of research has continued since then, hasn't it? I mean, haven't other scientists or doctors made even more progress? Why didn't you go to one of them?"

"No one else has had the same level of success regenerating injured neurons in a human brain. They've transplanted brain cells from donors, but damaged brain tissue usually has poor blood supply, probably because of swelling and scar tissue. So the transplanted cells don't get the nutrients they need to grow."

I want to ask him to skip the science speak and get to the point, but I tell myself to be patient. I have a feeling he's giving me the key to understanding my father and the choices he made.

"A lot of different studies have offered possible solutions, and animal testing has produced some good results," Ty continues, "but the standard protocol is to wait a certain period—years, even—to make sure negative side effects don't show up in rats or monkeys or whatever animal they're testing before trying something on humans."

"But Dad didn't wait. That's what got him into trouble, isn't it?"

Ty nods.

I sink inside. "He experimented on that little boy before he knew it was safe."

Watching me closely, Ty says, "Yes. But I believe he was right to do that. I mean, think about it . . . in certain situations, waiting could be a mistake." He sits forward. "Some people don't have time to wait around for a sure thing. Some people have nothing to lose and maybe everything to gain by trying whatever experimental procedures are available, even if there's no proof there won't be negative side effects or that the good results will last."

"Some people like Kyle," I say quietly.

"Yeah," he says. "And that other little boy. Even though this was back in the early nineties, your dad achieved something scientists are just now coming close to repeating. The serum he developed was packed with chemicals and stem cells that stimulated blood flow at the site of the injury. It was infused into the damaged brain tissue, so after the donor cells were implanted, they were able to receive the nutrients they needed to replicate."

I shake my head in disbelief. "This is my *dad* you're talking about."

Suddenly animated, Ty says, "It worked, Lily. It worked on rats and rhesus monkeys—and their brains are very similar to ours."

Rats. Monkeys. Animals in cages. I think of Iris and the man who scared her. "God, this is unbelievable."

He smiles. "Your dad's stem cell serum had a zero percent failure rate with the animals. No deaths, no deficiencies. In the rats and the monkeys, anyway. Like I said, until recently, no one's come close to repeating that success."

Wariness creeps over me. Iris quivers. "But Dad didn't have the same results with that little boy."

Ty blows out a long breath. "Don't judge him. You should be proud of him."

"I am, but it's hard for me to understand why he'd take that risk."

"The kid's parents wanted to go through with it. They knew it was their son's only hope, and it worked at first. The cells regenerated quickly. He got better, but only for a few weeks. Then some off-the-wall anomaly cropped up and he had a stroke and died."

I wince. "God, that's terrible. To come that close, and then to lose him."

He leans in across the table, intense. "But because of your dad, that little boy and his parents had a few really good weeks together. He was awake and alert. He could respond to their voices and smile. They could hug him and know he'd felt it. Before that, they couldn't even be sure he knew they were in the same room. Your dad gave him and his parents a gift, as far as I'm concerned."

"Thank you for saying that," I say. "But some people obviously didn't agree. The article said the boy might've lived for months or years more if not for Dad's serum."

"Maybe, but he would've spent that time lying in a bed hooked up to a bunch of machines and being fed through a tube. Is being unconscious twenty-four/seven really living?"

I realize he's thinking about Kyle now. And I understand why he'd want to try anything to bring his brother back, even if only for a short time. But there are still things I don't understand. "Why didn't Dad's team continue his research after he left?" I ask.

"It was his personal project. He didn't have government funding like he did for the studies conducted at Cell Research Technology, so he financed it himself, using his own money and private sources. None of his team from Cell Research worked on it." Almost as an afterthought, Ty adds, "I met one of them. One of his team. His name's Ian Beckett."

I'm aware of a tiny flinch at the back of my brain.

"Beckett said that your dad talked to him about the serum and his progress with it, but when your dad walked away from his old life, he didn't leave behind even a trace of his research data. Not on any of the computers at the lab, at least. Beckett didn't know if he took it with him on a hard drive or a disc when he left, or if he got rid of it completely, or passed it on to some other colleague." Ty reaches for his mug.

It hits me then just how much Ty's gone through to try to help his brother, even tracking down other scientists from Dad's lab, and I'm filled with compassion and respect for him. I say, "Tell me about Beckett."

He sets the mug down again and scowls. "Something about the guy bugged me. He still works at Cell Research and he took me on a tour of the place. Everybody there seemed really uptight around him."

Thinking of what Iris told me, I ask, "What about the animals? How did they respond to him?"

"That's weird you ask." Ty cocks his head to one side. "I hadn't thought about it before, but the monkeys went crazy when he walked in. I've never heard so much shrieking." He shrugs. "I figured that's how they are around everyone."

Iris winds tight. *No, they're afraid of him! Ian Beckett is the man! I remember.*

The fine hairs at the nape of my neck stand on end. Trying to stay focused on Ty, I say, "Did Beckett have any problem with you asking questions about Dad?"

"He seemed okay with it. But he couldn't help me, so finding your dad was the only other option I could think of." Oblivious to my unease, he continues, "There's a new gel out now that's similar to his serum, and they think the problems he experienced are worked out. It's still in the testing phase, though. It won't be ready in time for Kyle."

"What did Dad tell you when you met him here?" I ask.

"He wouldn't say anything. He didn't want me around."

"Because you knew about his past . . . who he was." He nods, and I add, "I still don't understand why it was so important to keep his real identity a secret."

Ty studies my face, then shrugs. "I'm not really sure. He told me to stay away from his family and walked out. I wasn't about to let him get away that easily, though. I planned to keep after him until he gave in. I just wanted his help; I didn't have any intention of exposing him. But I won't lie to you." Holding my gaze, he sits back. "I would've used what I knew as leverage to get him to cooperate if I had to. For Kyle's sake."

His admission flips my feelings around and sucks away the compassion I felt for him only moments ago. I hate that my father spent his last days worrying that he'd been found. Crossing my arms, I say, "And then he died and ruined your plan." The words taste bitter on my tongue. "So you changed tactics and got close to me." I huff a sarcastic laugh. "Did you think I'd be so flattered you were paying attention to me that I'd do anything you asked, like maybe give you Dad's files?"

The muscle in Ty's jawline jumps. "I didn't have a plan. I was fighting for my brother's life. After I met you, I realized you didn't know anything about your parents' past.

But I still couldn't leave Silver Lake until I tried to get my hands on that research data. I thought I'd do a little poking around the cabin and your dad's shop, and if I found it . . ." His voice drifts off. "I don't know what I thought I'd do with it. I realized pretty quickly that it was a waste of time and a stupid idea, but I still couldn't go home and face my family because I felt like I'd failed them. And then I got to know you . . ." His tone softens. "After that I had another reason for staying in Silver Lake."

A finger of pale morning light strokes the windowpane. Paula is grinding beans across the way. The machine buzzes and the earthy aroma of roasted coffee permeates the room. The bell on the door jingles and a guy in bicycling clothes and a helmet walks in. Paula pauses and looks over her shoulder, calling out a greeting to him as he unzips his jacket.

I don't know what to say to Ty, or how to feel. In some ways, he deceived me as much as my parents did; he pretended we were getting to know each other when, really, he already knew more about my family than I did. But it's hard to stay mad at him, because I know he did it for Kyle. I'd go to almost any lengths to save Wyatt or my mother.

"Everything changed after I got to know you," Ty continues, sounding desperate for me to understand. "*I* changed. I couldn't leave because I started to care about you. I wanted to tell you everything, but I didn't know how to start. And then when I found you playing the violin and you showed me the stuff you'd found in your dad's shop . . ." He pauses

240

for a breath. "I mentioned the possibility of the clothes belonging to someone close to your mom, hoping you'd ask her and that she'd break down and tell you everything."

"I wish you would've trusted me enough to tell me all this sooner," I say quietly, ragged with bewilderment over all I've learned in the space of twenty-four hours.

"It didn't have anything to do with trust; I was afraid you wouldn't believe me. Besides, you were so broken up over your dad, and I couldn't cause you more pain."

His expression is so honest, I have to turn away for a moment. "So, what now?" I ask. "What are you going to do?"

"I don't want to leave you, but I have to be with my family for a while. I'm heading out tomorrow. My car battery died, and I have to get a new one today."

"I know you must be anxious to get home," I say. I can't imagine how it must feel to know that he and Kyle are running out of time.

Ty takes a drink of his hot chocolate, then shoves the mug aside. "So, what do you plan to do with all this information?"

I shake my head. "I'm not sure where to start. I guess I'll call my aunt in Winterhaven today and ask if she has Dad's research or knows where it is. Maybe if we find it you could still take it to someone—another scientist or a doctor who could use it to help Kyle."

"It's too late," he says, sounding defeated. "It always was. I was just looking for a miracle when I came here. It would take too long for anyone to do anything with your dad's research. Even he wouldn't have had enough time."

"I'm sorry."

"Yeah. Me, too." He exhales noisily, then almost as an afterthought says, "Did I tell you your aunt owns a bookstore in Winterhaven called Purple Prose?"

"My *aunt Gail*." A short laugh escapes me. "I have family. Do you know how strange that is?"

He smiles. "You also have an uncle Matthew, her husband. He's a retired English professor. They know about you. There were pictures of you and your dad on your aunt's desk. One was the photo you had printed in the paper with your dad's obituary."

It's after ten when I arrive home. Ty and I agreed to talk later and figure out a way to get together before Wyatt's graduation tonight—after I've had a chance to call Gail.

Mom is in the shower when I walk into the cabin. I let Cookie outside, then make coffee for her. Soon, she comes in wearing her robe, a green towel wrapped turban-style around her head. She's pale and her limp is worse. I'm hit with a punch of guilt for some of the things I said to her yesterday. I hope the stress of our arguments didn't bring on an even worse flare-up of her lupus.

"You're home early," she says, moving more slowly than I've ever seen her walk. She shuffles past me, headed for the coffee pot, leaning heavily on her cane. "How's Paula?"

"Fine. She said to tell you hello."

"Nice of her to call you to fill in."

"I don't mind the extra money," I say, a little worried at how easily the lie rolls off my tongue.

Mom pours herself a cup, then heads for the table. "Who brought you home?"

"Rhonda," I tell her. "She was working the early shift, too."

I gather my nerve to tell her what I know. If she balks and says none of it's true, I can show her the information I found on the website. She won't be able to deny it then, and she'll be forced to confess the rest—why she and Dad told their friends and family that she miscarried, why they took on new identities and ran away to start over.

But my guilty conscience bites at me again. Seeing what yesterday's argument might've done to her health, I decide to talk to my aunt before confronting my mother. Maybe she'll provide the answers so I won't have to ask Mom at all.

I take a box of cereal from the cabinet. "Wyatt graduates tonight," I say, pouring corn flakes into a bowl and hoping I can repair any damage from yesterday's fight. "You want to go with me? He said we can ride in with Addie."

"Of course I'll go." Mom blows her coffee to cool it. "I wouldn't want to miss seeing him walk across the stage. He's been such a good friend to you."

Joining her at the table, I dig in to my cereal while she sips from her cup. But I can't eat. "I didn't mean it yesterday when I said I hated you, Mom. I'm sorry."

"I know you didn't mean it. I'm sorry, too." She smiles.

"Let's just forget all of that and talk about something else, okay?"

Swallowing a knot of regret, I pick up my spoon again.

Mom surprises me by saying, "We need to start thinking about getting you ready for college soon."

I shrug. "There's not much to do since I'm just going to Silver Lake Community."

"Have you ever thought about going away to school?" she asks, then purses her lips.

Surprised she'd even mention the idea, I say, "Yes, all the time. But now that Dad's gone, I thought I should stay close to home."

"If you want to go away in the fall, I think you should. I remember you mentioned O.U. once."

My surprise turns to shock. "I applied." I pause, then say, "I got an acceptance letter."

She draws back. "Really? Why didn't you tell me?"

"I don't know. I thought you'd be against it."

Mom's quiet for a moment, then says, "After all that's happened, I think it might be good for you to get away."

Encouraged by her mind change, I say, "I'm sort of having second thoughts about O.U., though. That's where Wyatt's going, and Dad said it might be good for us to do our own thing." I don't mention that I'm also worried about what's been going on between us. Everything's happening too fast.

Mom sends me a small smile. "I don't think having a friend you already know at school is a bad thing, Lily. I like the idea of you and Wyatt being at the same place. We should make a trip to Oklahoma to visit the campus. It's important that you blend in with the other students like an ordinary girl."

She flinches, like she's trying to jerk the words back in the minute they're out of her mouth.

An ordinary girl? I push my cereal bowl back and meet her wary gaze. "What do you mean? Are you talking about how I communicate with Iris? How I can play the violin like she did? What's wrong with me, Mom?"

With a nervous laugh, she says, "Don't be silly. Nothing's wrong with you. Of course you aren't ordinary, you're *extraordinary*. What kind of mother would I be if I didn't think so?"

Knowing she's hedging again, I look past her to the window. Outside, Cookie's sitting in a ray of sunshine. He's still not up to chasing squirrels, but he's better. Happier. "Look, Mom," I say, pointing at him.

"Thank goodness the medicine's finally helping," she says.

"I think it's more than that. He heard me play the violin, and he changed. It's like his depression lifted."

Mom rubs the swollen knuckles of her right hand and blinks at me. "You don't really believe that, Lily. It's only music. And he's a *dog*." She offers me another smile, but it looks forced. "That's a sweet thing to imagine, but you know it's nonsense."

"It isn't nonsense. You said Iris helped you. How, Mom?

With her music? Did it help you the same way it helped Cookie?"

Her lip quivers. "Why are you forcing this?"

I lean toward her. "Because I love you, and I think I can help you, too. I mean, I know the music won't heal you or anything like that. But if it could just bring you some happiness again . . . some peace of mind." My throat closes, and I finish in a whisper, "Even if it's only for a little while."

"Oh, honey . . ." Mom reaches for my hand. "I'm sorry if I've made you worry about me so much." She presses her lips together and looks away. After a long silence, she says in a soft voice, "Your sister gave so much of her energy to others, so much of herself, and I would never ask you to do the same."

The legs of Mom's chair scrape against the floor as she stands up. She turns her back to me and peers out the window, hugging herself.

I watch her for a long time before I head to the workshop for the violin. Carrying it to the deck, I sit at the patio table. Sunshine warms my face as I lift the instrument and bow and begin to play. The music swirls up from some secret place deep inside of me where it's been hibernating all of my life. I let the melody flow through me into the instrument, then out onto the crisp spring air, willing it to find my mother, hoping it will numb the pain in her heart.

An hour later, I'm upstairs in my room when I hear the screen door slam. I start downstairs, pausing midway when

I see through the windows that my mother is setting up her easel on the deck.

I stand perfectly still and hold my breath, afraid one wrong move might shatter the vision before me. As I watch, Mom pulls paints and brushes from a box and starts humming the song I played earlier. The sound of it pulls the air from my lungs and clogs my throat with tears. I know she's been lying to me about sketching, but now . . .

I hurry down the stairs, out the front door, and around the corner. "Mom?"

She looks up, then lays down her paintbrush and steps around the easel. Lifting both hands, she holds them out. I see the stiffness in her fingers and realize how brave she is to attempt to paint in spite of the pain.

Mom's voice is emotional, a quiet rasp. "I'd given up on ever making art again, but I'm going to try, Lily. Thank you."

I cross the deck and wrap my arms around her, thrilled that maybe I've helped my mother, but knowing that soon I'll hurt her, too. Because when Ty leaves for Maryland, I'll be going with him. If I can use my gift to give him, his parents, or Kyle one minute of peace, it will be worth it.

Positioning my chair so I can see Mom out the window as she paints, I sit at the kitchen table with my laptop in front of me. The Purple Prose website comes up right away and a link leads me to a listing of the staff, along with their photographs. Déjà vu grips me at the sight of Gail Withers.

She's an older version of the quirky young woman in Mom's video, but I have a weird sense that I've met her before. Her laughter echoes through my mind, and it's familiar. *My aunt Gail's laughter.*

Did she laugh in the video? Is that how I know the sound? I don't think so. When her image came on screen, I had the volume turned down so Mom could sleep. I think I know the sound of my aunt's laughter because *Iris* knows it.

A knock brings my head up. Wyatt is standing on the other side of the screen door. How can it be possible that only hours ago I was kissing him and wondering if we were meant to be together? What's wrong with me? So much has happened so fast, I can't keep track of my feelings.

"Hey, I didn't hear you drive up," I say.

"I walked over."

I tell him to come in, and he opens the screen door and steps inside. As he walks toward me, I smile and say, "So after tonight you won't be a Silver Lake Saint—or is it 'once a Saint, always a Saint'?"

He raises a brow and in a mock-whisper says, "I've never been a saint. I just had everyone fooled."

I laugh. "You didn't have me fooled."

Wyatt scoots a chair around to face me and sits. Leaning forward with his forearms on his knees, he says, "I'd really like you to go with me to the senior party after the graduation ceremony. It's an all-nighter. Should be fun."

Thinking of my plan to leave with Ty, I say, "I don't know, Wyatt."

"There'll be music . . . bowling . . . blackjack. A lot of other stuff, too." He pushes a loose strand of hair behind my ear, and a thousand tiny arrows shoot through me, followed by more guilt. "Come on. It won't be as fun without you." Wyatt's twinkling green eyes tug hard at my conscience. "Please?"

"Maybe. I'll think about it. You know I feel out of place with the kids from your school."

He makes a face. "They like having you around. Besides, I'll be with you the whole time." As if that's that, case closed, he gestures toward the computer and changes the subject. "You working on something?"

Excitement shimmers along the surface of my skin. I'm not sure if it's mine or Iris's or a mix of both. I glance to the window, and when I see that Mom's still occupied by her painting, I say quietly to Wyatt, "Look at that woman at the top of the screen. Does she remind you of anyone?"

His brow creases as he studies the photo. "Not really. Why? Who is she?"

"Gail Withers. My aunt in Winterhaven. The one Ty told us he met. He said the name of her bookstore is Purple Prose. I searched for it and this came up."

Wyatt frowns. "I don't remember him saying anything about her owning a bookstore."

"He told me this morning when I talked to him." I draw

my lower lip between my teeth.

"You talked to him on the phone?"

Preparing myself for his reaction, I say, "No, at the coffee shop."

Wyatt's eyes narrow.

Quickly, I say, "I knew he was holding out last night because you were there. I guess he didn't realize that I'd tell you anyway. He said—"

"I don't care what he said, because it's crap." Wyatt scoots back. "I'm sorry, Lil, but it just doesn't seem like you're thinking this through." Gesturing at the picture of Gail, he says, "What proof do you have that she's your aunt? He could claim that any woman her age is."

"She looks just like Dad, Wyatt. Exactly. Don't you see it?"

He stares at her picture for a long time, then shakes his head. "I don't see a resemblance."

I cross my arms. "Could it be because you don't *want* to see it? Because you don't want Ty to be right."

"You're imagining that they look alike because a part of you wants her to be your aunt." A spark of impatience flares in Wyatt's eyes. "I came over to help you figure all of this out. You don't need Collier. I don't trust his motives and neither should you."

I understand then that no amount of proof will convince Wyatt that Ty doesn't have some evil agenda. Wyatt's being protective, and I love him for that. He cares for me, and I know that he'll hurt even worse than Mom when they find out I've left with Ty.

Flooded with guilt, I say, "I'm going to call Gail Withers, Wyatt. If there's even a small chance she's who Ty says she is . . ."

Wyatt's jaw twitches and the tips of his ears turn red. After several moments, he stands, pulling his phone from his pocket. "Here. Make the call," he says stiffly.

"No, it's okay. I can do it later." I don't want an audience the first time I talk to my aunt.

Wyatt puffs out his cheeks and returns the phone to his pocket. "I guess there's no chance you'll be going with me tonight."

Suddenly realizing that the party will provide me the perfect opportunity to slip away with Ty, I say, "I'm not mad at you, Wyatt. I don't want to talk about any of this at the party, though, okay? I just want to have fun together."

He glances up. "So, you're going?"

I nod, feeling like the worst person on earth.

17

After Wyatt leaves, I go upstairs and call the Purple Prose bookstore. A clerk informs me Gail's out on an errand. I tell her I'll call back.

After ending the call, I pull up the Milano Lawn & Garden site. Iris's excitement crackles around me and my palms start to sweat as I punch the listed number into my phone. How will Jake react when I tell him who I am?

On the second ring, a guy answers and tells me that Jake doesn't work there anymore. "Would you like to speak to Adrian?" he asks.

Making a guess, I say, "Adrian Milano?"

"Yeah. Jake's mother."

"Um, yes, thanks. That'd be great."

Waiting, I stare out the window at the peaks and think of how Iris once told me that we're like them—the dark east peak and the colorful west one, unable to exist alone, a part of each other. I'm not totally sure what she meant by that. I only know that I'm doing this as much for her as I am for myself.

"This is Adrian," says a woman's voice on the line, breaking into my thoughts.

"Um—Mrs. Milano?"

"Yes?"

"My name is Lily Winston. I'm looking for your son, Jake. I was hoping you could tell me how to get in touch with him?"

"Could I ask what this is about?"

"I'm related to a girl he knew in high school, and I want to talk to him about her. Could I get his number?"

"I knew all of Jake's old friends," she says in a friendly tone. "They were such a fun bunch. Who are you related to, Lily?"

Staring at the east peak, I say, "Iris Marshall was my sister."

Over the next few seconds, I hear the background noises of the store—voices, a jingling bell, music playing. Jake's mother remains silent.

"Mrs. Milano? Are you still there?"

"I'm here." She clears her throat. "Iris Marshall didn't have a sister."

"I was born after she died."

Another long pause, then, "How old are you, Lily? I don't mean to be rude, but—"

"No, that's okay. I just turned seventeen."

"Dear God," she whispers so softly I almost miss it. "But you said your name is Winston."

"My parents changed their names before I was born. I didn't know that until recently. I didn't know I had a sister, either. Not until Dad died and—"

"Adam is dead?"

A creaking noise downstairs makes me jump. The door opening? Lowering my voice, I say, "He was killed in an accident a couple weeks ago."

"Oh, no. I'm so sorry to hear that. I admired Adam very much. How's Melanie?"

It takes a couple seconds for me to realize she's asking about Mom. "It's been hard on her," I say.

"I'm sure. Give her my best, will you?"

"Yes," I lie. There's no way I'll mention this conversation to Mom. Not any time soon, at least. "I really need to talk to Jake, Mrs. Milano."

"If you'll give me your number, I'll pass it on to him."

I recite the information, then hang up and sit on the bed, her whisper stuck in my mind. *Dear God.* Jake's mother was surprised that I'm seventeen. Why? Because my parents lied about the miscarriage? Or something else?

We're getting closer, I tell Iris, then shift my thoughts back to Dad. This morning when Ty told me about the little boy Dad tried to help, I started wondering if he might've attempted a similar experiment on Iris. In addition to his work on healing brain injuries, could Dad have also been using stem cells to try to cure leukemia? Is

254

that even possible? It would explain Iris's insistence that someone did something to her that she found frightening. She freaked out when Ty mentioned Dad's team member at Cell Research Technology, Ian Beckett. Since Iris was Dad's daughter, might Beckett have carried out the actual procedure in his place? If only she could remember the details. . . .

I'm so rattled by my thoughts and from talking to Jake's mom that I can't bring myself to try calling my aunt again. I punch in Ty's number instead, and when he picks up, I say, "I really need to talk to you about something in person. Can you meet me now?"

"Sure."

"If you're up for a hike, I'll meet you at the rock wall at one o'clock."

"I'll be there," says Ty.

I lean against the rock wall at the edge of the trail. The earth smells spicy and damp, and for a second, I wish I could stay here forever, alone with Iris where I've always felt safe—at least I always did until the morning of my birthday.

Closing my eyes, I listen to the gurgling stream on the other side of the trail, my back to the wall, my palms pressed lightly against the rock. I imagine the power of a hundred souls radiating through the hard granite and into me, giving me strength. I feel like it's time for me to tell Ty about my relationship with Iris. He might be able to help me figure out what happened to her. And I don't want any more secrets between us. But what if he reacts the same way Wyatt did?

"Hey," says Ty, and I jump and open my eyes. "Sorry, I didn't mean to scare you." As he walks up the trail toward me, sunlight filters down through the trees, streaking golden highlights in his hair.

"Hey back." I smile as he stops in front of me.

He reaches out a hand, then hesitates and withdraws it, eyeing me with uncertainty. "Are we okay?"

Ty's hopeful, narrow-eyed appraisal shoots a current of electricity through my body from my head to my toes. "We're okay," I tell him.

He drapes his arms loosely around my waist. "Do you have more questions about your dad?"

"Only about a million, but I want to talk about my sister right now." I twist the hem of his shirt around my finger, gazing down at my hand. "Have you heard any of the legends about this area?"

"Only the one you told me about the wall."

"There are plenty of others. One claims that people who sleep in the shadow of the peaks never die." I lift my gaze to his. "Maybe my sister was one of them. Maybe my parents brought her here when she was sick, or something."

Cocking his head, Ty frowns. "What do you mean?"

"Promise me you'll try to have an open mind, okay?" He nods, and I draw a long breath and tell him everything. As I talk, I try to interpret each subtle change in his posture, but can't. Ty listens quietly, and when I finish, his expression is alive with amazement, but not even a glimmer of disbelief.

"That's just—" He laughs. "God, Lily! How did you stay quiet about her? Hearing her voice in your head . . . feeling her *inside* of you! I would've gone totally crazy keeping something like that to myself."

Stunned by his reaction, I say, "You don't think I am? Crazy, I mean?"

He shakes his head. "Not at all."

"I thought you'd at least question me. See if I have delusions of persecution and all the other symptoms that go along with being schizoid." I laugh.

Ty studies my face. "Nope. I don't see it in you. Sorry." His mouth curves into a crooked grin.

"No apology necessary." I laugh again, amazed that he believes me. "I had to stay quiet about Iris. To me, she's as normal as breathing, but I figured out early on that other people probably wouldn't think so—even my parents. So I kept my mouth shut."

"You didn't tell Wyatt?"

"I just did. He thinks I've either lost it, or I'm making the whole thing up to explain why I kissed him the other day."

"You kissed him?" Ty squints at me.

"Sort of." I wince.

He smirks and draws back. "How do you 'sort of' kiss someone?"

"I'm pretty sure Iris made me do it. It was like he was someone else. Her boyfriend, Jake."

"She didn't have anything to do with you kissing *me*, did she?"

"We kissed?" I tease.

"If you've already forgotten, maybe you need a reminder." He lifts one arm from my waist, hooks his index finger in the neckline of my shirt, and draws me closer. Then his mouth lowers to mine, and I *do* forget. I forget everything except how crazy I am about him. He tastes like cinnamon and coffee, and I don't ever want him to stop.

When he does, I touch my forehead to his and say, "Don't worry. Iris didn't have anything to do with that. Or any of the other times, either."

He laughs. "That's a relief."

"Not half as much as the fact that you believe me."

Ty tilts his head back and shrugs. "It's a simple law of physics that energy doesn't go away, it just changes form. It makes a weird kind of sense that your sister's energy would attach to you."

A breeze swoops through, rubbing the branches of the trees together and making them creak. "If that's true, why doesn't it happen to everybody?" I ask.

"I don't know. There're a lot of things that can't be explained."

I twist a strand of his hair around my finger. "I think I missed out on a lot, by not having Iris in my life. As a real person, I mean. Like you have Kyle."

Ty's face darkens. "Sometimes I wanted to throttle him. He could really bug me, you know? It's weird, but the things

258

Kyle did that used to piss me off the most are some of my best memories now."

"I'm sorry," I whisper. "I know your parents are going to be glad to have you back. They need you right now." I take a breath, ready to tell him that I want to go with him, but before I can, he drops his head and squeezes his eyes shut.

"Not my dad," he says. "I don't know if he's ever going to be able to even look at me again."

"What? Why wouldn't he?"

"Because—" I hear his breath catch. He opens his eyes and looks at me. "The accident was my fault. I was driving the car."

"Oh, Ty. No."

"I was home for Christmas break. Dad and I had a fight. I don't even remember what about; that's how unimportant it was. Kyle was at a friend's and I'd gone to pick him up. The roads were icy, and because I was pissed off at Dad, I was speeding. When the light at the intersection changed to red I slammed on the brake, but I was going too fast to stop on the ice, and I slid into the oncoming traffic."

I lean my forehead against his again. "I'm so sorry."

"The guy in the other car walked away with a few broken bones. I had a gash in my cheek. Kyle wasn't so lucky."

I think of the scar on his face that I barely notice anymore. "Let me try to help you," I say quietly.

"I don't deserve to be helped." He pulls away from me. "Dad has every right to feel like he does. And Mom—" He swallows. "Well, she's my mother. She's already lost one son; I guess she can't stand the thought of losing me, too."

"She hasn't lost Kyle. Not yet."

"Yeah, and it's all up to me now—how much longer he lives. They're waiting until I get there to turn off the machines. Do you know what that feels like? I've been telling myself that if I stay away long enough, there'll still be time for a miracle. The problem is, the only miracles I believe in are the kind people make for themselves." He snorts derisively. "So there you go. All I have to do is figure out how to make one."

Cautiously, I say, "I want to go with you to Baltimore."

Surprise flickers across Ty's features. "Your mom isn't about to let you get in a car with me, much less drive all the way to Baltimore."

"I won't tell her. Not until we're already gone."

"She'll kill you. After she kills me first, that is." He shakes his head slowly. "Your mom's been through a lot. Have you thought about how worried she'd be?"

"I know she'll worry, but Addie and Wyatt will watch out for her while I'm gone. And once I explain things to her, she'll realize I had to go." I take his hand, lace our fingers together. "I want to be there for you and your family, Ty. Your mom was right about Iris's music. It helps, somehow. I can play for Kyle. I want to. Please take me with you."

After a long hesitation, he says, "Are you sure?"

I nod.

"Okay, then." He exhales loudly. "When can you get away?"

260

"I'm going to Wyatt's senior party after his graduation tonight. I should have plenty of chances to slip away without him missing me for a while. Just be ready to go and I'll call you when the time is right."

"If Wyatt gets to me first, you can forget what I said about your mom killing me. He'll have already done it. You sure you won't regret this?"

I think of Wyatt . . . of Mom . . . how upset they'll be. But then I think of Kyle and Ty's parents. Of Ty and what lies ahead for him. Shaking my head, I say, "No regrets."

A big flock of fluttering crows has invaded Silver Lake High's gymnasium. At least that's how it looks from my position in the bleachers between Mom and Addie as we watch the students gathered below us in their black caps and gowns. Folding chairs cover the floor in short rows, like corn in a field, and ninety-three seniors dart between them, hugging and nudging one another, laughing and calling out names as they move from one huddled group to the next.

I look through the binoculars Addie brought and zero in on a girl with neon-pink hair—Sylvie, of course. While most of the other girls are wearing sandals or heels, clunky leather boots peek out from beneath the hem of her gown. She's standing with a tall guy who's as skinny as a green bean. He leans down and whispers something in her ear, then nods to a group of girls a few feet away. Sylvie clutches her stomach and bends forward at the waist laughing, like she's about to pee her pants. I lower the binoculars and smile, hoping she'll be at the party later. No way it could be boring with Sylvie there. And I might need her help to make my escape.

I'm queasy just thinking about what I'm going to do. Queasy and guilty. Wyatt's going to think I used him to sneak out of town. I hope that he and mom will forgive me once I explain Kyle's situation. But I have my doubts about Wyatt.

More familiar faces appear in the crowd below. Wyatt's dorky friend Clinton. Some guys from the hockey team. A girl named Natalie that Wyatt went out with last year. I see Wyatt, too, standing with a group of guys, laughing. He's the center of attention.

This side of Wyatt is unfamiliar to me—at school with his friends—part of a world where I don't belong. It makes me realize how small and confined my own world has been.

On a makeshift stage at the front of the building, the school band begins to warm up and the black flock quiets as they migrate to the back of the room and line up. A couple minutes later, the music pauses, and then the band starts playing, "We Are the Champions."

In the bleachers, we all stand and watch the students file in and take their seats.

The next half hour is filled with speeches about working hard and following dreams and facing the future with courage and hope. I can't help wondering what surprises my own future holds. I hope I'm brave enough to handle them.

Finally, the students' names are called out alphabetically, and one by one, Silver Lake High's graduating seniors cross the stage to receive their diplomas. It seems like forever before they reach the letter *P* and "Wyatt Reid Pierson."

I look through the binoculars again. The black tassel on Wyatt's cap swings back and forth as he climbs the stairs to the stage and walks toward the waiting principal. I smile so wide my cheeks hurt. Beside me, Addie sticks two fingers into her mouth and whistles loud enough to pop an eardrum. I hand her the binoculars so she can get a closer look while Mom and I clap and cheer.

Wyatt takes the diploma from the principal's outstretched hand, then descends the stairs on the opposite side of the stage. Making his way back to his seat, he scans the faces in the bleachers, and when he spots us, he grins ear to ear. In that instant, I'm so proud of him. And it hits me like a brick that I've been afraid of losing him—that's what this change between us has been all about. We're graduating and the future is such a big, scary unknown. I think we've both been afraid that we'll grow apart now that high school's behind us. Maybe we thought we had to change in order to keep moving on together. But I can't mislead Wyatt anymore, even if it hurts us both. I do love him, but only as a friend.

"You should be with them, darling," Mom says, interrupting my train of thought. She nods toward the graduates on the floor of the gym.

"It's okay, Mom."

"No, it's not. You missed out by not going to school here. I'm sorry about that, but your father and I did what we thought was best." She surprises me by reaching for my hand. "I don't think I've ever told you how proud of you we've always been."

The compliment is so unexpected, I don't know what to say. I can only look at her and try not to burst into tears.

Mom's smile falls away. "I know there's been tension between us lately, and that there's a lot about my decisions you don't understand." She glances toward Addie, and when she sees that her attention is firmly fixed on Wyatt, Mom says more quietly, "There's a lot I don't understand, either, Lily. For one thing, how you play the violin as beautifully as your sister did." She sighs. "Maybe it's time we both just accept what is and put the past behind us. More than anything, I want us to move on with our lives."

I get her message. She's telling me to stop asking questions. I love my mother, and I hate causing her so much distress. But I'm not moving on from the past until I find out the truth. For myself and for Iris.

After the ceremony ends, Addie and Mom say they're going to dinner in Silver Lake, then to a movie. I'm glad for two reasons: Mom hasn't had an outing like that in forever, and in case Ty's delayed for some reason, it will give him more time to drive to the cabin and get Iris's violin. I didn't know how to bring it with me tonight, so I left the cabin door unlocked for Ty to grab it. He can take the violin from my bedroom and be gone before she gets back from the movie, with no problem.

Wyatt finds us, and we all take turns hugging and congratulating him. After pictures are taken with Addie's camera, Mom and Addie leave in her Jeep, and Wyatt and I head for the community college activity center for the party. The center is sort of like a gym for students, with basketball and racquetball courts, a small bowling alley, a swimming pool, workout equipment, and empty rooms for exercise classes.

"You all right?" Wyatt asks, sliding me a look as we follow the flow of students toward the rows of doors across the front of the building.

"Sure, I'm great."

He's not fooled; Wyatt knows me too well. "Relax, Lil. This'll be fun," he assures me.

Ahead of us, somebody tugs open the door. We follow them into the mouth of the beast and are instantly surrounded by blaring music, loud voices, and shrill laughter. Tingly heat floods my body and I throb head to toe with the beat of the music that's playing. I stay close to Wyatt as we weave through the congestion of people.

"Dude! There's a line," some guy barks. "You gotta sign in."

"Sorry," Wyatt shouts.

We make our way to the back of the crowd and take our place. The line moves quickly, and soon we're standing before two women. One of them gestures toward a clipboard on the table, saying, "Put your name there, please. Anybody leaving the building has to check out first. If your parents call, we'll want to let them know whether you're here or not." She wags a finger at us and in a singsong voice adds, "Once you leave, there's no getting back in!"

Wyatt signs our names, while the second woman—a stocky, stern army-sergeant wannabe—shouts, "Over here, ladies and gentlemen! Let's take a look in your pockets and bags."

I open my bag, hoping Wyatt doesn't see the clothes I stuffed inside for the trip to Baltimore. Luckily, he's too busy turning his pockets inside out to pay attention.

When the lady sends us on our way, I ask, "Why can't we get back in if we leave?"

"They don't want people bringing alcohol back," Wyatt explains.

Kids roam everywhere, relaxed now that the pressure of the ceremony is behind them. A dozen different activities are already underway. A coed basketball game on one of the courts, a volleyball game on another, dodgeball on a third. Both bowling lanes are occupied, and every racquetball court is full.

We make our way to the "Vegas" room, where blackjack tables are set up, and a couple of games of craps are being played. Wyatt spots some friends from the hockey team and they wave us over. As Wyatt, P. J., and another guy named Troy start playing blackjack, I stand back and watch, mentally devising an escape plan for later tonight. I'm so antsy I feel like I could jump out of my skin.

Iris is restless, too. I'm not sure if it's the crowd or worry about Jake or our upcoming trip that has her on edge, but she's like a tickle in my ear that I can't scratch.

Wyatt laughs and teases the blackjack dealer—the father of one of his friends—about cheating. I try to listen and act as if I'm interested in what's going on, but it's no use. A sense of urgency thumps through my veins. I wander over to a corner, lean against the wall, out of the way, and check my phone.

"Expecting to hear from someone?" a hoarse voice asks, and I glance up to see Sylvie approaching. She grins and waggles her brows. "Bet I can guess who."

Just as I'm about to reply, my phone vibrates. "Hey, just a sec. I want to take this in private," I say. "You know any-place I could go?"

She nods toward the door. "There's a bathroom down the hall."

"Thanks, I'll find you later," I say, and slip from the room.

18

I hurry down the hallway, my fingers fumbling across the buttons on my phone until I find the right one. "Hello," I gasp.

"Hi. Is this Lily Winston?" The man's voice is deep. Uncertain.

"Yes." I duck into the small restroom, lock the door, and lean against it, out of breath.

"This is Jake Milano."

Without warning, Iris rises up in me in such a dizzying spin that I have to reach out and grab the edge of the sink to keep from swaying. "Jake! Mr. Milano. I've been waiting to hear from you."

"My mother told me that you're Iris Marshall's sister?"

"Yes. I am."

A movement over the sink catches my attention. I look up to see my own reflection in the mirror, but for an instant I think I'm seeing Iris's excited face staring back at me. *You*

268

did it, I tell her. *You led me to him.*

"Um . . . this is . . . ," Jake stammers. "I didn't realize—"

"My sister passed away before I was born," I break in, talking too fast. "But I only found out about her recently. For some reason, my parents never told me about Iris."

"How did you know about *me*?"

"I was going through some of Dad's things and I found a note that you'd written to Iris."

After a long pause, he says, "My mother told me you're seventeen."

"That's right."

"Wow," Jake says under his breath.

"I'm hoping you can answer some questions for me. My mother won't talk about my sister. She won't even admit that she and Dad ever lived in Massachusetts. I don't have any idea why they changed their names and moved here after Iris died, or why they didn't stay in touch with anyone in Winterhaven. Do you know?"

"I have an idea," he says slowly. "But if we're going to talk I need proof that you're really her sister."

A little defensive, I say, "But I am. Why would I make up something like that?"

"Don't take offense. It's just—" Jake breaks off, and when he speaks again, his voice is thick with sorrow. "Iris was my first love. I was only eighteen when she died, and I felt like I died, too. It took me a long time to move on. And now, all these years later, here you are, calling me. . . ."

"I understand," I say, moved by his emotional response.

"I need to see you. Where do you live, Lily?"

"Silver Lake, Colorado."

"I think I know where that is. I live in Nashville now. I can see about getting a plane ticket out there to meet you. Where's the nearest airport to Silver Lake? Colorado Springs?"

"You'd come here?" I clench the phone tighter. "We'd have to be careful. My mom is so sensitive about Iris, and I don't think she could handle seeing you."

"I wouldn't have to see her. We could meet somewhere in town. I can be there in a couple of days."

"Wait. That won't work. I forgot I'm leaving on a trip tonight with a friend." I bite my thumbnail, thinking. "What if we meet you halfway?"

"Tonight?" he says with surprise. "You're driving?"

"Yes. Do you know where the midpoint would be?"

"Oklahoma City, probably." He pauses for two beats, then says, "I guess I could do that."

"Great!" I blurt out, nervous and thrilled at once.

"I can throw some things together and leave in a couple of hours, I suppose."

"How long do you think it'll take you to get there?" I ask.

"If Silver Lake's where I think it is, you should make it in around eight hours. It'll be a bit longer for me, but close enough."

His easy agreement to drive that distance tonight makes me realize Jake is as anxious as I am to meet. I'm glad that

Ty will be with me. I can't imagine he won't agree to make the stop.

"I have your number in my phone," I say. "We could stay in touch along the way and decide on a meeting place once we're there."

"Okay, Lily. I'll see you soon."

I tell him good-bye, then before he can break the connection, say, "Jake? Thank you."

"You're welcome." With a half laugh, he adds, "This is nuts, you know. If I'd known I was going to be driving all night, I would've taken a nap after work."

I laugh, too. "Yeah, it's sort of unexpected."

"I have one other request."

"Sure. What is it?"

"Drive safely, Lily."

I smile. "You, too."

See you soon, whispers Iris. *I've waited so long.*

After breaking the connection, I hear a tap at the door.

"Hey, Lily. You in there?" Sylvie rasps. "The Goob sent me to look for you."

"Yeah, just a sec." I open the door a crack and peek out. "Anybody else out there?"

"Nope."

I let Sylvie in and lock up again. "I'm not ready to see Wyatt yet."

"Don't wait too long. He's wondering where you are." Sylvie looks at herself in the mirror, wrinkles her nose, bares her teeth, and rubs her finger across them. She points at her pink hair. "What do you think? Should I have gone with green? Or maybe kept it black and put a white stripe down the center?"

"Like a *skunk*?" I ask, glad she showed up when she did so I won't dwell too much on my nervousness.

"Yeah, like a skunk. Why not?"

"Wyatt told me once that *moufette* means 'skunk' in French. Knowing Wyatt, he'd start calling you that, and you don't look like a Moufette to me."

With a bad French accent Sylvie flutters her eyelashes and mutters, "Ooh-la-la, Moufette." She faces me and frowns. "Good point. I'll stick with pink."

"Will you tell Wyatt that I'll be out in a few minutes? Tell him I have a stomachache or something."

"Do I have a sign on my forehead that says 'personal messenger'? Sheesh." Turning, Sylvie reaches for the door-knob.

"Wait." I grab her wrist. "Come back after. I might need your help."

She arches her silver-studded eyebrow. "Now I'm intrigued. What have you been doing in here?" Holding up a hand, she adds, "If it's gross, I don't wanna know."

"I was on the phone."

"Mister Intense?" Sylvie purses her lips and makes a smooching sound.

I roll my eyes. "No, someone else."

"You're juggling *three* guys now?" She looks impressed.

Making a face at her, I say, "He used to be my sister's

boyfriend. He must be, like, thirty-six years old."

"You have a sister?"

"Will you just go?" I give her a little shove. "I'll explain later."

While she's gone, I call Ty and tell him about the conversation with Jake. He's willing to take me to Oklahoma City, and he's ready to go whenever I am—he already picked up the violin.

I tell Ty to be here in twenty minutes and to park on the street behind the activity center. Then I put my phone in my pocket. Sitting down on the toilet, I bury my face in my hands. "Mom . . . Wyatt . . . please don't hate me," I whisper.

A few minutes later, Sylvie returns after buying me some time with Wyatt. She turns on the air vent, then sits on the sink and smokes, apparently unafraid of getting caught. Giving me her full attention, she listens while I lean against the wall and explain that I need to sneak out and meet Ty, and that we're leaving town for a few days, at least. She asks a million questions, but I tell her I'll have to give her the full rundown after I return to Silver Lake. If I tell her now and think too much about what I'm about to do, I'm afraid I might back out, and I can't do that.

"But how will you get back?" Sylvie asks, tapping ashes into the sink.

"I haven't thought that far ahead. Ty might be able to bring me. If not, I have enough money for a bus ticket." The acrid scent of the smoke gets to me. Coughing, I wave a hand in front of my face.

"Are you sure he's safe?" She squints at me. "I'd be on a permanent guilt trip if he hacked you up and dumped the pieces into some lake."

"Have you been talking to Wyatt?" I ask with a laugh. "You can relax. I trust Ty one hundred percent."

Blowing a smoke ring toward the ceiling vent, Sylvie says, "Go have some fun, then. You haven't had enough of it. What do you need me to do?"

"If you want to help, you'll have to leave the party and stay gone for a while." I bite my lip.

"Not a problem. This party's lame, anyway. I've got better places to be."

I grin at Sylvie and look into her kohl-smudged eyes. "We've got to hang out more after I come home."

"Yeah, no shit. You've been missing out." She bats her lashes at me. "I'm gonna hold you to that full report about all this."

"I hope it's not that my friendship with Wyatt came to a screeching halt, but I'm afraid it will be."

"No way. He's crazy about you. Whatever this is about, he'll eventually come around. One thing I'll say about the Goob—he has a big heart."

"I know. And I don't want to break it."

She flicks her wrist and scowls. "Don't worry. He'll get over it. Believe me, there'll be plenty of girls lining up to kiss him where it hurts and make him feel all better."

In a mock-whisper she says, "Don't tell him I said so, but Wyatt's looking sorta hot lately."

"I've noticed."

Laughing at my guilty expression, Sylvie flushes her cigarette down the toilet, then says, "So what's the plan?"

A few minutes later we find Wyatt pacing by the snack bar. Sylvie hangs back while I cross to him. He looks relieved when he glances up and sees me, which only makes me feel worse for what I'm about to do.

"You okay now?" he asks, his voice full of concern and a little bit of suspicion—or maybe I'm only imagining that part.

"Not really. My stomach's sort of queasy." At least *this* is true. "I think I'd better go home."

His worried expression doesn't hide his disappointment. He gestures toward the front of the building. "Let's go. I'll take you."

"That's okay. Sylvie said she would. She's leaving anyway, and I don't want to ruin your night."

"I can come back after I drop you off," he says.

"No, they won't let you back in, remember?"

As if sensing I need her help, Sylvie walks up. "Hey, Goob," she says to Wyatt. "No need to interrupt your merry-making. I've had enough of this lovely event and I'm headed toward Lily's, anyway."

Wyatt scowls. "You live in town."

"Yeah," says Sylvie, "but I hear there's a kick-ass party out Lily's way at Black Bear Pond. You might not have heard about it. Only the cool kids were invited."

Ignoring her sarcasm, Wyatt turns back to me. "I'll walk you to the door."

Sylvie and I sign out at the front table while Wyatt tries to convince the Gestapo moms to let him walk us to the car, then return to the party, even though it's against the Rules. He promises to be back in five minutes, and they give in.

Leaving the activity center, Wyatt and I follow Sylvie across the parking lot to a black Lexus.

"Whoa, look at you," Wyatt says in a teasing voice, eyeing the shiny new vehicle. "So Sylvie has a traditional side. Who knew?"

She gives him the finger, then opens the driver's-side door. "It's my dad's. My shitmobile is in the shop." Before sliding behind the wheel, she blows Wyatt a kiss.

Laughing, he walks me around to the passenger door. "Call me when you're home, okay?"

"Sure." I hug him. When we step apart, Wyatt dips his head to kiss me, but the moment our lips touch, I pull back.

His face falls. "Is something wrong?"

Struggling to control my emotions, I say, "I just don't want to give you my stomach bug."

He smiles. "I'll see you tomorrow. After I get some sleep, I'll come by your house and we can look over all that stuff about your dad."

I can't say anything because my throat has closed up.

276

Instead, I force the best smile I can muster and climb into the car next to Sylvie.

As she pulls into the street to take me around to the back of the building where Ty is waiting, I glance over my shoulder and see Wyatt standing in the parking lot, watching us. He lifts one hand in a wave. I press my lips together and wave back.

19

As we cross the northwest corner of New Mexico, the highway unrolls ahead of Ty's car like a strip of black tape, and the moon shines down like polished silver. I tuck my feet beneath me in the passenger seat and lean against the door, staring ahead. Ty doesn't try to get me to talk, and I'm grateful for that.

I bolt upright when my phone vibrates, and look at the display. *Great.* Pushing "Talk," I say, "Hey, Mom."

"Lily, thank God. Where are you? Addie called Wyatt to check in, and he said you went home sick."

"I'm okay, Mom. Is Addie with you?"

"Yes. What's going on?"

"Where's Wyatt?" I ask.

With a note of impatience, she says, "He's at the party waiting for me to call him back. He's worried about you."

"Everything's okay." Taking a breath, I say, "I'm with Ty."

"What?" Her voice drops. "I told you to stay away from him."

"Mom, I'm fine. He told me why he came to Silver Lake. I know all about Dad's work, and that Ty's mom used to be Iris's music teacher."

"Come home now, Lily," she says quickly, panic punctuating each word.

I take a breath and steady myself for her anger. "I can't. Kyle—Ty's brother—he's in the hospital in Baltimore in a coma. He's not going to get better. I want to be there for Ty, Mom."

"You're not going to Baltimore!"

"Yes, I am! You know how it is to lose someone you love. Ty needs me right now."

I wait for her to yell at me, or say she understands, or *something*, but she remains silent.

"I'm sorry, Mom. I know I should've told you, but you would've tried to stop me. I'll call you in the morning, okay?"

"I'm furious with you right now, do you know that?" She sighs, and in a strained voice adds, "Call me the second you wake up. I mean it. And be careful, okay? I love you."

"I love you, too." I end the call and lean my head back against the seat.

"I take it that didn't go well," Ty says grimly. "You want to turn around?"

"No, keep going."

Minutes later, my phone chirps a second time, and guilt and worry drop down on me like a bomb.

"Your mom again?" Ty asks.

"No. It's Wyatt." I answer the call. "Hey."

"I wouldn't be talking to you if not for your mother," he says, his words striking like bullets. "Hasn't she been through enough?"

I slump down in the seat. How is it possible for me to feel so miserable and selfish, and still not regret my decision? "I'm sorry I left like I did," I say. "I didn't know what else to do. You and Mom would've tried to stop me, and I had to go, Wyatt. I had to."

"You're right—I would've tried to stop you. But you know what? That was then. I don't care what you do anymore."

Tension crackles in the silence that follows, and when I speak, my voice is shaking. "I'm going to tell you where else we're going, but you can't tell Mom or it'll only upset her worse. Someone needs to know where we are, just in case something happens. Will you keep it to yourself?"

"I said I don't care what you're doing."

I watch the road markers skip past outside my window and try not to cry. "Ty's taking me to see Iris's boyfriend, Jake Milano. I found him, Wyatt. We talked on the phone. We're meeting him in Oklahoma City before we go to Maryland. That's where we're headed now."

"Why?"

"Because Mom won't answer my questions."

He huffs a bitter laugh. "And you think some guy you've talked to once on the phone can?"

"I have to find out," I answer, hating my pathetic, pleading tone.

"Don't you think that's dangerous?"

"I'm not alone. Ty's with me."

"So you said," mutters Wyatt, oozing sarcasm in my ear.

"I don't blame you for being mad, but for Mom's sake, please don't tell her I'm going to meet Jake. She would totally freak out."

The lights of some small town twinkle in the distance. The car engine hums. Wyatt says, "I'll cover for you on one condition."

"Name it," I say, then hold my breath.

"Hand the phone to Collier."

Apprehension sinks like a stone to the pit of my stomach as I extend the phone toward Ty. "He wants to talk to you."

Ty takes the phone. "Hey, Wyatt."

I nibble my cuticle, watching him.

"I'm listening," Ty says, then, "Loud and clear." He hands the phone back to me.

Pressing it to my ear, I say, "Wyatt?" but he's already gone. I frown at Ty. "What did he say?"

"It's between Wyatt and me," he answers, his focus narrowed on the road.

"That's not fair."

Ty's mouth twitches. "Let's just say that if anything happens to you, my anatomy's going to suffer a radical transformation."

Sometime later, we stop at a gas station at the side of the highway. A fast-food restaurant is attached, so I buy burgers, a couple of soft drinks, and snacks while Ty fills the tank. We eat on the move, and when we finish, the road lulls me to sleep.

I wake to the sound of Ty talking into his phone. Rubbing my eyes, I sit up and stretch. The Incubus song "Black Heart Inertia" flows from his iPod and through the car speakers.

"We should be there the day after tomorrow at the latest," says Ty into his phone. "Probably early, but if something slows us up, I'll let you know." A pause, then, "No, Mom. I don't want to talk to him. Just tell him . . . tell him we'll talk after I'm home, okay?" Another pause. "I love you, too." He puts the phone away.

"How are your parents?" I ask.

"Hanging in there." He stares ahead. "Mom said to tell you hello."

I nod, unable to imagine what she must be going through. "How's Kyle?"

"The same."

"Do you think we should go straight there? I can postpone the meeting with Jake."

"No, it's okay. This is only going to sidetrack us a few hours. Kyle will hold on for a long time if he's hooked up."

Hearing the guilt and remorse in his voice, I remove my seat belt, lean across the console, and kiss his cheek.

"Put your seat belt back on," Ty snaps. "I'm scared shit-less as it is driving you anywhere after what I did to Kyle."

I sit back and buckle up again. "It was an accident, Ty."

His jaw clenches.

"You're human. You made a mistake. You didn't mean for anyone to get hurt, least of all your brother. He wouldn't want you to blame yourself."

"There's no one else to blame. Just ask my dad."

"Has he said he holds you responsible, or are you just assuming he does?"

"He doesn't have to say it, I see it in his face." Ty swallows, and his fingers clench the steering wheel. "After it happened, he couldn't even look at me, much less talk to me."

Softly, I say, "But he wants to talk to you now, doesn't he? Isn't that what your mother was trying to get you to do just now?"

When he doesn't answer, I decide to give the subject—and him—a rest. I watch a cloud pass over the moon. We're in the middle of nowhere, and I can't see much of anything to clue me in to our location.

"Where are we?" I ask.

"In the Oklahoma Panhandle. We just left Guymon."

I stifle a yawn. "Are we getting close? I can drive if you're sleepy."

"I'm okay. We're not even halfway."

"I can't wait to get there," I say, twisting sideways in the seat to face Ty. "We're going to see Iris's boyfriend! Don't you think that's amazing? She led me to him. She made this happen."

He reaches over and tugs my hair. "It's more than amazing. But Iris had some help from you."

"Only a little." Watching the scenery roll by, I gesture out the window. "This is the farthest I've ever been from home."

"Not very scenic so far, huh?"

"It's pretty bleak. What's it like in Winterhaven? You've been there, right?"

"Yeah, I went to your aunt's bookstore, remember?"

"Yes, but you never said why. How did you even know my dad had a sister?"

"One of the scientists who worked on your dad's team at Cell Research Technology told me. That eccentric old guy, Dr. Beckett."

Iris rouses with a start, instantly on full alert. Her reaction makes me wonder again if Dad and Beckett might've used some untested method to try to save her, like Dad did with that little boy. I've read the articles about Dad's work at least a half-dozen times, and each time, I became more sure that could be a possibility. Only, I'm not so certain they were trying to find a cure for leukemia. I'm afraid they had another way of saving her in mind. If I'm right . . .

I swallow hard. "Yeah, you mentioned Dr. Beckett," I say to Ty. "So what do you mean by eccentric? Is he crazy, or what?"

He lifts a shoulder. "I don't know. There was just

something weird about the way he looked at me that made my skin crawl."

"Iris keeps telling me he did something bad to her, but she can't remember what it was. She was afraid of him."

Ty's forehead creases. He turns to me, searching my face.

He's wondering the same thing I am, I think, and dread tightens my chest. "I hope Jake can tell us what he did," I say quietly. I'm not ready to voice my dark suspicions that Dad might've also been involved.

Ty looks back at the road, blinking. I get the feeling he wants to say something, but isn't sure he should.

"So what did Beckett tell you about my aunt?" I ask.

"Apparently, he called her a couple times right after your folks disappeared. All she'd say was that Adam had left a message that he didn't want her to try to find him, and that he and your mom were fine but wanted their privacy."

"If she wouldn't say more than that to Beckett, what made you think she'd confide in you?"

"I didn't know if she would or not, but I had to try. I showed up at the bookstore, and by a stroke of luck, there was a Help Wanted sign in the window, so I applied. The clerk put me in your aunt's office to fill out an application. That's when I saw the photo of you and your dad standing next to his van with the two peaks in the background. It was on her desk."

I recall how upset Mom became when I put that same

photograph in the paper with Dad's obituary. Her reaction finally makes sense.

"How did you know it was Dad?" I ask, baffled by how he was able to put it all together and find us.

"I recognized Iris."

"Iris." I blink at him. "You thought I was her."

"At first. But something seemed off. The picture didn't look old enough. I mean the clothes you were wearing . . . your hair . . . and then I gave your dad a closer look." Ty glances at me. "My gut told me it was him, but it was you I couldn't figure out."

"Did you ask Gail about me?"

"I didn't get a chance. After she came in and interviewed me, I reached for the picture and asked if the man was her brother."

"And she said yes?"

"Are you kidding?" he says. "She jerked it from my hand and told me to get out. But I'd already gotten a good look at it." Pausing, Ty adds, "Remember I told you it was Kyle's goal to climb all the fourteeners? I recognized the two peaks as some we'd seen in books. They're pretty distinctive."

Amazed, I say, "You tracked Dad to Silver Lake just by seeing the peaks?"

"Well, it was his van that cinched it. In the picture you can see his logo on the door. I did a search on the internet for Winston Carpentry in Colorado and his website came up with the same logo and your address. When I saw the name Adam, I knew I was right." Ty's brows lift.

"I took a chance and came."

I shake my head and give a short laugh. "Wow. That was some good detective work."

"I hoped it would pay off for Kyle," he says quietly.

I feel Ty's sadness like it's my own. "I wish Dad could've helped you," I say.

We grow quiet. The music on Ty's iPod surrounds us. The dashboard lights emit a muted glow that illuminates the angles of his profile. Ty grips the steering wheel, still tense.

I think of Ian Beckett again, and fight down a surge of fear. "I know you have your own theory about why Mom and Dad left Massachusetts. Why won't you tell me?" I ask.

"Let's talk to Jake before we jump to any conclusions," Ty says.

"It would take something pretty dramatic to make my parents change their names and break contact with everyone they cared about."

My mind races with all I've found out in the past few days. I know Ty's right and I shouldn't jump to conclusions, but I keep circling back to the same shocking possibility—an untested procedure . . . and what that procedure might've been.

"I've been thinking about Dad's work with the animals at the lab," I say slowly, apprehension fluttering in my chest. "He and his team were trying to replicate endangered species, right? In order to save them."

Ty glances at me. "Yeah, in a nutshell."

"When you think about it, Iris was sort of like that after she got leukemia. Endangered, I mean." I hold very still, letting the implication sink into him.

It doesn't take long. Ty's head jerks toward me. "Don't go there, Lily," he says sharply.

"Why not? You've been wondering the same thing, haven't you? Maybe it's time we got it all out in the open. If I'm right, do you know what that means?" I press my palm against my stomach and cringe. "Oh my god, I think I'm going to be sick."

"Stop, okay?" Ty sits straighter. "What good is it going to do you to get upset over something that's probably not even true? Like I said, let's hear what Jake has to say."

I give a quick nod, then crack the window to let in some fresh air, hoping it will clear the outrageous thoughts from my mind. Ahead of us, a truck's red taillights stare back at me. Iris is so withdrawn that I don't even sense her presence. I wonder if she's worried about seeing Jake, or lost in memories of him.

Returning my thoughts to Mom and Dad, I tell myself that they were just grieving. That's the only reason they wanted to leave the past behind. It held too many memories of Iris. But then, the article that Dad wrote about his work scrolls again through my mind. . . .

Experimenting with specialized DNA technology . . . trying to produce multiple exact genetic duplicates of endangered species of animals . . .

And suddenly I hear Mom's voice saying, *"It's important that you blend in with the other students like an ordinary girl."*

A trembling sensation starts deep in my core as my uncertainties about Iris's intentions join all the other fears in my ever-growing collection. All my life, Iris has told me that she can't leave because she's waiting for someone, and I'm sure now that the person is Jake. She said she had to watch over me, and I think I might have figured out why. I'll find out soon enough if I'm right. We're getting closer to the truth—and Jake—with each passing mile.

Iris . . . ? I wait, but she remains silent. In a way, I'm relieved. I'm too afraid to ask her what's on my mind.

"Hey," Ty says. "Are you okay?"

I shake my head. "When I was a little girl I thought Iris was my shadow," I say in just above a whisper. "I could hear her, so I should be able to see her, too, right? Sometimes when I'd see my shadow, I was afraid she might break away and run in the opposite direction." I smile at my younger self, but I still understand that fear. "And then when I got older," I continue, "I never thought of her as a ghost or a spirit in limbo or anything like that. She's always seemed more like an extension of me." I take a breath and face him. "But maybe I'm an extension of *her.*"

Ty sends me an uneasy glance. "Quit torturing yourself, okay?"

I want to stop, but I can't. I wish he'd pull over and wrap his arms around me and make this all go away. But that's not possible. "What if after we find Jake and learn the truth, Iris doesn't need to stay here anymore?" I say, asking him what I can't bring myself to ask her.

Ty blinks at me. "I don't understand what you're so afraid of."

"What if that's what's kept her here all along? Her need to see Jake one last time, and her need to remember the truth, so I could know it and protect myself."

"You think after she does those things she'll disappear and you won't sense her again?"

I press my lips together and look away. "Maybe she'll think I don't need her anymore."

"That's not going to happen. Everything's going to be okay." Ty's voice is warm and caring, but less than convincing.

"How do you know?" I ask.

"I just do."

Suddenly, I think of Kyle and shame slams into me. "God, Ty, I'm sorry," I say, facing him. "Here I am worrying about losing Iris when your brother—"

"No, it's fine. I'm okay. But are you sure you're ready to meet Jake? If you can't handle it, I'll call him and tell him it's off for now. We can talk this out first, just you and me, then see him tomorrow. Or we can go straight to Baltimore and forget all of it."

I draw a deep breath. Either I want the truth or I don't. It takes only seconds to decide. "Keep going," I say.

20

The sun is pushing up from the earth like a bloodred bulb when Ty shakes me awake. My head is resting against the door, and the chest strap on the seat belt rubs against my cheek.

Yawning, I sit up. "You want me to drive for a while?"

"No, we're here."

"In Oklahoma City?"

"Yeah."

I look outside. The traffic is almost bumper to bumper, and industrial-type businesses line both sides of the interstate highway. I've never seen so many eighteen-wheelers in one place.

"You're getting a call," says Ty, pointing to my quietly buzzing phone on the console.

I pick up without looking at the display.

"Hi, Lily. I'm pulling into Oklahoma City," Jake says. "I broke a few speed limits and made good time."

"We're here, too," I tell him.

"There's a Denny's ahead of me at exit eighty-five. Should I wait for you there?"

"Denny's at exit eighty-five." I glance at Ty, and he nods. "That's fine."

"I'll go on in and get us a booth," says Jake.

"How will I recognize you?"

"If you're Iris's sister, I'll recognize *you*."

His statement sends a shiver through me.

I tell Jake good-bye and end the call, so nervous I'm queasy. Without a word to Ty, I reach for my bag on the floor and dig through it until I find a brush. I pull the sun visor down and look at myself in the mirror, working the brush through the tangles in my hair.

Thank you. Iris's whisper sweeps through me like a puff of warm wind.

My hand stills. *We made this happen together*, I tell her. *I'm so happy you're finally going to see Jake again and we're going to get to the truth.*

I wait for her to reassure me that I'll be able to handle whatever it is. But there's only a frail, soft hiss in my head—the constant white noise that's Iris—tremulous now. Excited, but also fretful.

I break away from my reflection in the mirror, unable to meet my own terrified gaze as my fingers fumble to weave my hair into a braid. What will Jake think of me? Who will he see? What will he tell me?

292

"This is it," Ty says quietly.

I look out at the road, see the exit, and beyond it, the Denny's sign.

"It'll be okay," he says, noting my expression. "I'll be with you every second."

Only three cars are parked outside the restaurant. A dilapidated gray van. A shiny red Toyota Prius. A white Chevy Tahoe. The Prius has a Tennessee license plate. As Ty pulls into the parking space next to it, I secure my braid with a band, then reach into the backseat for Iris's violin case, thinking Jake might want more proof that I'm who I say I am.

Ty cuts the engine and faces me. "Ready?"

I nod, my heart pounding so hard I can't speak. We climb out.

I have a memory of my mother on her knees beside the tub, shampooing my hair when I was around four years old. I remember a yellow rubber duck and frothy white bubbles on the water's surface. I can still smell the lavender scent of the room and hear Mom singing.

I tilted my head back and squeezed my eyes shut while she poured clean water through my hair. When she finished, I looked up at her and said, "Mommy, when are we going to see that boy?"

"What boy?"

Scooping a mound of bubbles into my palm, I blew them

toward the faucet. "That big boy with the pretty blue eyes. I miss him."

Mom slipped her hands beneath my armpits and lifted me to my feet beside the tub. "Do you mean Sean? The man who helped Daddy in his shop last summer?"

"Nuh-uh." I shivered as she wrapped a fluffy white towel around me. "You know who. He gave me a music box. And flowers sometimes. White ones with yellow in the middle. They made me sneeze."

Mom fell silent. She rubbed the towel against me so hard and fast it stung, saying firmly, "We don't know any boy like that, Lily. You must've dreamed him."

I didn't ask again about the boy with blue eyes.

I grew older and forgot about that night in the tub, my questions about the boy, and the white flowers with yellow centers. But as Ty opens the door to the restaurant, the memory rushes back in such vivid detail that I feel the sting of the towel on my back.

I'm clutching the handle of the violin case as we walk into the warm, bright diner. I skim my attention over an elderly couple at the first table, a young man in his twenties wearing a baseball cap at the counter, and a man with short dark hair and glasses studying a menu at a table in back.

"Good morning! Be with you in a sec," a waitress calls out to us as I search almost frantically for someone else—someone familiar.

And then I jolt and I'm drawn again to the man at the back table. He looks up at us. At me. I hear his gasp from

294

across the room. He stands so abruptly that he knocks against the table, sending a fork and spoon sailing to the floor with a clatter. The man reaches for something in the chair beside him. A bouquet of daisies.

"Is that him?" Ty whispers.

I can't answer him. Iris has risen up inside of me, and her heart beats in time with mine. She leads me to Jake . . . one step . . . two . . . until we're standing so close I could touch him. He's wearing glasses, but his eyes are that piercing shade of blue I could never forget.

"Oh my god," he whispers, and Iris gasps, *Jake! Oh . . . look at you.*

I have the strongest urge to kiss him—to lift up onto my toes and press my mouth to his. Something tells me it would feel like coming home. But I understand that the desire belongs to Iris, not me, and I don't want to scare Jake away. Not when she's finally found him again.

I set the violin at my feet, and lift my hand toward the daisies. "You remembered," I say, but I'm speaking for Iris, not myself. Because she can't.

"Iris loved daisies." His voice is deep and wavering, so soft I barely hear him. "I thought you might, too."

I take the bouquet and we stare at each other, speechless.

Ty walks up beside me and clears his throat. "Hello, Mr. Milano. I'm Ty Collier."

Jake shakes Ty's hand, saying, "Call me Jake."

Motioning toward the table, Ty says, "I need coffee."

"Oh—sure." Jake waves the waitress over, then pulls out a chair for me. I sit, placing Iris's violin in my lap and the flowers on the table, off to the side.

Ty takes the chair next to me. Jake sits across from us. The waitress brings coffee and menus, then leaves again. I have a thousand questions, but I don't know where to start. Jake also seems tongue-tied. He watches me with his mouth slightly open.

I understand his shock. It's difficult for me not to gape at him, too. I don't know what I expected—that he'd still look like the face in my dreams? I knew he must be in his midthirties, but it didn't occur to me how much he would change in eighteen years.

"I'm sorry," Jake finally says, shaking his head and smiling. "I know I'm staring. It's just—it's uncanny how identical you are."

I smile, too. "I've seen a video of Iris. We do look alike."

"Exactly alike." He examines my face.

The waitress comes back. I order toast and juice. Jake says he's fine with coffee. Ty gets the works; clearly his stomach isn't tied in knots like mine.

When the waitress leaves, I say to Jake, "I thought you might want to see something of Iris's. For proof that I really am her sister." Sliding the violin case from my lap, I extend it across the table, using both hands.

Jake's eyes never leave my face. "I don't need to see her violin. I know who you are."

I place the case on the floor beside my chair. I don't

know what to say. Where to start.

Ty saves me from having to decide. "Lily and I have a lot of questions," he says.

Jake blinks and clears his throat. "How much do you know?"

"I know that my parents lived in Winterhaven before I was born," I say, "and that their last name was Marshall. I know Mom taught art at the high school and Dad was a research biologist. Mom told me that Iris died of leukemia when she was seventeen. Is that true?"

"Yes." He closes his eyes. "My god, they did it. They got her back."

My body turns to ice, and I start shaking; but I tell myself that I'm prepared to hear the truth, that I already know it.

Ty looks at me for one long moment. I nod, pressing my lips together. Beneath the table, I grab his hand and hold on tight.

He faces Jake, and in a quiet voice says, "We know about Adam's work with animal cloning. Are you saying that Iris was Lily's . . ." He swallows. "Is she her original?"

"Yes," Jake whispers.

My stomach lurches, and my chair legs scrape the floor with a shriek as I push to my feet. I thought I was ready to hear the truth, but maybe I was wrong. It didn't seem real, or even possible, until I heard it spoken. "I'm her *clone*? Dad did that to me?"

"Lily," Ty says, reaching for me.

I jerk my arm from his grasp and push past the table, then bolt toward the ladies' restroom at the back of the restaurant, praying it's empty. Just in time, I push through the door and drop to my knees in front of the toilet, retching.

I'm at the sink washing my face when I hear the door squeak open behind me. "Are you okay?" Ty asks in a worried voice.

I turn off the water, keeping my back to him and my head lowered. I can't bear to see his face and read what he thinks of me. "No, I'm not okay. I'm a freak!"

"Don't say that." His hand grips my shoulder, and for several long moments, my erratic breathing is the only sound I hear. "I want you to know that when I came to Silver Lake, I knew about your dad's work," Ty finally says. "But I didn't know about this."

I face him. "But you suspected, didn't you? You saw me in that photograph on Gail Withers's desk . . ."

"Lily . . . you've suspected it, too. You know you have."

"Suspecting is one thing. Hearing it confirmed is another." I lean back against the sink, not trusting my legs to support me. "I'm just a carbon copy of my sister. An experiment." My voice breaks.

Ty is silent for a long time. Then he nods toward the door. "Let's go get some air, and then we'll talk to Jake. That's why we came here, isn't it? To get answers?"

I don't know why I'm striking out at Ty. None of this is his fault. Avoiding his scrutiny, I pull a paper towel from the dispenser on the wall, wipe it across my face, and toss it into the trash bin. Then I follow him outside to the parking lot. He's right. I'm tired of trying to piece together the fragments of Iris's life, and mine. I wanted the truth, and now that I have it I can't pretend it isn't so.

I'm my sister's clone. That's the reason we have a psychic connection, and why I glimpse her memories. She's not a ghost, she's a part of me—no, I'm a part of *her*. I never would've existed without Iris.

"You want to talk or just walk?" Ty asks as we step outside, a breeze ruffling his hair.

"Walk," I croak.

As we start around the perimeter of the parking lot, I breathe in the warm, humid air. It bathes over me, washing away my denial. The roar of city traffic on the highway sounds as peculiar to me as my life has become. But no matter how strange or frightening it is, I can't hide from it.

It takes three laps before I'm finally cried out. "I'm ready," I tell Ty. "Let's go back in before he decides to leave."

Ty ducks his head to capture my attention. "You sure?"

"Yeah." I push his hair back, let my fingertips linger. I'm so glad I have him to lean on. "Thank you," I say.

"Anytime." He smiles and takes my hand.

We go back inside the restaurant and I slump into the chair across the table from Jake, shaking from head to toe. He looks ragged as he scrubs a hand across his face and drags it back through his hair.

"How could Dad do that to me? To *her*?" I ask him, my

voice breaking again. "He used his own daughter! He made me a freak."

Ty's arms wrap around me. He holds on tight, but not tight enough to still Iris. I sense her energy inside me more strongly than I ever have before. She's the fluttering in my breastbone, the sinking sensation in my stomach, the press of dread surrounding my heart.

Crying again—for her, for myself—I sink into Ty, but it's Iris I cling to. She's the only one who really understands how I feel. The song from the music box flows through my veins as she hums it, trying to comfort me.

Our food arrived while Ty and I were gone. Jake pushes his coffee aside, his face flushing red. "I'm sorry," he says. "I don't know what to say."

I sit up and sniff, staring down at my plate of toast. "Have you always known about me?"

"No," Jake says. "I knew they tried, but I didn't think it worked." Looking from me to Ty, he adds, "You said you suspected . . . how?"

Ty explains the events that led him to me as I sit numb and speechless beside him.

"Adam and Melanie must have been afraid that Ian Beckett wouldn't keep their secret about the cloning," Jake says. "He was in on the whole thing. It was his idea to begin with. But he was an egomaniac with an agenda. If he knew the cloning was a success, he would've leaked it to the media. I'm sure the Marshalls didn't want you to become some kind of sideshow phenomenon." I flinch, and Jake sits forward, wincing. "Lily, I'm sorry. That was insensitive."

"But that's what I am, isn't it? And what's worse, the experiment wasn't a success, it was a disappointment. *I* was a disappointment."

"That's not true," Ty says gently.

"I think I was to Mom. She'd get so unhappy. And the way she looked at me sometimes." I grab a paper napkin from the dispenser, wipe my eyes, then clutch it in my hand. "She probably wanted a perfect duplicate of Iris, but instead she got a poor imitation."

"Why would you think such a thing?" Jake asks.

"I've seen Iris play the violin. I found a video online. She was amazing."

"But so are you," says Ty.

I shake my head. "I couldn't do it in front of an audience like she did. She was so calm. So perfect. The way she looked . . . everything."

Jake sits straighter, his eyes going wide. "You can play?"

Ty nods. "Yeah, and she's incredible, whether she'll admit it or not."

Pride blooms inside of me, sweet and soft and unexpected. Maybe there is something good in all of this. My sister's talent somehow became mine, and it's a wonderful gift. "Thank you," I say. "Not that I had anything to do with it."

Jake smiles. "I'd love to hear you play sometime. Iris's music meant everything to her. Whenever she'd hear from a fan about how much joy it brought them, she'd be so happy. There was something special about it. Something soothing and powerful."

The waitress appears and refills Jake's coffee. As she leaves, he says, "I hope I'm not speaking out of turn, but I want you to know that I was close to your folks, Lily. Iris and I were together for two years—from the time I was sixteen—so I got to know them pretty well. People don't tend to change all that much. They loved Iris more than anything, and I can't imagine they didn't feel the same about you from the moment you were born."

"I know," I say. "I'm just upset. And I'm having a hard time understanding how Dad allowed any of this. I mean, I've read about animal cloning. There can be problems. Defects. A lot of the cloned animals die young." A shudder rifles through me. "How could he take that risk with his own child?"

"They loved Iris so much, and your mom just couldn't let her go," Jake says. "When the doctors said she wouldn't survive, Beckett approached your parents with the idea, but Adam refused because of those very reasons you mentioned."

"I thought they found the solution to those problems," Ty says, picking up his fork. "I remember reading about a breakthrough in the research. Didn't later testing produce animals without any abnormalities?"

"Yes," Jake confirms. "But human cloning raises a whole other set of concerns. Apparently Beckett didn't have any moral or ethical issues with it, but Adam did."

An old man shuffles to the table behind us. As he passes by, I smell cigarette smoke on his clothing and the scent triggers a memory. A voice crackles at the back of my mind and a memory flickers before me . . . Iris's memory . . .

"Think about it, Adam." The cigarette trembles between my mother's fingers. "We don't have to lose her. Iris could live again. Please. Ian wants to help us."

The vision fades along with Mom's voice. Blinking, I say to Jake, "My mother was on Beckett's side about the cloning, wasn't she."

"Yes." Watching me with a curious expression, he adds, "Beckett told your dad that if he was uncomfortable taking part in the actual process, he could do it alone. He promised that no one else would ever be told. But Adam wouldn't hear of it. He refused to allow Iris to become Beckett's first human subject. His guinea pig, so to speak."

The scent of the cigarette smoke still lingers, drawing me back to fragments of Iris's memories. I still don't know how I have them, how it's scientifically possible that they transfer to me. But I can't come up with another explanation for what I'm experiencing, any more than I can make sense of the other aspects of our connection.

"So Mom arranged to go behind Dad's back," I murmur, seeing into my sister's past.

Jake nods. "Beckett came to the house one day when your father was away. Iris overheard their conversation, and she told me about it. She was really sick that day and it was all she could do to take the stairs down. She hid in the hallway and listened to Beckett tell your mother that he didn't need Adam's help to carry out the procedure, or Iris's cooperation, for that matter. It was almost as simple as drawing blood and about that painful."

"Did Iris understand what they were talking about?" Ty asks.

"Not at first, but then Beckett started trying to ease Melanie's mind about problems that had occurred in the past with animal cloning—things like physical and mental defects and increased speed of aging and shortened lifespans. He mentioned the success they'd had at the lab over the prior couple of years cloning red kangaroos."

Agnes, Iris whispers. *She was afraid of him.*

My breath hitches. "Was one of the kangaroos named Agnes?"

"Yes!" Jake gives a short laugh. "I'd forgotten that. Adam took Iris and me to see her once at the lab. She was fine until Beckett walked in, then she freaked out. Iris was convinced that he was mean to the animals when no one was looking."

They were just experiments to him, Iris whispers harshly. *So was I.*

"Beckett mentioned Agnes to your mother that day to plead his case," Jake continues. "How Agnes was healthy and normal, and the fact that she and her original looked exactly alike, right down to their markings."

"She let him turn her against Dad." I shake my head, disgusted with my mother.

"She was desperate to save her daughter," Jake says.

"But it didn't work out like she planned." I look away, trying to tamp down my anger at Mom, then turn to him again. "Did Iris confront them? Mom and Beckett, I mean?"

"Not Beckett. She came to me first, and I told her she should talk to your mother. So she told Melanie what she'd overheard, and that she wasn't willing to let him do the cloning. That he was just trying to take advantage of Melanie's grief to get what he wanted. There was no way he could bring her back—the clone wouldn't be the same person she was."

I see the instant Jake realizes he's referring to me. He shifts uncomfortably.

"Why didn't Iris go to Dad?" I ask him.

"Your mother promised she'd forget the whole thing since it upset Iris so much. She asked Iris not to tell Adam because he'd be angry that she'd considered going against his wishes."

"She lied." I stare outside at the cars in the parking lot. "I don't know how to feel about any of this. Who am I? *What* am I?"

"You're you," Ty says. "The same person you've always been."

The rubber soles of the waitress's shoes squeak as she approaches. She sets our bill on the table, then takes off again. "So you didn't know Mom and Beckett went ahead with the procedure until I called you?" I ask Jake.

His brows cinch together above his glasses. "I knew. When I heard that Melanie was pregnant, I was suspicious. I went to Adam, ready to tell him everything. But Melanie had already confessed what she and Beckett had done. Later, Adam told me she'd miscarried, but I was never completely convinced." He removes his glasses and pinches the bridge of his nose. "After Iris died and your folks disappeared, I got really depressed, and I told my mom everything. A part of me was hoping that they'd lied about the miscarriage. I knew that Beckett had convinced your mother that Iris and her clone would be the same person. That you would want the same things Iris had wanted. That everything . . . your feelings and interests, your very soul, would be identical. Iris didn't believe that, and neither did I. But after she was gone, I wanted to think that some small part of her might've lived on." A pall of sadness surrounds us as he lays his glasses on the table and picks up his coffee mug.

For the first time, I notice the wedding ring on his finger. "You're married?"

"For six years now." With pride, he adds, "I have a three-year-old son and a new baby girl."

I'm sorry, I tell Iris. But she seems content, not upset. She wanted to find Jake to learn the truth, but I think she also needed to see him to make sure he's happy. To know that his life is good.

Road weary, Jake twists his neck from side to side.

"As much as you look like her, Lily," he says, "and despite all the things you have in common, I can see that you're your own person; you aren't Iris. The two of you are completely separate. I think she'd be relieved to know that you have your own life and identity."

I brace my forearms on the table and lean forward. "That's not exactly true—what you said about Iris and me being completely separate, I mean."

Jake frowns. "I don't understand."

"We're something in between."

Confusion wrinkles his brow. "What I meant is, you'd realize if you'd known her that—"

"I *do* know her," I break in. "Iris sent me to you."

Jake draws back, glancing between Ty and me. "Sorry. I'm not getting this."

"She's been insisting that I find you for a while now," I say.

"Iris talks to you?"

I nod. "I hear her thoughts and she hears mine. She's with me now."

The color drains from his face.

Smiling, I say, "You think I'm crazy."

"I don't know what I think."

"It doesn't matter. Iris worked hard to make this possible. The two of us meeting, I mean. I'm not leaving until she has the chance to tell you whatever it is she needs to say."

I sit back, wait. And then I hear her, as quiet as the

flutter of a moth wing at the base of my brain. I smile. "She says that knowing you're happy makes her happy, too. And that even though the two of you didn't get your forever, the time you spent together meant everything to her."

"Our forever . . ." With a stunned expression, Jake puffs out his cheeks and exhales a long breath. "Iris always said that."

A short laugh slips past my lips. "Oh, and one more thing. She wants you to know that she loves the daisies, but they make her sneeze; they always did."

21

We follow Jake to a hotel. He insists on paying, and we don't argue. While Jake talks to the lady at the front desk, Ty and I sit on the sofa in the lobby, holding hands, our bags and Iris's violin case at our feet. A few minutes later, Jake walks over, slipping one card key into his pocket and holding two more out to us.

"I'm in three-twelve. You guys are in three-oh-eight and three-oh-nine. Get some sleep, then give me a call and I'll take you to lunch." He laughs. "Or dinner. I'm exhausted."

We reach our rooms and part ways. I miss Ty the minute I close my door.

I draw the curtains to block out the day. Placing Iris's violin in the corner chair, I carry my bag to the bathroom and take a quick shower. Minutes later, propped up against the pillows on the bed, I text Sylvie: *In okc. Mom & Wyatt know I'm w/Ty. Will call w/details soon.*

I lower the phone, worried about Wyatt and wondering if he'll ever forgive me. Knowing I won't get any rest until

I touch base with him, I text him and tell him we made it and that I'm okay. I ask about my mom and Cookie, then wait five minutes for a reply, staring at the phone. When he doesn't respond, I make up excuses for his silence: It's early and he's still sleeping; he's in the shower; he stayed at the all-night party even after what happened, and he's having breakfast with friends.

Just when I'm about to give up on him, he texts: *Gran is w/ your mom and Cookie. They r ok.*

I text back: *Thanks.*

I stare at the painting on the opposite wall—a vase of red flowers. What am I going to say to Mom? I'm sort of mad at her about everything—especially the cloning, which is totally weird, when you think about it. If she hadn't gone behind Dad's back, I wouldn't be here. I should probably thank her for being a liar.

But what if I had been born with health problems, deformities, or other terrible defects, instead of an amazing ability to play the violin and communicate with my "original"? Would she deserve my thanks then?

Original. The word gives me a sick feeling inside.

To steady my nerves, I picture Ty in the next room and imagine looking into his beautiful dark eyes. They've calmed me so many times since we met, and just the thought of them calms me now. Taking a breath, I lift the phone from my lap and call Mom.

"Lily!" Her relief flows through the phone. "Are you okay?"

"I'm fine, Mom. Ty and I are in Oklahoma City."

"Oklahoma? But why?"

"Is Addie there?" I ask.

"Yes. And Wyatt. What's going on?"

"We made a short side trip so I could meet Jake Milano."

"Jake?" Mom's voice drops. "Oh, no."

"Iris and I needed to find him and talk to him so we could finally know the truth about what happened. She'd forgotten everything, Mom." I pause to gather my nerve, then add, "Even what you did to her."

I hear her quick intake of breath, and then she says, "There are things you need to know."

"I know what you and Ian Beckett did to Iris against Dad's wishes. And against Iris's wishes. I know what I am, Mom."

"Please come home and we'll talk about this," she says in a broken voice.

I take a moment to get control of my emotions, then say, "I think I finally understand why you've always been so unhappy. You wanted Iris back, but instead you got me."

"No! No, Lily. I love you more than anything. I just— losing Iris destroyed something in me."

I stare at the ring she gave me for my birthday. The one she and Dad made especially for me. I know Mom loves me. But I can't help feeling bruised.

"I haven't been fair to you," Mom continues. "I know that. I didn't give you what you needed from me. What you deserved. I tried, but I couldn't let go."

I suddenly hurt so much for her. For all of us. Mom and Dad. Iris and myself. "I don't know how to help you," I whisper. "How to make you happy."

"It's not up to you." I hear the tears in Mom's voice and Addie in the background, asking if everything's okay. "What are you going to do now?" Mom asks. "Will you come home? We need to talk face-to-face, not over the phone."

"I'm still going to Baltimore with Ty to see his brother. After that, I don't know. I need you to answer my questions first. I'm so tired of secrets."

"Anything," she says. "Anything . . . just ask me."

My voice is strangled and harsh. "Are Iris and I the same person or two separate people or what? I mean, if I was reproduced from her cells, is she my sister? My mother? Jake called her my *original*. God—am I even human?"

"Lily, listen to me." Mom sounds steadier now. "You're the same as everyone."

"Then why did you and Dad run away from Winterhaven and change your names before I was born? Was it just to hide me from Beckett? I mean, you didn't even let our family or your closest friends get to know me. Were you ashamed of me?"

"Ashamed? No! Your father was sure that Beckett had ulterior motives. That's why we left," she says, confirming Jake's thoughts. "Adam was convinced that if I carried you to term, a healthy baby, Beckett would try to turn you into a specimen to be studied and probed, with no privacy or anonymity. We had to create a new life for ourselves. A normal life for you. We had to protect you. And that meant not even trusting our closest friends to keep the secret. You were too important to take that risk."

I want so much to forgive her, to understand, but I'm still so confused. "Why didn't you tell me when I was older?"

"For the same reason we left our past behind. We wanted you to feel normal. And we were afraid you wouldn't. But you *are* normal, Lily," she says firmly. "Please believe that."

With an incredulous laugh, I say, "How is my relationship with Iris normal? Or the way I play the violin? How is it even possible when I've never had a lesson?"

"I can't say why you have the connection to Iris that you do, but as for the violin . . . Ian had been dabbling in genetic engineering. He told me he might be able to transfer Iris's abilities to you. I said I only wanted a healthy child. I didn't care about the music. I only wanted you."

We grow quiet, and when I finally speak again, I sound calmer than I feel. "Today is the anniversary of Iris's death, isn't it?"

"Yes. Eighteen years ago today," she murmurs.

"Did you plan for us to be born on the same day, eighteen years apart?"

Sounding regretful, she says, "Yes. At the time, I was so obsessed with everything being as much the same as possible, and Beckett encouraged that. We tried to time the pregnancy, but of course babies only come when they're ready, unless they're induced. So, I told my doctor in Pueblo that I wanted to have you on the sixth of May, and he agreed to it because I was far enough along and he didn't think it was risky."

"And Dad was okay with that?"

"He thought it was completely obsessive of me, and it was," she says with a note of self-derision. "But I'd made the appointment and I refused to change it. I worried about doing everything just right, but I should've listened to your father. I should have trusted that he knew what he was talking about." After a quick pause, she says, "Please come home."

I hear a bump against the wall in Ty's room. "No, Mom. Not yet. Ty saw me through this, and I'm going to see him through the hard stuff ahead with his brother."

"And after that?"

"I'll come home and spend some time figuring out where to go from here." My last ounce of energy drains away. I yawn. "I need a nap, Mom. I'll call you before we get on the road again, okay?"

"Okay." Softly, she adds, "I'm sorry, Lily."

I don't say anything. I can't. Not yet.

"Before you go," she says, "if you have Jake's number, I'd like to call him."

"I'll only give it to you if you promise not to get mad at him. He didn't do anything wrong."

Mom makes the promise, so I give her the number, then put the phone aside.

Iris's sigh soothes me as I lay my head on the pillow and curl into the fetal position. We sleep.

Exhausted from their night of driving, Jake and Ty sleep the day away, giving me some time to myself. After a two-hour nap, I try calling Wyatt a few times, but he never picks up. I watch television in my room, then call Mom again. There's so much we still need to say.

"I talked to someone today," she tells me. "This may come as another shock to you, but we didn't hide you from *everyone*. We have family in Massachusetts, and they know about you."

I can't help smiling. "You mean Dad's sister? Gail and her husband, Matthew?"

"How do you know them?"

"We have a lot to talk about when I get home," I say.

"That's what Gail and I discussed—you coming home. She lives in—"

"Winterhaven, I know. And she owns a bookstore, right?"

I hear a hint of humor in Mom's voice when she says, "I suppose you know what Gail and I decided?"

"Nope. I don't have a clue."

"Since you're going to be close to her, anyway, we thought that when you're ready to leave Baltimore you might go to Winterhaven and I'll meet you there. We could stay for a week or two. I think we both need a change of scenery, and Gail and Matthew are anxious to meet you."

"Wow," I say, more than a little nervous about meeting my extended family for the first time.

"Gail and I also talked about me selling the cabin and moving there."

"You'd sell the cabin?"

The thought of it is like a punch in the stomach. My first instinct is to worry about Iris, because it's hard for me to imagine her living anywhere else but in the mountains. I used to be afraid that when I left home, she'd stay behind. But maybe *I'm* Iris's home. She lives where I live. She goes where I go.

I feel her at this very second, as warm as the sunlight sifting through the window. She's extra quiet though. *Iris?* I say. *Am I right? Will you go with me if I move?* I listen and hear her steady hiss, but she doesn't answer. Maybe she's trying to sort everything out, too.

"I know how much you love it here," says Mom, breaking into my thoughts. "You could always come back to visit." She's talking fast, as if to convince me. "But I think I'm going to need family around me when you go away to college."

I nibble my fingernail, happy and sad at once, wanting so much to reach out to her like she's trying to do with me. "We'll talk about all this at Aunt Gail's, okay?" I say. "We'll figure out the best thing to do."

Sounding hopeful, she says, "Okay, Lily. We'll decide together."

I tell myself that maybe she can change. Maybe our relationship can. Maybe my mom can finally move on and be happy again.

"I love you, Lily," she says. "Call me again when you're on the road. And be careful."

"I will, Mom. I love you, too."

I end the call, torn between excitement about the possibilities for a new life in Massachusetts and sadness over what I'd be leaving behind. The peaks. The forest. My home, and all the places that remind me of Dad. And, most important of all, Wyatt.

Jake takes us to an early dinner at the Spaghetti Warehouse in Bricktown, a refurbished area of Oklahoma City with a river walk and old brick buildings that now house bars and restaurants and shops.

"Your mother called me," he says.

I glance at Ty and raise my brows, then ask Jake, "What did she say?"

"She thanked me for telling you the truth. She said she could never find the courage to do it."

"I want to thank you, too," I say. "And so does Iris."

Jake's face pales. Coughing, he shifts in his chair. Maybe someday I'll convince him I communicate with Iris, and he'll cast his doubts aside. But not yet. That much is clear from his uncomfortable reaction.

Still, when the waiter brings our iced teas, Jake toasts Iris for bringing us together, and we make a promise to stay in touch.

After dinner, we say our good-byes, and Ty and I start off for Baltimore. We have a twenty-two-hour drive ahead and want to put as many miles behind us as possible before we stop again to sleep.

By silent mutual agreement, for the next few hours we don't discuss any of what we learned from Jake and my mom. Instead, we listen to the radio and sing along.

And we talk about his brother.

As Ty describes him, I begin to think Kyle has a lot in common with Wyatt, which makes me feel close to him instantly. They're both funny, both well liked. Kyle can dribble a basketball like nobody else, and he likes to tinker on cars, just like Wyatt. He loves the mountains. And his family.

We stop for gas a few hours into the trip, and when I come out from the restroom and climb back into the car, Ty hands me a sack. "Room service. The midnight snack you ordered is ready."

I open the sack. "It's only eleven."

He starts the car and pulls out of the station. "I had a craving for something sweet. I hope you like Fudgsicles."

I take the wrapper off one and hand it to him. "Here you go."

"So," he says. "It's been a wild couple of days, huh?"

"Yeah. It's not every day a girl finds out she's a modern-day Frankenstein's monster."

He scowls. "I wish you wouldn't talk about yourself like that."

A drop of chocolate plops onto my knee. I wipe it off and lick my finger. "Don't tell me you aren't blown away by the whole clone thing. You wouldn't be human if you weren't." Though nothing about being a clone seems funny to me, I force myself to grin and add, "You'd be like me!"

"There you go again." He finishes his Fudgsicle and stuffs the stick into the car's old ashtray. "I've never met anyone more human than you," he says. "Thank you for deciding to come to Baltimore. It means a lot to me."

"You're welcome. Thank you for trying to help me understand all this crazy stuff about myself. I'm sorry I had my doubts about your intentions. You've really been someone I can count on from the first day we met."

"That's because I fell for you the minute I saw you."

My Fudgsicle isn't the only thing melting. I wipe another drop from my knee and study his profile. "Did you fall for me at first because I look like Iris? You said you were intrigued by her music. So maybe it's her, not me."

He shrugs and smiles. "She's part of you, so I guess that's true in a way." I almost stop breathing when he lifts my hand from the seat and kisses the back of it.

Glad all of our secrets are out, I say, "Today there were times when I thought I understood all this and I was okay with it. Then the next second, I'd get this panicky feeling, like I don't know who or what I am anymore. That's how I feel now. Am I Iris? Is that voice in my head I've been hearing all my life really mine? And if I'm not her, what do I owe her? I mean, the only reason I'm alive is because of her."

"Maybe you should think of Iris as your identical twin. Twins have a lot in common, but they're two different people."

I consider that. But then it occurs to me that maybe the answer of what I am and how I was made doesn't matter. Maybe it's more important that I just enjoy this life Iris gave me and be happy for it. In a way, wouldn't that be giving her a second chance? It's the only way I know to repay her.

Sighing, I say, "Iris has been so quiet since we met Jake and found out the truth. It's like she's pulling back or something. What if what we talked about before is right? What if her purpose for staying around is finished? What will I do if she goes?"

"I can't believe she would leave you. Have you asked her?

I nod. "She didn't answer." Ty brushes my knuckles with his fingertips. "First thing in the morning, we're going to watch the sunrise together. You, me, and Iris. After seeing Jake, she probably needed some time to herself."

I nod at him, hoping with everything in me that he's right.

At three in the morning, we get a hotel room. I'm so tired I don't even know what town we're in. Ty opens the curtains over the window so we can watch the sunrise, like he promised. Then he sets his "mental alarm clock," as he calls it, and stretches out on the bed. I lie down beside him, tucked into the crook of his arm, my head on his chest. My pulse slows to match his heartbeat, and soon I can tell that he's fallen asleep.

Even though I've never been this exhausted, I lie awake,

staring at the window. Afraid to close my eyes. Afraid to stop listening for Iris's faint hum.

Ty is snoring softly when I slip from beneath his arm a few hours later and tiptoe over to the corner chair where I propped the violin case when we arrived. I think I must've dozed for a while because I feel more rested. It's almost morning, and I realize I sense Iris more strongly than I have all day.

The city lights flowing in from the window make it easy for me to see without turning on a lamp. I stare at the violin case. I haven't held the instrument since I played for Mom, and I'm suddenly afraid to try again. I don't want to wake Ty, but I need to talk to someone to settle my nerves.

I grab my cell phone, then slip into the bathroom, leaving the light off and closing the door. I lean against the sink and text Wyatt. He won't see the message for a couple of hours, but I just need to make contact with him. I can't leave for Baltimore with so much left unsaid between us.

I text: *Guess Mom told u our plans. Miss u. So much more to tell u. Pls call. Luv u.*

As I'm starting to leave the bathroom, my phone buzzes. I guess Wyatt can't sleep, either.

Your mom told me more than your plans. Always knew something not rt abt u. Crazy stuff. U ok?

I choke back tears and smile, relieved by Wyatt's teasing tone. Then I text back: *I'm ok. All the times u called me a freak u were rite. Who knew?* I send the text, then before he can respond, send another one: *U still upset?*

A minute passes. Then another quiet chirp sounds. *I'll get over it.*

Wincing and biting my lip, I text: *I'm sorry, Wy. U are part of all my best memories. Pls call.*

Need time.

I swallow my disappointment, then text: *I can't lose u.*

Five full minutes pass without a response. Feeling forlorn, I reach for the door just as my phone chirps. I look down at the display.

90% of male students @ Columbia develop chronic halitosis by age 20. That's serious bad breath, in case you don't know. Tlk soon. Nite, Lil.

A half sob, half laugh bursts from my throat. *G'nite, Wy.*

I slip back into the room. It's quiet.

Too quiet.

Going still, I whisper, "Iris?" I listen for her, exhaling my relief when I hear her sigh. Why did I ever take her for granted, like my heartbeat, my breath? I was wrong to think she was my shadow. The truth is, in so many ways, I'm hers. Without Iris, I would've been nothing.

Gathering my courage, I ask, *Iris, you're staying, aren't you? Tell me nothing's going to change between us.*

I'll always be here, she whispers. *You're strong enough alone now, but if you need me, look inside. Listen . . . the west peak can't exist without the east. We're a part of each other.*

I understand what she's trying to tell me. I think that, all my life, Iris has been haunted by a lost love and a past full of secrets she couldn't remember. Secrets she feared might hurt me. She stayed alert to watch over me, while struggling with the vague notion that she had to find her way back to the boy she'd once loved. Now that she knows Jake's happy and we've uncovered the truth and I'm okay, Iris can relax. She's not going away, she'll only be sleeping.

Forgetting that Ty is in the room, forgetting I'm in a hotel and everyone is asleep, I cross to the corner and take the violin from the case. Tonight, I'll play for Iris, so she can experience her music again through me, like I've experienced so much through her.

I walk to the window, lift the bow to the strings. The music in me unwinds and the violin cries out, one joyous note bleeding into another, then another. The song is a new one I've never heard in her memories or my dreams, one she's never hummed in my ear. It comes from a place deep in my center where Iris resides, where she always has and always will.

The melody expands, and the air stirs slightly. I feel Ty at my side and end the song. Lowering the bow, I lean against him.

As light peeks over the eastern horizon, he puts his arm around my shoulders, and Iris pulses next to my heart. We've never seen a more beautiful sunrise.

EPILOGUE

The air changes when I step inside Kyle's room behind Ty and his parents. The sterile antiseptic scent of the hospital disappears, replaced by the fragrance of hundreds of flowers. The room is filled with them.

I'm carrying Iris's violin and a bow, and I'm more nervous and fearful than I've ever been in my life. After I play, someone will come in and turn off the machines that are keeping Ty's brother alive. I can't stand to think about it.

Mr. and Mrs. Collier block my view of Kyle as they approach him and, one at a time, lean over to kiss him while Ty walks around to his opposite side.

Holding my breath, I make my way to the foot of the bed. Machines wheeze and tick as I settle my gaze on Kyle. He's pale and fragile. So frail. Like a broken bird.

"Lily, this is Kyle," Ty says with love and pride in his voice. "My brother."

I want to be strong for Ty, so I hold my emotions in check as our eyes meet. Ty nods, and I shift my attention to his mom and dad, relaxing a little when they offer me teary smiles of encouragement.

On the table beside the bed, I see a photograph of Ty standing with Kyle on a mountaintop. I recognize friendly mischief in the younger boy's eyes. He looks so much like Ty. So full of life.

As Ty takes one of his brother's hands, and his parents take the other, I lift the violin to my shoulder and close my eyes, holding in my mind that image from the photograph, thinking of everything I've learned about this boy. The people and the places he loved. The things he liked to do. Each quirk and quality that makes him unique. I want so much for the power of the music to flow through him and fill him with happiness. I want it to touch his parents, too, and Ty, and bring them peace.

But the bow I hold is shaking, and anxiety rises up to choke me.

Just as I'm about to panic and think I can't do it, Iris's words sweep through my mind: *You're strong enough alone now, but if you need me, look inside. Listen. . . .*

Blocking out every other noise in the room, I search my soul for the ceaseless, rhythmic whisper of her breathing, and when I hear it, a deep wave of calm washes over me, along with a certainty that the music will reach Kyle, and he'll live on, no matter what.

I inhale, and with a steady hand, touch the bow to the strings.

ACKNOWLEDGMENTS

This book would not exist without the following people, to whom I owe a huge debt of gratitude:

My wise, wonderful, and patient editors, Sarah Sevier and Tyler Infinger, who helped me over the bumps and through the valleys, and pointed out all the things I didn't see.

The fabulous HarperTeen team, who created a beautiful book around my story and presented it to the reading world.

My agent, Jenny Bent, who asked for more time when I desperately needed it, and saw me through a difficult period.

Anita Howard, April Redmon, Linda Castillo, and Marcy McKay, who read and reread, again and again and again, and never complained. (And who, miraculously, love and support me no matter how much I whine!)

The folks at Roasters Coffee & Tea Company on Soncy in Amarillo, Texas, who provided me with a friendly, comfortable place to work (and great coffee!) whenever I needed to be out of the house.

My good friend Joe Kitchens, who shared his expertise as a flight paramedic by walking me through the details of a mountain rescue mission. Even though the rescue scene was cut from the book's final version, his insights helped me get things straight in my own mind so that I could move forward.

And last but not least, my husband, Jeff, for too many things to list here.

THANKS to all of you!

Every ghost has a story to tell.

The last thing Tansy Piper wanted was to move to the middle of nowhere in Cedar Canyon, Texas. Once there, her life takes a chilling turn when she finds a pocket watch, a journal of poetry, and a tiny crystal in her new home. The items belonged to Henry, a troubled teenager who lived in the house and died decades ago. Tansy soon discovers that through the crystal and the lens of her camera, she can become part of Henry's surreal black-and-white world. But the more time Tansy spends in the past, the more her present world fades away. . . .